ANCIENT ENEMIES

Elizabeth North

ANCIENT ENEMIES

JONATHAN CAPE
THIRTY BEDFORD SQUARE LONDON

First published 1982
Copyright © 1982 by Elizabeth North
Jonathan Cape Ltd, 30 Bedford Square, London WC1

For permission to reproduce the poem 'Touch and Go' by
Stevie Smith, from *The Collected Poems of Stevie Smith*
(Allen Lane), the author and publisher are grateful to
James MacGibbon, Stevie Smith's executor.

British Library Cataloguing in Publication Data

North, Elizabeth
Ancient enemies.
I. Title
823'.914[F]   PR6064.0764

ISBN 0-224-02052-8

Typeset by Oxford Verbatim Limited
Printed in Great Britain by
Mackays of Chatham Ltd

For Jo

TOUCH AND GO

Man is coming out of the mountains
But his tail is caught in the pass.
Why does he not free himself
Is he not an ass?

Do not be impatient with him
He is bowed with passion and fret
He is not out of the mountains
He is not half out yet.

Look at his sorrowful eyes
His torn cheeks, his brow
He lies with his head in the dust
Is there no one to help him now?

No, there is no one to help him
Let him get on with it,
Cry the ancient enemies of man
As they cough and spit.

The enemies of man are like trees
They stand with the sun in their branches
Is there no one to help my creature
Where he languishes?

Ah, the delicate creature
He lies with his head in the rubble
Pray that the moment pass
And the trouble.

Look he moves, that is more than a prayer,
But he is so slow
Will he come out of the mountains?
It is touch and go.

STEVIE SMITH

ONE

When Bentley's father threw him out, on discovering Bentley's leaning towards homosexuality, Bentley's father threw an ornament at him. It was a really disgusting kitsch china naked nymph that Bentley's mother had been given by an aunt. It smashed, having missed Bentley.

When Jane failed biology O Level, her father tore a banister out and brandished it at her. Half-way through his cries of anger and despair at not having produced a brilliant daughter, he decided he was after all complaining about modern workmanship which had made it possible for him to tear banisters out of their brand-new staircase.

Today in English we were talking about the tempest scene in *Lear* and I quoted both those instances for everyone's benefit. Some of the class had been saying that they thought the way that Lear behaved was silly and irresponsible. I said that men got angry men got angry men got angry period; and Mr Forbes asked me what point I was making.

I said I wasn't making any point, just commenting about experience. At which he looked disappointed, wrinkling up his nose as he does when I, his brightest spark (at any rate among the girls), have let him down.

Some of the boys said that anger led to war and was dis-

1

graceful, but I've seen them playing pool in pubs around town and jostling each other for a place at a table and getting very tight-lipped when they lose. And even Bentley owns up to frequent violent feelings, but he left school last summer and could not support me in my argument.

Thinking about other boys, there's Giles, my cousin who's at public school, but he says they have to play so much sport that they're too shagged out for much violence on the whole.

The other girls in class said nothing of course, except for Maxine who said that her father did get angry. Perhaps, she said, like her father, Lear really had an ulcer but they hadn't discovered that in medieval times.

Mr Forbes said we were discussing Shakespeare's times and not times in general. He was wrinkling up his nose at the whole discussion by that time and told us to begin our essays on 'The role of parenthood in *Lear* with particular reference to the Gloucester sub-plot'.

And while we got out pens and paper he sat and bit his finger-nails and stared out at the playing-fields from time to time. I stared out too and thought of Giles, but not that much, more of the playing-fields themselves which lead towards the park which leads towards our house – or rather flat – beyond the park and wondered how my mother was. Dire gloom would still be with her probably, I thought. Dire madness even possibly, and how we all might deal with it if it arose.

Mr Forbes, in addition to biting his nails, was ruffling his thick brown hair and looking fairly agonised as well. As soon as the bell went he collected all his books into his briefcase and bolted for the door. We'd heard that his wife had had twins in the night.

I'd rather hoped we'd have one of our little chats. On madness possibly today. But maybe twins are an excuse for rushing off. At least he had been spared one of my raking stares which have been known to make him blush. Jane used to say before she left she thought that Forbes was 'rather sweet' and I was hard on him.

2

But anyway, I am dozens of essays in arrears, so I got my book-bag and I sprinted out along the corridor. There is this weird girl Liz, who hardly ever speaks though when she does it's always relevant. She gets up my nose because, if she's so bright, she's not revealing it. She only sighs and looks as though she thinks the lot of us are dim. Well, maybe some of us are. After the class, as I was sprinting off because I had a lunchtime plan, she caught up with me and said didn't I think women could be angry too?

'Of course I do.'

'Well, then? Why make a special case of men?'

'Because we were dis*cuss*ing men.'

'My mother throws things. She is actually mad,' she said.

This Liz has a lot of style. She had a flying suit months before I did, but mostly wears ex-US Army stuff. Her hair is shorter than mine – like two millimetres long, close to her head, and her eyes are small, which somehow in her case is quite enviable. She is, I suppose, good-looking in a cold way. I've always guessed that she's a lesbian and considered, somewhat intolerantly, this to be a good reason for avoiding her.

'You mean your mother's really mad?' I said. We'd got outside by then and I was unlocking my bike padlock. 'Enough to be in a mental home?'

'Sometimes,' she said. 'The trouble is that her mother, my grandmother, told her that she'd tried to get rid of her. You know – abort her and failed, because it wasn't easy to arrange in those days.'

I could see that it could be quite a blow to someone, that sort of thing, but I couldn't see that it would necessarily send you mad. Liz leaned against the bike-shed breeze-block wall and lit a cigarette and offered me one. I was in a hurry, but it seemed she wanted to talk, so I took the cig and she lit it for me, cupping the match flame in her hand very competently since it was quite windy.

'My mother's mother even fell downstairs deliberately,' she said.

3

We hadn't even discussed the wisdom or otherwise of smoking within the college grounds, and I liked this Liz for not giggling about how naughty we might be being.

'My mother thought of getting rid of me as well,' she said.

I thought a bit. I haven't talked a lot about my abortion, though it is no secret to a good few members of the class. I thought of mentioning it to Liz, but then decided that she was so cool, accepting things, she might not be impressed. If she was to become a friend of mine, then it might be better to wait and see and maybe knock her out with the revelation at some later stage.

'It's interesting,' she said. 'My mother's mother thought that she was mad and shouldn't pass the madness on, and so she told my mother endlessly that she, my mother, might be mad, and now my mother thinks she is, and so she is, sometimes at any rate.'

'A kind of self-fulfilling prophecy, you mean?' I said, quite pleased with this remark.

'No, kind of very pissing-off,' she said and stubbed her cigarette out, grinding it into the tarmac with her trainers, me still wondering what on earth she'd told me all this family saga for. I stared at her and was mostly envying her looks, her incredibly clean face with its complexion of even paleness, which I'd never really studied before.

'Why don't you talk more in class?' I said.

'No point.' She lit a cig, not offering me one this time. I was astride my bike by now.

'There's *only* talk,' I said. 'What else is there?' And I wondered why if she didn't think it worth discussing things, she had followed me and seemed to want to talk to me? Or was she after me?

It wasn't until I'd shot across the yard and on through the gates that I realised that, if she was lesbian, it could be because she had decided, in view of the chancy mental or unstable background of her mother and her grandmother, that she must not procreate herself. My mother, were she in a normal frame

4

of mind, would be quite fascinated by all this.

But Liz had at least made me feel a sort of warmth inside, a sort of being-wanted warmth, as though I had more options in the world all of a sudden. As well as that, the sun was out. I cycled round the college railings and along beside the playing-fields. I reached the smooth road going through the park.

She was, it seemed, intelligent and interestingly ruthless too: if I am to hold my head up high and go on holding it that way, I should make friends with people who will challenge me, rather than dodge the issue by knocking around with Bentley and with Jane who are both like ever open doors. And if it means, with Liz, cool little hands inside my clothes, I should be up to dealing with that.

It's all needing to be wanted, isn't it? My mother could be going mad, if mad it is, because she is afraid she isn't wanted after all.

It isn't spring as yet. Not really spring. No leaves on trees. Sometimes you see a kind of hazy green surrounding trees, suggesting spring. But it was mild at lunchtime and I got off where there is a wood and leaned my bike against the railings, still putting off the thing I'd promised myself I'd do. And went up through the trees a bit and wondered how bad I'd feel if I failed to do it, even though I'd made this contract with myself first thing today.

My mother was quite helpful about madness when we started doing *Lear*. She would say things like 'Mad? Yes, temporarily so maybe', and then: 'Americans use mad for angry anyway.' And later on she said: 'It's losing certainties sends people mad, I think. You build up certainties through life and then they go kaput and there you are . . . before a hovel on the heath.'

'You're always saying that you never had any certainties,' I said.

'I suppose I must have *some*,' she said, looking rather distant and a bit too tearful for my liking.

For the last few weeks she hasn't really talked of *Lear* or any of my other set books or asked about my sociology, except to enquire, because she thinks she ought to know I suppose, what grades I get, but, having asked, forgets and asks again, which really sets my teeth on edge.

I even find it hard to look at her sometimes. Her hair needs doing at the roots. She piles it up on top of her head as she's done for years, but it keeps escaping the pins and falling everywhere. She's developed a nervous twitch which is feeling round the back of her neck how many strands have fallen recently.

'How are your certainties?' I said to her the other day, testing her memory of past conversations.

'What certainties?' she said vaguely. I would rather she had lashed out at me. At least that might have warned her that her control of herself was slipping. And I can't really tell her she is going mad, since that would be tantamount to making her go mad. If Liz's mother is anything to go by.

This smallish wood in the park: it slopes up, reaching the highest point that there is round here, since the town is in a flat-bottomed river valley. From the wood you can see one way to the back of college and the other way towards the Portsmouth Road, on which we live, the top windows of our flat being visible.

I found a lowish tree with a branching bit near enough the ground and hooked myself up and squatted there and found a Yorkie bar in my pocket. I couldn't sit because the tree was dampish and these were my new red dungarees.

I saw the top two windows of our flat: my bedroom and my mother's bedroom. Rather, hers is really Henry's room and hers. I have to think of it as Henry's room as well and wish that he was in it still. At nights, for her sake anyway.

Sun, nearly spring and about one month to the equinox. Sun eases everything. Well, while you are not thinking about everything, that is. Our flat: the sun would be on the back of it, on

6

Daisy's room and on the cobbled yard, on the tubs of daffodils. My mother would be in the shop or studio. But I would not go home just yet.

Same street, same block as us, same windows looking out across the park: my uncle's shop. Well, not a shop like ours, but a room with books and dust, tobacco smoke and Patrick sitting at his desk, not expecting customers and closing a book hurriedly. Probably one from his filthy section which I guess he calls erotica – from the shelf high up in the far corner, to which only a few chosen people are directed.

I had decided I would ask him if he'd anything on *Lear*. Not that I wanted such a book, although I might just borrow it or look at it and give it back. This wasn't why I came, however.

'Hullo,' he said and I said 'Hi' and gave him time to hide the book he had been reading under some paper on his desk, while I sauntered round the shelves. Perhaps it had been mean to take the stairs so lightly in my new trainers and catch him off his guard. He's like my mother, private, shy and inward to the point of absurdity. They are both Leadbetters, and the family motto is 'Constrain, conserve and be consistent' which brings us to another instance of a self-fulfilling prophecy. This is my mother's theory, to do her credit. She says naturally a motto does not order you to follow it, but if you live with it, live under it as it were, you get to be the way it tells you that you are.

'Have you anything on *Lear*?' I asked Patrick.

'Of course. Yes, plenty,' he said. He has my mother's rather classy voice, her thin dark hair. He's a year or so older than her though. He claims he understands her mind and she claims to understand the way his works, although to me they don't seem close. They seem quite uptight in their dealings with each other on the whole. Perhaps there is a subtext of incest somewhere. And both have fairly fucked up sex lives anyway.

'How's everything?' he said.

'Oh fine,' I said, lying in my teeth, but reminding myself that I'd have to get round to the gritty topic before long.

7

I walked along the literature section, pulling some books out and looking at them, turning pages and re-turning them. I felt him watching me. He's never quite forgiven me for sucking lollies in his shop and spilling raspberry-flavoured juice on a first edition of something or other when I was twelve or so.

'Try . . . L. C. Knights,' he said, still watching me. I felt his gaze kind of boring into the back of my neck.

'You've had your hair cut, haven't you?' he said.

'Some weeks ago,' I said, not wishing to frighten him off by reminding him that he'd commented on my short style at least ten times recently. I think he possibly fancies me or fantasises over me. I've heard him talk with Henry about schoolgirl fantasies they have, the gymslip fetish. Although I never wore a gymslip since our uniform up to sixth-form college was a pleated skirt. I wore mine shortish and he was always staring at my thighs.

'There's nothing to make up for reading round the topic, is there?' Patrick said. He seems to think I'm very academic like he was, and that I'll go to Oxford or wherever it was he went. He's often been on about how my mother should have gone to university because she's got what is called an objective mind like he has or is supposed to have. My mother went to a college of education but never became a teacher on account of getting married to my father at an early age, for a variety of reasons she never goes into with her usual accuracy.

'I am dozens of essays behind,' I said to Patrick to show him that I am not dedicated to the world of study in the way he is. 'Which is a sod,' I said.

But at the sound of the word 'essay' Patrick's eyes lit up. He stood looking down across the park, puffing at his pipe, asking questions, seeing himself no doubt as the highly literate guru offering his wisdom to the young upcoming brain of Britain.

Poor Patrick though, we often say; he hasn't got much going for him, Henry and my mother say, what with having lost his first wife to a lecturer and having pursued several girls recently without success. And having given up the academic life because he couldn't seem to get round to finishing the thesis which would have given him a PhD. There is a strand in all the Leadbetters, or said to be in all the Leadbetters, which comes from somebody called Lazenby, of laziness. All mythical of course, although my mother argues that it could be scientific, something in the genes perhaps, a kind of metabolic apathy.

'Did you say parenthood, in *Lear*?' he said. He was standing in between the literature and history shelves and fairly close to me. I rather stared back at him and so he wandered back towards the window with his back to me.

'I can't remember now,' I said, 'and anyway . . . ' His back view at the window with the light behind: a little man with a bald patch like a monk's bald patch, a lonely man perhaps, my mother thinks, a rather selfish man she says or used to say, or self-absorbed because of living on his own these past five years or so. And if she's right and he was really so self-absorbed, I was thinking that he wasn't going to be much use to me for what I'd come about.

The only other person to whom I'd spoken on all this was Jane. At lunchtime yesterday. I meet her these days at this cocktail bar in town, which she says is the in-place for people in the Rugby Club and Young Conservatives.

I have forgiven her this lapse of taste because the cocktails are delicious, the one I usually have is called a Pina Colada and stuffed with lumps of things like cherries, pineapple, bits of coconut. At lunchtime the place is full of businessmen and Jane is, after all, a kind of business person now and it is fair enough that she has to fit in with the life she leads these days since picking up with Geoff who's hoping for a Hampshire trial.

'Oh Petra, no!' said Jane in her usual tone of wonderment. 'How terrible! Your mother will be so upset!'

'You could say that,' I said.

She's very easy to impress. That's been the case with Jane ever since first year of middle school when I came late to join the class and really needed her. And she is loyal. I think that loyalty really is a quality or an almost abstract entity. I feel on firm ground when I speak of loyalty, just as I feel on firm ground when I am with Jane.

'I mean I know that Henry has been – well – not always very nice to you, but still I don't suppose you'd want him dead or anything like that.'

I've said already that she's had her brushes with male violence in the shape of the brandished banister from her father who is in local government but a most uncivil servant frequently at home. But Jane, who is big and blonde with something of a shining innocence about her, describes such incidents but never seems to aim to draw conclusions from them.

'At least my father's hardly ever late coming home,' she said. 'Five minutes is quite rare for him. Two weeks! Has Henry really been away two weeks?'

'Well, some of it he was supposed to be away,' I said and rather wished I hadn't started on the Henry thing. The muzak in the cocktail bar was cheerful, bouncy and well recorded, and the place was rich, all red and plush and in a shiny bulbous thirties style. A spurious optimism was seeping into me along with the Pina Colada.

Jane's voice is musical as well. It has a singsong tone. 'You'll have to go to the police,' she said.

The sandwiches were good as well. Smoked salmon; she had bought me one. Expensive, but she earns a lot at Pevensey's and gets things at cost price like scents, Tampax, shampoos and eyeshadows.

'What does your mother say?'

I speared a cherry, ate it, then a piece of pineapple, because, although the sandwich had been quite sustaining, I was ravenous. My mother's cooking has been minimal these last two weeks, consisting of warmed-up freezer meals and things that Daisy particularly likes like fish fingers, and although I've said I'd cook some evenings, she doesn't seem to welcome it that much.

10

'We haven't really talked about it properly,' I said.

'There is amnesia, you know,' said Jane. 'I read about this man who disappeared for months and months and was found working on this farm, believing he was someone else. Amnesia is quite a well-known clinical condition.'

I speared and ate a square of pineapple and then another square of pineapple and tried to think of Henry on a farm believing he was someone else and couldn't think of Henry thinking he was anyone but Henry Harrison.

'It can come on quite suddenly,' said Jane. 'It can come on very suddenly, because of strain, I think. It's an escape, you see. The person doesn't like their life, but is too good to walk out of their life and family. We talked about it once in human biology I think.' She took a drink of Campari at the thought of her failure at O Level. Although I'm sure her present life-style is some compensation for that disturbing memory.

I sucked the last of the Colada into a straw, which made a gurgling farting sound, although this was drowned by the muzak which was a number from a Busby Berkeley movie which I'd seen on TV with Henry once. The vision came of Henry pulling my mother by the hand as she came into the room and dancing around with her.

'I'm not suggesting that your family . . .' said Jane.

'Amnesiacs can't do something totally out of character, you mean?' I said and wondered how you could define his character. My mother once said that Henry moved like God in mysterious ways. I thought that was quite witty of her at the time, but have heard it said of other people since, so must assume it was not original.

'He's blown,' I said to Patrick in the shop today.

He wasn't listening at first, still standing with his back to me and lost in thought and rising pipe smoke and in speculation possibly on spring, the park and the traffic passing up the Portsmouth Road into the main street.

It would be easier to leave things unsaid since he hadn't

heard, but it would niggle me and in the end I'd have to come back and repeat the message. I had given Henry days and days to ring up, write, break cover, surface, and I'd checked the post, my mother's desk and earholed phone calls whenever possible. But each day she looked worse, more miserable, more choked, more inarticulate.

'He's blown, bunked off, disappeared,' I said, and Patrick, with his hands stuffed into the pockets of his cardigan, which he kept on twisting and stretching, turned round in a flash. His pipe fell out of his mouth and ash scattered down his front. But he caught the pipe in one hand which he seemed to have burnt and kept on shaking in the air thereafter.

'Oh come on, Petra! Henry disappeared!' He looked as incredulous as I'd expected that he would. He looked embarrassed too. His great brain, quick brain had perceived that here was something very personal and to do with someone purported to be close to him and in which he'd have to be involved.

I went on looking at pages of this book on Thomas Hardy and said: 'I mean he didn't come back from British Interiors Biennial.'

He blinked, still brushing hot pipe ash off his cardigan: 'I saw your mother yesterday. She didn't say . . . she didn't seem . . .'

'She wouldn't say. It hasn't been acknowledged.'

'And Daisy; she was perfectly all right.'

'She's always perfectly all right. She's protected from anything that isn't perfectly all right.'

He plunged his hands into the pockets of his trousers and, with head down, began to pace around the outer shelves, looking at the floor, putting one foot carefully in front of the other as if he was treading the white line to have his reflexes tested for alcohol.

'Don't tell her that I told you though,' I said. 'Just go in, couldn't you, and see if she reveals or needs to talk or anything.'

12

I suppose it isn't until you've done a thing you've planned to do that you realise just how useless it was doing it. Patrick can't even keep himself together. He was not the man for coming to in times of trouble. His old suede shoes were going where the uppers were coming away from the soles and showing the shape of his feet. Seeing someone quite so messy makes you realise just how easy it is to go downhill. Although he's not bad looking in a way and I used to think him fairly admirable.

Henry once said that the trouble with people like the Leadbetters is that, although they are a gloomy bunch, they can't deal with the gunge of life, and here was Patrick acting true to form. But who else in the family could I have gone to for advice? Not Uncle Gerald certainly – he is too dim. Not Mavis, Gerald's wife, because she'd rush round organising and make us go to the police, as well as generally sigh or else condemn outright. At any rate they wouldn't understand. While Patrick might, I hoped.

Although it must be said that he has cause for feeling less than total warmth towards Henry, since in the case of girls they usually prefer Henry to him.

'I just thought you ought to know,' I said and left.

'I'll think about it anyway,' I heard him say as I ran downstairs and cursed him for being so like my mother in that he thinks that the answer to all things can be found by thinking. She's always saying 'I'll think about it' as if that's bound to bring the solution.

She told me once that when I was very small I had this illness, gastro-enteritis, and was on the brink of death and so on and wouldn't take the medicine or drink anything. She sat and thought and held me. She described the way I was like a tiny bag of bones, thin and feverish, so hot that the teaspoon she was offering me seemed to conduct the heat into her fingers. Then she thought about a plastic spoon which would be soft and easier for my mouth. So she found this plastic spoon – and magic – I was well again. She claimed that she had 'thought me into being better', and thought she had made

13

me better by her thoughts. I've never questioned the story but it occurs to me that most medicines are supplied with plastic spoons already. She doesn't reminisce about my early childhood very much as a rule.

I wheeled my bike along the pavement which is set above the road with white railings at its edge and felt the wind blowing up towards me from the southwest, encouraging me to keep away from college this afternoon, although the thought of catching up on essays was not in my mind by any means. But I was hungry so I'd have to go home briefly.

When Henry's there I can't go in through our shop. I shouldn't say *our* shop perhaps. The name above the door is Harrison – and that's not mine. When Henry's there you know he's there, simply by standing in the shop and testing for his presence. That sounds silly maybe, but it is a fact. I am not over-sensitive. In fact he's always or often said I am not sensitive at all, but Henry's presence is so vibrant that it fills the space. It can be sensed.

The space is elegant: door-fittings of polished brass; doorframe, oak. Above my head as I walk into the high part of the shop are hangings: patchwork quilts, wallhangings, some from India embroidered with tiny mirrors which catch the spotlights further into the shop. Also wallhangings of softer materials which my mother makes. All these hang like sumptuous washing, swaying slowly as the door is shut.

Maybe I could tell by the way my mother stood by the cash desk speaking to a customer, that Henry wasn't back. Perhaps the way she held her shoulders tense? Although her hair was properly held in check by pins this afternoon and she was wearing her Laura Ashley green check top and skirt which suits her reasonably well. And she had done the flowers; new daffodils, narcissi with some sticky chestnut buds on the low round brass table in the centre of the shop.

My mother didn't acknowledge my presence, but she knew that I was there. She went on listening to the tweedy woman customer reading out a list of wedding presents by the till. As if

14

listening intently, but she wouldn't have been listening. She can pretend intense interest most convincingly. But she would have seen me slipping through the shop and up the spiral staircase where they keep the oriental carpets and soft furnishings. She would have known that I stood there watching her and listening. I saw the tweedy woman follow her across the shop towards the corner full of pottery. I heard the woman's raucous county voice and saw my mother lift a pot and hold it to the light and the woman looking at my mother's face more than at the pot.

I went on through the door into the flat and along the corridor and checked all rooms for any signs of Henry, such as the fur-lined yellow jacket which he must have taken with him. I checked their bedroom for his overnight bag or for him or for the smell of him. Then went into the kitchen where the sun was pouring in and grabbed some cheese, an apple and some orange juice. Then I opened up the door out onto the steps down into the back yard. And sat there, eating, looking at the tubs of daffodils, the shed, the twiggy trees in our garden and in other people's gardens, sat there hearing sounds of birds close to and busy people on the edge of town and traffic on the road behind.

But still just heard the shop bell go as the customer left; and tiptoed back along the corridor, back into the upper floor above the spiral stairs and stood there, practised in my silent listening and heard her telephoning once again, enquiringly. She would be crossing names off her list as she drew yet another blank. It was the usual thing.

TWO

It's a pity that Henry and Mr Forbes never really met because they have a lot in common. But Henry never wanted to know anything about Forbes or what Forbes said and would start yawning the moment I ever mentioned his name or referred to any discussions we'd had in class. The moment I'd start to say 'Mr Forbes thinks . . .' or 'Mr Forbes said . . .' Henry would put his hand over his mouth in a pretend yawn and cross his eyes. Like Mr Forbes does when I go on about theories of mine in class about people and books and the world and that.

Henry's dislike of Forbes began when they met in town one day. I hardly ever walk with Henry into town, but if he's going in that direction and so am I, it's silly to walk on different sides of the street. So once, this day about a year ago, I was walking with him. Although he says I don't walk *with* people. He says I walk alongside them, but not with them. He says I behave as if I am conducting people. Anyway we were walking more or less beside each other or parallel to each other and Mr Forbes was coming towards us, pushing his older kid in a push-chair. His only kid at that time in fact. I suppose, like Jane was saying yesterday, they'll have to get a double push-chair for the twins. Anyway this must have been about a year ago and I said 'Hullo' to Forbes and he stopped and seemed to want me to look at the baby, shoving the push-chair to and fro under my nose as if it was a display or something, so I stopped and Henry slowed down as well, and I said quick as a flash: 'Mr Forbes, this is my stepfather,' and Henry looked like he could murder me for introducing him to any friend of mine at all, but smiled his kill-you-with-politeness smile, which Mr Forbes took to be a genuine friendly welcoming grin. Like customers do.

But when customers have left the shop, and if they haven't bought anything but look like they could have afforded to buy something, Henry puts his two fingers up and says 'And the best of luck!' He even does that sometimes when they *have* bought something. Some people think he's a bit like Basil Fawlty, offering a service but despising those who want to make use of it.

On this day on the pavement outside the tobacconist's Forbes must have missed the second part of my introduction, viz. the stepfather bit. It was a fairly windy day and my words may have got blown away. Unfortunate, that. Forbes put out his hand – rather, he had to get his hands sorted out by changing them on the push-chair handle because his right hand was holding it at the time. So, having shifted hands, he shot his right one out with a cheerful 'Oh hullo, Mr Frobisher' and Henry's grin got even more homicidal or suicidal and he took three steps back.

So I said as plainly as I could: 'No, he isn't Mr Frobisher actually,' and Henry said: 'Well, never mind and I must rush,' or words to that effect and tore into the tobacconist's for the cigarettes he'd come out to get. Though I'd have got them for him if he'd asked, but he never wants to be obligated.

So that was the nearest they've been to meeting properly, which is a pity because they are in a sense each other's idea of a good person. Both hard workers, both living by their intelligences, both fond of kids and interested in ideas. Both funny with it, making people laugh a lot. Both like a drink and are not purist in their attitudes, i.e. both like ordinary pleasurable things like ice cream or a pint of beer and do not reject what they'd call pop culture totally, although deploring areas of it.

'Did I say something?' said Forbes that time, looking somewhat surprised when Henry dashed into the tobacconist's. One difference is that Forbes doesn't smoke and Henry's on thirty a day but is pretty healthy with it most of the time.

'Oh no, it wasn't you,' I said. 'He does a lot of that,' I said. 'Running away from people. Basically, he feels trapped easily I think.'

Another thing they have in common is that they both disapprove of people saying 'basically'. Henry reacts violently against it and Mr Forbes explains it is what he calls a 'nothing' word and you might just as well clear your throat instead or say 'er'.

Mr Forbes is better at explaining why he doesn't approve of certain words, etc. Henry reacts. He doesn't go in for explanations or self-justifications. Henry's kind of what you might call raw in many ways. When you ask Henry to explain something or, if you dare, try to explain something to him, he's quite likely to say 'There is no answer to that' or sometimes even 'Arseholes to that'. His language is probably what a lot of people would think of as filthy, but he is so clean in himself and so kind of private about bodily functions and that, that his language never seems shocking. Not to me at any rate, though obviously I'm used to it.

When I told Mr Forbes about Henry feeling easily trapped, he said 'Well, don't we all?' but at the time he, Mr Forbes, seemed more concerned in getting me to admire the baby, whom you could hardly see so muffled up was it in quilted covers and a hood, its cheeks a pounding bright red which Mr Forbes explained was caused by teething.

But I don't think he feels easily trapped. Not Mr Forbes. Nor is he, like Henry is, frightened of women as well as loving to them. In fact today when we were discussing *Lear* again, he more or less convincingly claimed that he wasn't. Frightened of women, I mean.

18

The essay topic he was setting was going to be something like: 'Pernicious daughters. Do you agree?' and he made us read the bit in *Lear* where Albany says to Goneril that he'd like to tear her flesh apart, or words to that effect. 'Proper deformity seems not in the fiend so horrid as in woman.' That bit.

'It's a proper ding dong doodle of a castigation, isn't it?' said Forbes when we'd read that speech.

'He was probably frightened of her, I think,' I said. 'A lot of men are frightened of women.'

'Oh you think that, do you?' he said. He seemed really genuinely surprised. 'Surely in this case the man's rage was justifiable. We don't have to bring the sex war into this, do we?'

'I wasn't trying to bring the sex war into it,' I said. 'I was only saying that he might just get angry not because of her double-dealing or whatever, but because of being frightened of her.'

Then Liz pointed out that Albany was saying that it was worse if women were evil than if men were evil, which implied that only men were entitled to be evil and not women, as if people expected men to be evil and women good, and if that wasn't a sexist attitude then what was? Like I said, she hardly ever talks in class except when there are sexist issues at stake.

The boys, although none of them as individuals are that dim or yobby, jeered and leaned back laughing, tipping their chairs.

'And are you saying that all these lads are laughing because they are frightened?' Mr Forbes asked both Liz and me.

The other girls aren't tuned in to twigging sexist remarks yet and were getting fed up too, so the discussion more or less ended there. Tracey was saying could she be told exactly what the essay topic was because there were some people who did want to get work done and handed in.

'Yes, Tracey. Of course, Tracey', said Forbes. 'It never ceases to amaze me that those most keen to get the essay topics down tend to turn in the least stimulating essays. Never mind . . . yes, certainly . . . I'm only here to serve your zest for work of course . . .' and went on quite a bit sort of digging at her.

19

'Would that your demands for work were equalled by the standard of your thought...' and looked out of the window in a saddish and disparaging way.

Tracey went all sulky then, though why she should mind about being told she is unthinking I can't imagine. She's only bothered about getting essays in on time and making her hair all frizzy. On the way out afterwards, she was still fuming and saying that she wished she'd joined the other English set who had Miss Jameson who wasn't cynical and that set had got much further through the syllabus. Nor were there so many argumentative people in that set.

'Why don't you join it then?' I said.

'There's some people,' Tracey said, turning back to sneer at me, 'some people won't get kept in any set I've heard.'

'So?' I said.

'I've seen Forbes has got it marked on the register that you haven't done any essays, not since last October. Some people might be for the chop or for a warning from the Principal...'

'Well, anyway,' said Susan. 'He wouldn't dare do anything, would he, being as he would be frightened of you anyway, if you consider yourself female, that is.'

'And someone's Daddy is going to pay for her to go to college in America,' said Tracey, 'isn't he, if he's not scared of her?'

'They'll be dead scared of her in America,' said Susan, toadying along not very originally.

'And the best of luck to you!' I said, but under my breath said 'Arseholes to the lot of you.'

The college I might go to – that is true: my father made the offer in the summer just as I was leaving Colorado where he lives now; Denver, Colorado where he teaches business studies. Not that I suppose I'd take the offer up unless I failed my A Levels or got kicked out of college for not doing essays or whatever. Or really got pissed off with everything.

I kept on thinking arseholes to the lot of them and went to ride my horse instead of going back for General Studies in the afternoon. King's Radlett is the real place, the Leadbetter domain, the rolling acres where I gallop. I mounted Troy and headed out towards the chestnut avenue.

Troy is bulky, black, heavy and broad at the withers. He's a bit splay-hooved, i.e. his hooves are massive, verging on the carthorse scale and his canter is wild, off true. His neck is thick with a touch of Morgan horse. His pedigree is far from immaculate, but full of good ingredients. I hardly ever ride him now, so he wasn't in good condition, panting like hell and I had to whack him to get him to shift himself along the avenue and towards the monument.

The place was deserted. It's more fun riding there on Saturdays when people park their cars on the green and buy ice creams and walk along the chestnut avenue. Then I get going on Troy, leaning forward in my crash helmet, throwing up clods of turf at them from his pounding hooves.

My main reason for going there this afternoon was need of cash. I remembered that Uncle Gerald owed me £18.50 for some tough work humping sacks of fertiliser in the cold some weeks ago, and while there I took the chance to exercise poor old neglected Troy. And it helped to work my anger out. Tracey and Susan and the rest of their lot could take a running jump up their mini-kilts as far as I was concerned.

'Oh, horse-riding, is it?' Tracey said once. 'Well – you know what they say . . . makes up for all sorts, doesn't it?'

Henry once made the same suggestion, although he knows bloody well I've never been that short of sex. Not in the past at any rate. He knew, for instance, about Giles, my cousin, and about Kevin. And anyway I don't suppose any girl ever had an orgasm on horseback. Maybe after dismounting as in the past with Giles in hedges round about; in stables, which I recall with some degree of hankering these days.

No, pleasure in riding is more to do with speed, with being in control, which is sometimes worth the tedious business of grooming and feeding. Still worth it sometimes, though for ages now, I've been thinking of selling Troy and spoken frequently of selling him.

My mother doesn't seem to want me to part with him. 'No, don't! Not yet,' she says as if he is some precious relic from the past, and I say 'Why?' and she says 'Don't' and won't explain. Once, after such a conversation, she offered to drive me up to the village to save me cycling. I used to think she thought that riding kept me out of sexual danger, but now I reckon it was more to do with keeping me out of Henry's way, because it was pretty certain Henry wouldn't come near Troy – or rather me on Troy. And anyway, I presume my mother knows I'm on the pill, since she shows a basic lack of interest in my sex life.

I got the horse when I was eleven; he was huge and a pretty silly idea of my mother's at the time. Now I'm quite a bit too big for him, although when people are in the avenue, they turn impressed and stand well back. The monument, when you get to it, is pinkish brick to match the Manor and has a carved stone ball on top. There's a photograph of me which my father took when I was four. I'm sitting on the monument in red shorts, clutching it as if trying to break it between my knees.

OK, so I've grown out of most of the pleasures of riding now, but there's still the listening to the hooves on soft, damp ground, the flashing past of the chestnut trees, Troy's pricked ears, the patchwork fields, the well-timed slowing down before a jump, even sometimes the fantasies (non-sexual) that I am being filmed, perhaps as a hussar of the Light Brigade, charging head down against terrific odds. Great movie, that.

Last summer in Colorado my father paid for me to rent an appaloosa horse and the rent included buckskins and boots; I felt like Eastwood or Wayne in *True Grit*, great ace old movie that, a favourite. Henry's favourite movie is not to do with horses at all: it's *Casablanca* probably, but he goes moony and nostalgic about a different movie every week.

When Troy moves well I feel like a cossack taking in the distance of the steppes *à la* Zhivago. In the first photograph Henry took of me I look a bit like Julie Christie, someone said. Then, when Troy's obedient, I do the *haute école* bit slowly round the paddock, making him prance and buck and rear. I

22

remember the look in Henry's eyes the first time he came close when Troy reared up. At that time no one thought I'd manage him – Troy, I mean.

So today there I was at the monument, looking down the spur of hill towards the south and seeing, more or less, the whole of Hampshire spread before me. Should make Leadbetters feel good. But why was it, I was wondering, that suddenly everyone was interested in Henry's whereabouts? Like Patrick had stopped me on the way to school this morning to ask if Henry was back. And now my other uncle, Gerald, had been quizzing me, asking me to give Henry a message. He, Gerald, is selling some cottages and wants Henry's advice on doing them up.

'OK,' I said to Gerald. 'I'll give him the message – Henry, I mean.'

'Right-ho,' he said and I got on Troy. Luckily anyone can run rings round Gerald, although he's had to turn himself into something of a businessman to keep the place together. Henry, incidentally, sees him as effete, but basically harmless. Harmless, I mean.

From the monument you see not only southern Hampshire but further west to the New Forest and on clear days into Dorset, over Bournemouth and beyond and feel like all the Gulf Stream air is coming into your lungs across Cornish cliffs. I reined Troy in. The Leadbetters, the lot of them, have gone commercial now, as Patrick says, lighting his pipe. They've kicked their heritage, their shameful heritage, and are working for their livings now. But Henry often argues that, since they owned it all to start with, they had it made, whereas he, a self-made man, as he tends to state with boring regularity, has nothing but his energy. 'We couldn't have given it away, could we?' says Patrick in their arguments. 'We didn't have a proper revolution here. We've tried to live up to some socialist ideal. At least I have and so has Alison,' he says, defending my mother as well, and he continues, with equally boring regularity, to claim that he has rejected what he calls patrician qual-

23

ities, has never given orders to anyone and was miserable at public school to boot. 'Whereas you,' he says to Henry, 'like giving orders, don't you?' Then, before Henry boils up and seethes over, Patrick adds that Henry can't argue from a working-class standpoint because his mother was in show business. Henry says: 'But the downmarket end of show business – in the chorus line.'

'Nevertheless show business,' Patrick says, 'which is a truly classless place to be.'

Henry painted a landscape view from the monument, but never finished it because he said he felt uncomfortable sitting there, as if he had become a Leadbetter or a tourist. He doesn't want to be either.

Last time he came here, there was this row. My birthday it was. A picnic it was. So I got away from them all and saddled Troy and then there was this thunderstorm. I didn't ride along the chestnut avenue that time, but behind the Manor, round the edge of Gerald's raspberry fields and on up north towards the beacon where there is this hollow in the ground where I sheltered.

The row wasn't between Patrick and Henry that time and was much, much more than an argument. The thunderstorm: I could hear it coming, see the lightning, time the gap between the lightning and the thunder on my watch. An arc of clouds was closing in, looming from all sides as if intent on getting me, as if I was the centre they were aiming at or focusing upon. The world was negative, all black, and everything that was not black was white, dead white. My riding mac looked almost silver.

Thunder does not clap. It booms, reverberates and fills your ears and yet it's soft; you're under it. The bang begins and grows and grows and dies away. My hands looked luminous.

Curled in the hollow so that the lightning could dance around the edge, but wouldn't come down into it, I knew it wouldn't come down into it. Troy of course was going absolutely loony, tethered to a bush, freaking out, doing his nut.

The hollow is like a bomb crater from some war or other. It

is steep and scattered with chalk stones. They were like pearls or opals when the lightning flashed.

The lightning found where it was going to. The clouds closed over completely. Nothing was coming nearer me, so I stood up, knowing this and climbed up to the edge and thought; if I stand here and stand up in this thunderstorm, I know I'll be all right. Like someone, almost like someone asking to make sure that I stayed all right. Almost like having a bargain made with me.

With me and Troy perhaps.

'All well?' said Gerald as I was unsaddling today.

'Yes, fine,' I said.

'Your mother well?'

'Yes, very well.' I kept my head down, pressing into Troy.

He hovered, seeming to want to say more, but went away in the end. He said he had some early newborn lambs to feed, but I guessed what he had been wanting to say. He wants the paddock, doesn't he, to grow more raspberries in and wants me to move Troy or sell Troy or simply get rid of Troy. I pay him for the rent of the paddock, don't I? And for hay.

Troy is a hunk, a chunk of life. He's massive in the loosebox where I rub him down, not talking to him, but surmising, as I often do, what he weighs, but not for the reasons of the meat on him. Particularly not for the reasons of the meat on him. When I first had him, my head came up to the top of his withers and I used to have to struggle to get the saddle on him, almost throwing it across his fat back. No, it wasn't fat. It was and is all muscle. Muscle under his rippling glossy coat, so where you pat him there is this satisfactory solid sound. His mane grows thick like clumps of spring grass bursting upwards from embedded roots. The bones of his head, the ruler-straight nosebone ending in the soft skin round his muzzle, the silky material of his ears and the warmth of the inside of these, the thumping of his heart if you bend and listen, the amazing speculation on the thought of the guts of Troy, the weight-

25

lifting exercise of raising a hoof against his will, the horizontal extent of the underneath of Troy, the removal of the blanket and the clopping walk to lead him back by halter along the track to the paddock where the rooks are always cawing in the elm trees and there is the slope down to the stream.

No other Leadbetters are into horses any more. Gerald's into sheep and raspberries, Patrick is definitely anti-equestrian and my mother once said that not being interested in horses was, she sometimes thought, the only thing she had in common with my father.

From the paddock across the stream is Rad Cottage where we lived until Henry arrived and my father left. Rather my father left and Henry arrived. It's not a cottage, more of a long house and made of stone, not brick, stretching sideways on to the stream and there's a footbridge you can reach it by. I guess it will be one of the properties Gerald will sell this year.

From the paddock you can see the side of it, the outbuildings where Gerald's wife, Mavis, keeps doves. You see the doves flapping on the far side of the willow trees which line the bank that side. The footbridge is a narrow one and slippery with moss. I used to cross it in wellingtons and later in riding boots. Also I used to see Henry and my mother walking hand in hand on the far side of the willows. Before he came to live with us, that was. When people knew but didn't know and didn't say anything, except that my mother had said she was going to be away that day.

'Come on. Come on!' I was calling to Daisy in the park this evening. 'What time is it?' she said. She seemed to think we had gone there to meet Henry off the London train.

'Twilight,' I said.

'That isn't a time,' she said.

'Then lighting-up time,' I said as the street lights came on, but she'd shot ahead of me up the hill on this short and fairly springy grass towards the wood, beyond which is the station. We'd come up between the two converging rows of fat round conifers. The trees looked black in the half light.

'Half light, half light, half dark, half dark,' she was calling out ahead of me. She has this irritating habit of saying everything twice, but she is a pretty bright kid, having learned to speak grammatically at an exceptionally early age. At two she sat in our posh lounge saying 'Please switch the television on, Petra. I want to watch *John Craven's Newsround*.' She did watch it too and has always been very well informed.

'Wait, Daisy!'

At the top of the hill the conifers converge and there's this single thick round tree. She was cavorting around it in her thick white sweater and her winter kilt. As well as having Henry's incredibly long legs, she is altogether a very narrow shape with dark thin hair like my mother's and Patrick's, dead straight to her shoulders.

'Half light, half dark and we're half sisters.'

I looked back down at the lit-up shop, which had just closed. I could see Patrick's shape and my mother's shape, still talking they were and I'd have to keep Daisy out for a few minutes longer.

'Do you think Daddy will . . .?' she began to say.

'Knock knock,' I said. She's always collecting knock knock jokes.

People were walking past us up and over the hill on the tarmac towards the station and other people would soon be walking away from it after coming off the train.

'Who's there?' she said.

Silhouettes of people moving and dogs in the park, scurrying nose-down in search of something, people letting them off leads, dogs throwing themselves sideways, curving their spines in the air to catch a ball.

'Avenue,' I said, not being able to think of a better one.

'Avenue who?'

'Avenue heard this one before?'

It was dead still all around us suddenly as though everyone had stopped moving.

27

'Weedy weedy that old thing,' said Daisy.

'Weedy weedy yourself.'

It was three-quarters night and one-quarter day now and we sat on a bench, me smoking, wanting to think, telling Daisy not to talk so we might hear the moment when the blackbirds stopped their twittering. A train sounded its double note in the distance.

'Do you think . . .?' she began to say again.

'Hey, listen . . .' I said, not exactly sure what I was asking her to listen to. She wriggled on the bench and swung her legs. She is a hyperactive child, or nearly hyperactive like I'd been. My mother hasn't had much luck with kids that way.

'What am I listening to?'

'Keep listening.'

I was thinking how, if Henry happened to come up from the station in this nearly dark, how we'd recognise him first by his hair which is fair going white and thick with it. It might be either fair or white at a distance. If we have to describe him as a missing person, that might be useful.

'I can't hear anything,' Daisy whispered.

So I told her how I sometimes think about twilight, that it could be dawn, that if you sit in the park or walk in the park or anywhere outside in a certain light, you wonder how you know whether it is the end of the day or the beginning of it.

'But it's scary, isn't it?' Her voice is weird, sometimes low and fruity, but when she panics it begins to swoop up like a soprano. 'It's dead scary,' she repeated, 'like you once said there were things you couldn't see or hear or smell but were always there.'

'I never said anything of the kind,' I hissed.

'You did. You said there were people you couldn't see or hear or smell looking after you like Mrs Thatcher and the Queen and the Prince of Wales have people like private detectives following them, protecting them . . .'

'I don't know what you're on about,' I said. 'You're loony, you!'

28

Sometimes I can shut her up by rolling her on the grass and fighting her, although these fights are never proper fights like I used to have with Giles years ago and like Jane says she had with her older sisters. My fights with Daisy are only half fights: half sisters' half fights. Daisy's screeching must have drowned the nearer sound of the London train, but I went on holding her down on the grass, which wasn't all that damp, and told her, clenching my teeth at her: 'There is nothing in existence which you can't see or smell or hear.'

'I am not loony,' she was yelling all the time I held her there. 'You're the loony one. You told me all those things. You did. You did.'

Seven-eighths night and one-eighth day and we were on our feet again and near the wood and this black dog shot towards us, leaping on us, prancing around us on its hind legs with its front paws up. Taller than Daisy it was as it leaped, higher than my head sometimes.

'Get it away from me,' she howled. She was up on a park bench now, dancing up and down in her navy blue kneesocks. 'If Daddy comes, that dog will send him bananas, totally bananas.'

I got the dog by its collar, dragging it away from her. It was pulling against me, growling, but only in play. It's never bitten me. It's a mongrel – half labrador–half sheep dog probably and not a bad dog, though naturally it senses when people don't like dogs.

Daisy was calling out from the bench: 'Where are you, Petra? Don't leave me here. Don't desert me. Oh, please don't! They'll get me, won't they?' Only her white knees were visible and I was some way from her.

'They'll get me. You said people got people and only you knew how to keep them away.'

I found this stick and threw it for the dog. The stick flew from my hands up into what was total darkness now and vanished. Then I heard it crash against the trees at the edge of the wood. The dog dashed after it.

'I want to go home now,' Daisy called as the dog came bolting back with the stick in its mouth, and I held it again, the dog I mean – at a distance though – to keep its face and foul breath away from me and made it sit beside the single conifer, saying 'Stay!' and backed away from it, Daisy calling out still. Yes, I could see the dog staying, only see its white teeth now, but could hear its desperate whining still.

I suppose it isn't Daisy's fault that she can't deal with animals on account of Henry not liking to have them in the house. Then I shouted to her to wait for me and she stood at the bottom where the street lights are.

My father had a dog at Rad Cottage, a spaniel called Noggin, which he took with him. But Noggin died and now he has two alsatians, or German shepherds, as he calls them.

I was thinking of those dogs, thinking of my father I suppose, thinking of the Colorado thing again this evening when walking back along the road with Patrick later, wondering as well if the black dog was still there beside the conifer. Patrick was saying that my mother wouldn't talk to him about the thing I'd told him yesterday.

'Well, since she won't talk to me about it either, that's it, isn't it?' I said.

'Do you know anything?' he said.

'Of course I don't know anything,' I said.

'I have a theory,' he was saying, shambling along beside me with his hands in the pockets of his tatty old parka jacket. 'I have a theory that, as often as people go towards things – they go away from them.' But he was saying this cunningly, pretending that he was just airing views rather than questioning.

'Oh really!' I was saying.

'Only a theory,' he was saying.

Patrick was enjoying himself. He was expressing what Mr Forbes would call Schadenfreude, which is what people have when they enjoy other people's misfortunes. Well, that's what Forbes says it is anyway. 'A theory worth exploring,' Patrick went on. 'Possibly . . .'

I began to feel angry again like I had this morning. I wasn't going to show him though. 'Cheers, goodbye,' I said and crossed the road back into the park. The dog had gone and it was dead quiet everywhere. Think of something else, I told myself, but the only idea that occurred to me was that there was a thing which you could neither smell nor see nor hear, but which could kill you, namely radiation.

Arseholes, I was thinking, knowing Patrick would keep on at me, asking me again about the Henry thing, keep on keeping on about the Henry thing, keep on like he does when solving crosswords every day, keep on arseholing about what started it and how I'd have to get my head right and my story right.

THREE

It's always been hard coming home from my father's place in Denver, Colorado where he lives. Not because I much mind leaving him or my stepmother, but because I come home high with jetlag and with bursting to talk about what I've been doing in America and no one at home really wants to hear. I mean my mother pretends she does and maybe is actually fairly interested, but there's always the subtext that she's likely to resent the goodies I get there – not so much material objects and clothes, but more things like a superb sun tan and stories of mountains and magnificent sights and scenery and weird, weird people. But because of what she might be thinking I have to kind of hold back on everything, because she could be dead scared that I'll be seduced and leave and want to go and live there. It's possible that she feels like that. Maybe in some ways she'd be relieved if I did. I am of an age to choose, you see.

But playing safe I've never yet told her about the private college, which, incidentally looks pretty OK from the outside and where you can major in any subject or topic that you choose. Although I must say that I met a girl who'd been there majoring in something like silk embroidery, which seemed pretty daft. She seemed pretty daft herself, but she may have been an exception to the rule.

I don't know what I'd major in, but maybe a few modern languages, a bit about art and that and how to argue interestingly and with force. Which might be asking a lot.

So I came in at Heathrow and the sun was pretty amazing for England and my mother met me. It really was hot and a Sunday and I remember wondering why Daisy hadn't come with her. Not that I minded Daisy not being there since it meant we could talk a bit without screeching interruptions. And my mother kissed me like she always does, kind of formally but you know she means it and is somewhat pleased to see you. And we drove and it went on being hot. The fields, once we got away from the motorway, were all cut corn and dark green trees and the air was such that it made me want to have it brushing against my cheeks as I leaned my face out of the car and I remember trying to work out why the sun here, even though hot, was of a different quality of sun from Colorado sun where it kind of slaughters you – explodes your head if you're not careful.

So we drove with open windows, exchanging news – about my time in Colorado mostly, though I have to play that down a bit since, like I said, she might think that's where I want to be all the time. She did once say that, from my glowing report of it, she could understand why people wanted to be there and thought America was God's Own Country, whereupon I said, carefully, that it wasn't God's Own Country at all really, but what it was lacking I couldn't say precisely, but it seemed to me that people were too positive for my liking. Like people there are never hesitant. Or seldom hesitant.

We were getting near home, getting near fields and hills which were familiar, but had changed since I left in August and had been harvested and that. Maybe the thing about the gentle, rounded English countryside at its best is that it's unspectacularly beautiful while Colorado is all grand and dramatic and enormously high or dead flat.

I kept trying not to talk too much and to ask questions about the holiday in France which they'd had while I was away, but she was on the reticent side about all that, except to say that the weather had been great and they'd all got tanned. She may have been reticent on account of feeling guilty that I hadn't been with them, in fact had almost certainly organised the holiday to coincide with my absence, so there could be no question of my being included in it. Well, that was, as my father says, par for the course. If I go on holiday with them, something always culminates with Henry in the end, however good everyone's intentions are at the start.

Like Henry's crazy about holidays and gets as excited as a kid, even more excited than Daisy does. He goes off and buys beach clothes for everyone and lashings of Ambre Solaire and says he's going to give people the best holiday they've ever had. Then half-way through he decides it is the worst holiday he ever had because people aren't leaping about and clapping their hands with unconfined joy all day every day.

'So France was OK?' I said.

'Yes, fine,' she said and seemed to be searching around for something non-controversial she could say and told me Daisy had learned to swim while there.

'Oh good,' I said. 'About time,' I said. This meant that if I ever went to the sea with them again Daisy wouldn't have to be watched full time, being a reckless kid where water is concerned. Aged two she just waded into the sea till it went over her head and this has always been considered my fault – by Henry at any rate. Although it was me who fished her out.

'She played with some French kids, learned to say "bonjour" and "Mitterrand" and even "Giscard d'Estaing" . . .'

'The villa that you took. What was that like?'

'Idyllic actually,' my mother said. We were coming to the final hills before the town and the grass verges were incredibly dusty. My mother seemed to be slowing down as if she wanted to tell me more before we reached home, kind of wanting to make me feel more part of things again.

'So where's Daisy today?' I said.

'Oh, she stayed to keep Henry company,' my mother said,

and for the last few moments of the journey I went back to talking about Colorado again. Because it is amazing and it kind of gets to you so you have to keep on telling people, like the Ancient Mariner, about the time, say, when you walked down-town in Denver and the skyscrapers sent the sun back into your eyes, because the newest ones are finished in silver colours and brilliant golden glass colours and in between there's a Boeing 747 cruising in the staggering blue sky.

'You went camping, did you?' she said.

'Yes, in the mountains. That was OK. But it wasn't like camping. It was, you know, in the Winnebago, a sort of huge camper.'

I would have gone on to tell her about the day we took the camper up to over ten thousand feet near Mount Evans and Echo Lake and Squaw Pass where the ground we parked in was scattered with shards of mica which glittered like broken glass and when you picked it up you could shred it into layers. I would have gone on to tell her all that, about the altitude and the view down Independence Pass and standing on the conti-nental divide where I'd had my picture taken wearing my Denver Broncos peaked cap which kept the sun off my head and out of my eyes and how on the peaks the snow had already started to fall. I hardly ever tell her things like what was said between me and my father and Laura my stepmother and their friends – unless it was especially silly or naive and would make her laugh. They never say anything really interesting anyway.

'No, France was interesting this year,' my mother said. 'It's very clean and prosperous-feeling, we decided . . .'

Always *we* decided, I was thinking. Always, basically, what Henry thinks, I was thinking. But my mother had got on to this story about how Henry had got over-charged for drinks at a café and had held up two fingers to the waiter and said some-thing like France would never get into the Cup Mondiale – the world cup – and told the waiter where he could put the Entente Cordiale and arseholes to the Common Market and all that.

But in most ways I was still reeling with thoughts of America

35

as we got near home and knowing that, if Henry was around, I'd have to keep these thoughts to myself. I'd have to be careful that I didn't use my temporary American accent in front of him. The last time I came home from Colorado years ago – soon after my father got married out there – Henry accused me of putting on the accent and saying things like 'kind of' and 'you guys' and 'have a nice day' for effect. Which was unfair: you have to talk that way when you're over there or you sound stupid, stick out like a sore thumb and people stop and stare and laugh as if you were something out of an English B movie about the war. It only takes twenty hours or so to get home and you haven't slept that much and you're short of a whole night's sleep usually, and like I said you're kind of high with first-stage jetlag, so it stands to reason you're still talking the way you talked over there. It's the same day for you.

The dumb thing is that Henry is terrifically keen on America and Americana and people there like Hunter S. Thompson and American movies and the standard of their design industry and, if he'd ever been there, he'd just have gone over the top with talking when he got back and it would have been disasters-ville for anyone who didn't sit wide-eyed and drink in every word of it. But he doesn't go in for listening to other people a lot, especially not to me. So there you are, as my mother sometimes says. Or, to use Henry's own phrase: there's no answer to that. All of which is to do with the fact that things are generally insoluble as far as Henry is concerned.

So the beginning was my homecoming and was to do with the presents I'd bought people. Which were as follows: for Daisy a Denver Broncos hat like mine – that is, a blue and orange peaked cap which she'd seen me wearing before and had been asking for. The Broncos are a pretty hot team who nearly reached the Super Bowl one year. For my mother, a flat sailor hat like Jack Nicholson wore in *The Last Detail*, but a large size so she could turn the brim down and use it for a sun hat. In fact I'd got it out of my airline bag and given it to her at the airport, so she was wearing it and looked pretty good in it as we drove. She kept it on as we got out of the car in the yard. It was about 11 a.m. on this Sunday morning and I guessed Daisy and Henry would be in the garden, which they were. There stood Daisy in the gateway to the garden, leaping up and down in her shorts with her legs still pretty brown from holiday.

'I can swim! I can swim!' she was squealing. She jumped at me and put her legs round my waist, fastening them behind me by entwining them at the ankle and gabbling about a hundred things. I shoved the Broncos cap on her head and it fitted and she said it was ace and other typical Daisy adjectives.

For Henry I'd got this printed T shirt. Well, I know you can get printed T shirts anywhere in England now, but this one had a message on it that I hadn't seen over here. The moment I saw it in that T shirt shop in downtown Denver it reminded me of Henry. I'd chosen a white shirt with black printing. It said 'Have a nice day until some bastard louses it up', which is just what happens to a lot of Henry's days. But although at the time of purchase it seemed entirely appropriate to him, I'd had passing doubts since. It would depend of course whether he was having a nice day when I gave it to him.

It felt weird to be home and about to see Henry again. The sun on the cobbles and on the virginia creeper which hangs down the back of the building and which was now bright red; the sudden blast of English birds singing their heads off made me feel even more out of focus than I'd felt before. But he hadn't come out of the garden yet. He maybe wouldn't, I was thinking. Come out of the garden, I mean.

Daisy was still gabbling. If there were bad vibes around she wouldn't probably have noticed them anyway. She's grown up with these variations in the general mood, though I suppose the time will come when she does begin to respond to the old inter-familial aggressions. Being outside in the open air it was difficult to feel how things might be and my Henry-reading antennae were dulled by absence I suppose.

But Daisy had to show him her hat of course and she

swaggered back into the garden. I followed her. I was wearing these white jeans I'd got in Aspen where I went with my father and a red and white singlet suntop and my Broncos cap of course. And my mother was behind me wearing hers. But Henry's present was still in the airline bag which I had in my hand.

Well, he didn't get up. He was lying in his shorts reading the *Observer* colour supplement, I remember, on one of the red canvas loungers. He looks good stripped to the waist and has a fairly flat stomach for his age and not that much hair on his chest. He's not an exhibitionist about his body, but likes to get the sun on it when he can and I suppose Sundays is the only day he can really relax, so I didn't really expect him to get up. But he turned his head and said 'Hullo' and I said 'Hi!' Well, maybe I should have said 'Hullo', that being more English and, in my case, acceptable to him.

My mother, standing near me in her Jack Nicholson hat, said 'Look what I've got!' and he looked up at her and smiled and then went on reading the colour supplement. 'Yes, nice,' he said.

To kiss or not to kiss is always the question. But it wasn't a question any more. I mean – the moment had passed: I would have had to lean down very deliberately to get my face near his.

'Saucy, isn't it?' said my mother about her hat again.

He nodded, not looking up and turned another page of the supplement.

'Don't worry,' I said. 'I've brought you something too.'

'Oh, how nice,' he said, or rather murmured or he may have even said something like 'You shouldn't have', but I always always bring him something and I bloody well always will bring him something even if I have to stuff it down his throat. After all he always brings me something, even if he hands it over with an expression which suggests it's bound to be wrong. In fact it hardly ever is. On the whole he brings me pretty nice things. Last time on a business trip to Germany he brought me a super leather shoulder bag which I always use and was in fact beside me on the grass beside the airline bag that Sunday. While he kept on turning the pages of the colour supplement.

It didn't show too much that he wasn't asking me how I'd got on because Daisy was chattering and my mother was talking and saying she'd go and get us all a drink of juice or whatever.

I sat beside him on the grass – a few feet away from him. The grass felt good and cool and soft and had been mown. I remembered sprinklers in America watering lawns round people's houses the day before as my father drove me to the airport and as I was trying to make conversation before saying goodbye, because although I don't mind leaving him as I said, it can be embarrassing or might be embarrassing for him if I didn't speak.

'Would you like a cigarette?' I said to Henry. 'I've got lots.'

But Henry shook his head. He did at least stop reading advertisements in the supplement for a second and put it down across his knee. My mother and Daisy had gone by then I think.

'So it was all right, was it?' he said.

'Yeah,' I said, trying not to sound too American by saying 'yup' or, like a lot of people had said to me this year, 'All righty then.'

'Good flight?' he said.

'Yes, fine,' I said.

And that was all that he ever asked. He lay back trying to look as if he was as relaxaed as he'd been before and closed his eyes and folded his arms across his chest. The birds were singing amazingly and it seemed to echo back at me from the wall around, which enclosed only him and me in the garden like we were the only two people in there, like even if we had been the only two people in the world there was no way we could do anything together to survive except to fight till there was only one of us left.

I had my head down a bit and I got my new dark glasses out of the airline bag. My hand rested on the paper which had his T

39

shirt wrapped in it, and I thought, have a nice day, you bastard. Have a nice day, knowing I couldn't give it to him because the handing over would exactly express what he must be feeling, i.e. that he'd been having a nice day until I'd come home and loused it up. And the guy's supposed to have an amazing sense of humour, isn't he?

I remember I gave the T shirt in the end to Bentley who still wears it pretty regularly.

Maybe if there was no limit to what you could major in I'd choose to major in an art or craft that made you able to smooth things over and attract people. Or even to cast a spell on people and make them believe you thought they were all right and you were all right and meant them no harm and didn't hate them but were afraid of them. Not just tell them, but convince them I mean. Bit of a silly idea, I guess.

My father had been talking about the college when he drove me to the airport the afternoon before, about how it would be easy to get in and he could now afford it, having sorted out his tax problems and the rest of it. He lectures at another university – which might be more difficult to get into – lectures on business studies which was a subject he took up and trained in after having been a fairly successful businessman himself, in England, here in Hampshire in the motor trade.

So the college was in my mind, though I hadn't told anyone at home yet. It would be nearly two years before I knew whether I'd get A Levels in England and I was set to start in the sixth form in a few days' time – the next day in fact. That very Monday as ever was. So it wasn't as if I was going to be around getting up Henry's nose permanently – only for as little of the evenings as I could manage.

But I did mention it to Jane when she came round later in the afternoon. I'd given her this T shirt which said 'If God had meant Texans to ski he would have made bullshit white'. Which wasn't really her sort of thing, but she would be tactful about wearing it like my mother was about wearing her hat for the next few days. Though to be fair to Henry I never gave him the chance of rejecting his T shirt, did I?

In the sun, which was getting lower and coming at us sporadically through the willow tree, I was explaining to Jane how Coloradans didn't think much of Texans like we didn't think much of Irish people, but that on the whole Americans seemed to me to be an over-optimistic, cocky lot, making you think they can put everything right. Like my stepmother Laura who is a professional counsellor to people who have been in prison, seems to believe that she's really going to change them by what she says to them.

'You never know,' said Jane. 'People are such queer fish, aren't they?' and asked me if I had met any interesting blokes over there.

'Not really,' I said, but I did mention the guy I'd met who'd been climbing Mount Evans and who had danced with me one night at a kind of disco at this mountain resort. 'He was fairly dishy,' I said, but didn't tell her more. Maybe I wanted her to think that things had gone some way with this bloke, whereas in fact he hadn't seemed to want to do more than talk about mountains and different ways of climbing them. Also I wasn't going to admit to Jane that I'd come over nervous suddenly, being the only English person there.

I should add in my own defence that Laura came to collect me early from that disco place and hung around looking bored out of her mind, which made things difficult for me and the next day we'd moved on in any case.

'And you?' I said to Jane.

This was before she got it together with Geoff and she'd been with her family on a package to Benidorm and this bloke had been after her and she'd said no to him, but he had had practically every other girl in the hotel.

'A frog,' I said.

'Oh no, he was English actually,' said Jane.

'I meant like the frogs in that television programme – *Life On Earth* with David Attenborough where he showed those

41

frogs on a log, crawling all over it, fucking the logs and each other and everything . . .'

'Oh, he wasn't anything like as bad as that,' said Jane.

Then I told her more about America, bits that she'd be interested in – like clothes and drive-in banks and drug stores where you could buy almost anything. Jane sat and listened and it was OK then. My mother and Henry were inside and Daisy was playing with her friend in the next-door garden. We could hear their voices. I began to feel quite sleepy and relaxed. Like I can do when, say, Henry is indoors and I am out or he is outside and I am indoors.

When Jane had gone I went to sleep on the lounger in the garden with my Broncos cap shading the low shafts of afternoon sun. Funny how any day in the sun remembered seems good in spite of previous vibes and that. Funny how anything seems better than cold spring which isn't coming in yet.

Then I heard Henry's voice. He'd gone in next door to fetch Daisy and I could hear him talking to the neighbours, telling them stories about France and everything.

I can't describe how he talks. No one could I don't think, if it came to getting an investigator to track him down as Patrick has suggested that we should. Henry was telling the neighbours how some of the people on this beach took their clothes off, Germans probably they were. Henry called them Krauts but he isn't really racialist. I don't think anyway. 'All the Brits,' he was saying, 'all the Brits in their Marks and Spencer's shorts were gawping at them through binoculars . . .'

They were howling with laughter next door. He often does that: goes and showers his energy and wit over other people when he feels he isn't appreciated here. Used to do that, I mean, used to feel he wasn't appreciated here.

Funny how things fade and you forget your stories of America and remember things like Laura not liking you to smoke in the camper and making you stick to the law about age-limit drinking in bars. I hardly had one Pina Colada in America.

Funny that I can remember my mother's voice coming down from outside the kitchen door across the wall and me lying there and hearing her say: 'Did you say you were going to unpack before supper?' Typical that: she doesn't ever say: 'Unpack, will you!' Rather she manages to suggest you'd said you were going to. When you had done nothing of the kind.

Then more came out about the holiday in France. Did I mention that Patrick had been on it too? Well, he was, and apparently there was this French girl whom he'd fancied no end and followed around on the beach for hours. My mother told it as a joke because we've always had this joke about Patrick being like those frogs in *Life on Earth* and like Jane's Englishman in Benidorm.

'But she liked Daddy better,' Daisy said.

'I don't remember that,' said my mother.

'Daddy talked and talked to her,' said Daisy.

This was the next day after school. Henry had gone away – to the carpet fair in Harrogate – and we were in the kitchen – my mother making a quiche for the party we were having later in the week when he came back. The French girl can't have been a threat or my mother wouldn't have mentioned her.

'So who won?' I asked.

'There wasn't any contest,' said my mother rather stuffily and seemed not to want to talk about it any more. But I could just imagine it, Patrick letching away, trying to ingratiate himself and Henry coming along and giving the girl one look, one long yearning look into the eyes and slaughtering her with charm like he does and ruining it all for Patrick.

'She kept wanting to help him teach me to swim,' said Daisy. 'He made her eyes go funny like he did Karen's.'

Karen was a Danish au pair we had earlier that summer who kept on saying how lucky I was to have such a smashing stepfather and how he was the nicest person in the world. Well, she wasn't here all that long, was she? Karen it was who told me that I talked like Henry, used his language; she wondered why I hadn't fallen in love with him myself, which made me laugh a lot.

In the kitchen Daisy was still going on about the French girl and my mother was having trouble getting the pastry fitted into the fluted sides of the huge quiche tray, so she left this unfinished and began to fry onions and mix eggs for the filling.

'Me and Daddy taught her lots of new English words and Daddy told her endless things about herself . . .'

That's how 'Daddy' does it, isn't it? Telling people all about themselves, things they didn't know about themselves, like he used to tell Danish Karen she was stunning and sensational and must stop worrying that people didn't like her. That's how he does it when he approves of people.

'So history repeats itself and poor old Patrick didn't get his girl once more,' I said, trying to make the whole thing back into a joke again. Patrick had fancied Karen like mad as well.

'Oh well,' my mother said vaguely, 'it didn't spoil the holiday.' She lit a cigarette and stuffed the dead match down into the soil of one of the pot plants on the window sill, which is an infuriating habit of hers. The cigarette was one out of a packet of my Marlboro Lights we were sharing. 'Good, aren't they?' I said.

'Yeah . . . great.'

We usually agree about brands of cigarette.

She was quite matey that day and I told her what Mr Forbes had been telling us and she told me about a wallhanging she was planning. There was sun outside and this reflected on the virginia creeper which grows over the shed and flooded reddish warm light into the room.

I never heard more about the French girl and it seems a long time ago. There are so many people whom Henry's attracted to him that it must be quite a job for my mother remembering them all and making a list of them for present purposes. The French girl didn't even get put on the list, so she was no big deal. Karen did, but her name's off it now: she wrote a friendly letter just the other day. Anyway Henry didn't take his passport and I'd say was more into older women anyway. He often says he doesn't really like young people: which is maybe on account of I am one.

FOUR

Patrick, as I said, will fuck anything, the younger the better, but Henry's different and it's my theory that he doesn't screw around that much. It's the way he looks at women always makes people think he does and, I suppose, they get hopeful. That look! You can see their eyes getting round and soupy, kind of oily maybe: at any rate spellbound. Like even Daisy noticed it with the French girl, didn't she? Personally I've never been the recipient of this long yearning glance, although the first time I spoke to him, I do remember realising even then how very hard he was trying to make me think him marvellous.

There's a background explanation to this which may be relevant. Henry, you see, worries about people being against him. I overheard my mother once explaining to Patrick when there'd been some row or other – explaining that Henry from time to time thinks he is a particularly nasty slug inside and that people see him like that – with revolting protuberances and antennae and an awful smell. Which is why he has to make especial efforts to charm people. Patrick said that reminded him of a story he'd read once about a man who stayed in bed for years and years because of being hopeless about life and finally

46

decided that he'd turned into a slug and firmly believed that people in his family didn't like to tell him that he'd turned into a slug. Nothing would change his mind. They brought him meals in bed, but he was still totally convinced that they did this out of kindness and were only pretending to his face that he was normal. All the time he knew for sure he was a slug.

But Henry didn't come home feeling slug-like from the carpet fair last September. He was, at the time, terrifically into carpets. He gets crazes for things as well as for people. Carpets were the big new thing in the shop and the balcony was to make room for selling them. These crazes; years ago there was the stripped pine craze, then the craze for wickerwork, then brass wickerwork followed by stained glass, stained glass boxes, miniature greenhouses – all that stuff. But last year was the year of the oriental carpet. We were selling tons of them. It's lucky that Henry's crazes run with trends in marketing. Even when they don't, my mother gets left-overs from crazes sold off at not too great a loss. But I often hear her say that the best years may be over and the shop is now running on its fat to some extent.

So he was on his way home – in good time for the party you see, the party which was to celebrate the opening of the carpet and soft furnishings balcony, although it had already been in use for several weeks. Autumn was coming in ever so gradually and it was still warm outside that evening. I have a diary, though I don't write much in it, but it shows that lighting-up time on that date was 6·30 p.m. and I took Daisy into the park as usual so that she could meet him coming over from the station. So he can't have taken the car that time. He didn't take it this time either. He doesn't like long car journeys on his own.

Henry coming home isn't like me coming home. It's a cause for celebration and people sit around and listen to the stories of the people that he's met at sales, trade fairs and trains and everywhere. Henry is always meeting literally zillions of people.

And always has. He worked his way up from window-

47

dressing in this chain of department stores, got extra qualifications from night school or day release school or whatever they
call it. Then he was a buyer some of the time, then a boss of
other buyers. His stories of those times are stories of rows with
other bosses who bossed him or thought they could. All his life
he wanted his own business and now he's got it he is bloody
miserable. Well, some of the time he is. My mother says that's
life: you think you want something and you get it and then find
it is all the same old thing. Henry says she is too patient and
accepting of the disappointments, too much what he calls the
willing victim. I'll drink to that, as Henry would say.

So I was in the park with Daisy and, like I said, I can always
sense him coming, but I waited until I was quite sure it was him
on the way up the hill and left Daisy to greet him. I bunked off
on the principle that I owed him no greetings and must have
gone in home about half an hour later by which time he was
well into stories of the people he had met and smiled upon in
his progress up the country. And there was drink as well. He
nearly always has a bottle of gin in his briefcase for my mother
and some scotch for himself and for Patrick if Patrick's there,
since he, Henry, is unfailingly generous with drink when it's in
the house. Even for me on such occasions and that evening he
poured me one as if I was the same as everyone else.

So I remember the start of that evening particularly well.
(Not that I'm likely to forget the rest of it.) He'd even said
'Hullo' and I'd said 'Hi!' Hullo hullo, I thought to myself, a
new beginning – not without foreboding. But you can't really
spoil a happy scene like that by looking suspicious. Not when
the kitchen is bursting with this burgeoning warmth. The blue
and white stripy blinds were drawn down and spotlights lit up
the centre of the long table where we were all sitting round.
You could almost feel the pot plants loving it and thriving with
such a bonhomous atmosphere. The thing on such occasions is
to stay calm and keep your fingers crossed.

It's easier to describe Henry up and cheerful. His profile, for
instance, is considered to be rather special and magnetic. He is

said to have a look of a younger Kirk Douglas, but is never thought of as vain and never wears medallions round his neck or any other butch male display symbols. But that aside, you have to acknowledge that Henry generates good moments like there was that Saturday. He really does exude what might be called generosity of spirit – and I don't just mean with gin and scotch – I mean the thing that Mr Forbes is always going on about – generosity of spirit of certain characters in literature, e.g. Edgar in *Lear* and Gabriel Oak, the good shepherd in *Far From the Madding Crowd*, which was another new set book of ours last autumn.

So there we were and everything amazingly OK and I had some scotch and it was like Henry had forgotten that he hadn't been pleased to see me back from America the week before.

My mother got up from the table to go on cooking. The big quiche was out of the freezer and in the oven and my mother was chopping parsley and other herbs to go on the top of it and I was making mayonnaise. But whenever my mother had a hand free, Henry would catch hold of this and she would fasten her fingers round his wrist and stand near him for a moment or two. Or sit down and they would grip each other's wrists across the table. They often do that. Did that I mean.

The table is a Leadbetter relic – supposed to have eighteenth-century legs or whatever, and the kitchen is designed round that. There is a dresser with brass hooks and handles on it and the plants are pale green against the window blinds. There are cleverly shadowed recesses. Sounds a bit *Homes and Gardens* maybe, but somehow what Henry has designed and my mother has agreed to and they've both chosen – always looks like it is all their own idea and never copied from anyone else.

Generosity of spirit of whatever it is which causes other people in its range to smile and laugh and talk a lot: I remember wishing, as I went on working on my mayonnaise, wishing that such bonhomie could be bottled up or put in a plastic bag and sealed in the freezer like the quiche had been, the only trouble

49

being that when you took it out the atmosphere might be too icy to thaw it.

So for at least an hour there was a hum about the place. A real hum in fact, coming from my mother who always hums when getting ready for a party. She'd had her hair properly put up that morning and was walking around holding her head very steady, humming. She was, as we say, getting her party head on.

This is a reference to a joke Henry made years ago when my mother was going through a very absent-minded phase and kept on doing things like putting tea in coffee-jars and vice versa, driving Daisy to play school when she was meant to be taking her to the dentist: that kind of absent-mindedness. All of which led Henry to say things like: 'You haven't got your coffee-jar head on, have you?' or 'You've forgotten to put your driving head on again, haven't you?'

The silliest mistake my mother ever made was years ago – to do with Noggin, the dog my father had. She took him shopping in Salisbury which is miles and miles away and tied him up outside a supermarket and left him there and drove home. He got taken to the RSPCA and it was only by chance we got him back. Mind you, she never had much sympathy for him.

None of which is to say she isn't needle-sharp in other matters, like remembering telephone numbers, filling in tax forms and knowing exactly how much money should be in the till at the end of each day. Although at the present time of writing, her usual degree of accuracy in most matters is, to say the least, pretty impaired.

Except in Henry's case: she makes calculations about him all right. Witness the diary I have found locked in a drawer. There are hieroglyphics in it referring to last autumn and on several dates since then. So maybe she's always done that kind of speculating or calculating about him. In fact that must be what she was doing that evening when he came home from the carpet fair. In spite of humming and looking animated. Something built the tension up to start with and it wasn't me.

No, I was still reflecting on Henry's ability to spread good cheer and the rest of it and how, when he's like that, it's like whatever happened, even the holocaust, wouldn't affect a place where there was someone with a socking good measure of the old expansiveness. I even began to wish I'd given him that T shirt after all and trusted him to be pleased with it.

My mother said something. I'm trying to remember what. It was just after she'd said it that she broke the crust of the quiche as she took it out of the oven. She'd asked him something, something about the carpet fair: like what the hotel was like and he said it was lousy and he couldn't even lock the door of his room, and added: 'Not that I needed to . . .'

I should try and remember it because it might have relevance to where he is now, seeing as, according to the diary, whatever happened in Harrogate may have been the beginning.

I do remember that she was using a tone of voice she uses when she's saying something as if it wasn't important but it is, important I mean. It's a carefully casual voice I suppose, and I do know she'd been asking him who he'd seen there and he'd reeled off names of people they both knew through the business and she was kind of nodding as if ticking people off in her mind.

Anyway, I didn't need to remember it at the time. I wasn't in the least bit bothered what he had been up to while away, because of planning what to wear at the party. It seemed I was expected to be there and Henry's cheerfulness had got me in an obliging mood, although there were dozens of other things I could have done and in some ways now I wish I had. Definitely wish I had, I mean.

But that's neither here nor there and irrelevant to how the vibes began to turn a little threatening. I think it was when Henry said about the hotel room door and not being able to lock it, when he added 'not that I needed to' that Patrick said something like 'No, no, of course not . . .' saying this with

51

sarcasm in his voice as if he really wanted to get at Henry but not seeming to be doing that.

Or it may have been a general joshing from Patrick about what the form was like at the fair, meaning girls available presumably and Henry saying 'What would I be wanting with a girl?' and putting his arm round my mother as she was on the way to the oven to get the quiche out. I know I'd said: 'I think the quiche might be ready now' because I could smell it pretty well cooked.

It may not matter if I can't fix events exactly, but anyway what happened more or less was that Henry had his arms round my mother and she was trying to get to the oven, so she was delayed and hurried once she reached it, then used a thin cloth instead of the oven glove, burnt her fingers and had to bang the quiche down harder than it could take, so the crust fractured in several places in the baking tray and she said 'Fuck fuck fuck' and Henry grabbed at her again to comfort her and suck the burnt finger for her and she buried her face in his shirt, half giggling, half crying possibly, although I couldn't see her face to tell which.

Anyway by that time I was trying to push the quiche together again and I don't remember the immediate aftermath except that when I looked up Henry had gone to have a bath. And it's only that Patrick keeps going on at me about what I did remember about Henry and what he said about the carpet fair that I've tried to recall the incident. 'You were there,' I've said. I haven't, mind you, told him about the diary in the locked drawer in the workroom and the coded hieroglyphics in it which refer to that time.

Funnily enough I remember more about Patrick in the kitchen that evening. While Henry was in the bath, Patrick was sitting on a high stool by the sink and getting in our way no end. So he dodged around, moving the stool from place to place while talking to us all, trying to interest us in some theory of food of his and telling a story about a Leadbetter ancestor who had gone in for the healing property of plants, growing unusual flowers in the old conservatory at King's Radlett and finally getting it wrong and poisoning himself.

'I never heard of him,' said my mother.

'Just a typical example of the English gentleman having time to dabble, I suppose,' said Patrick. 'Did you know, incidentally, that we had a great-grandfather who was a friend of Arthur Sullivan's? They used to put on operettas in the drawing-room?'

He's like that, always knocking the Leadbetters, but going on about them endlessly; how this grandfather was musical or that grandmother was said to have second sight. The nutty healing one, he said, was married to a Lazenby.

I suppose he may have been trying to edge the subject away from Henry's possible misdemeanours at the carpet fair. He kept on helping himself to more of Henry's whisky and was drunk for that stage of the proceedings. I have seen Patrick very drunk, particularly when he is on good terms with Henry, coming back with Henry from the pub, their arms around each other, Patrick sprawling on our long settee and telling Henry he is the best thing that ever happened to the Leadbetters, bringing fine new blood, new hope, the only hope in fact.

Daisy was in one of her whiny moods by now. She'd been as excited as anyone earlier on, but now she was saying that she'd had a boring boring lousy lousy day with everyone being busy and her friend Rosie from next door not coming round to play because of having a grandmother to stay. 'It isn't fair,' she kept saying, 'I don't have a grandmother.'

'Of course you have a grandmother,' my mother said.

'I don't count her; she's horrible and she's in Australia.'

This was Henry's mother, the one who visited us a year ago and whom Daisy took against, Henry's mother who used to be in variety and was married for the third time to this man from Adelaide.

'Rosie says that if I have an Australian grandmother, I must be Australian or partly Australian.'

Henry's mother is called Ginny. I think she was some kind of dancer in a 1940s version of Hot Gossip or Legs and Co. Her real name is Virginia, but Ginny's suitable because she soaks up gin.

'So am I any part Australian? Am I? Am I?'

We'd been too busy to answer her, but now my mother said 'Nonsense' and explained at great length that Ginny had married Roy from Adelaide long after she had given birth to Henry and therefore no one was Australian excepting Roy himself. And Patrick added that in fact Daisy was as much Scottish as anything because of the McLarens and because his late mother, my grandmother Leadbetter, had been an Orr from Inverness. The Orrs, I've often been told, had the motto: Oblige! and therefore were obliging people.

Daisy climbed up on another high stool she'd dragged beside me at the table. 'Ginny didn't like me anyway,' she said. 'She only liked Petra. She went bananas over Petra.'

There was some truth in this. Ginny did seem to take to me, but only because it was so many years since she had seen Henry that she wasn't sure who was his kid and who wasn't, and as I've got the same blonde hair he had as a young man, maybe it is understandable. Plus gin making inroads on her perspicacity, of course.

'Of course Ginny liked you,' my mother said, switching on the coffee grinder – to grind some nuts to go on a trifle she was decorating.

'She didn't like Daddy either,' Daisy said.

My mother went into all sorts of details about relations not necessarily liking each other, but feeling close to each other, bonded to each other, but quarrelling sometimes which was inevitable. Daisy wasn't listening at all, and kept putting her fingers into my bowl of mayonnaise and licking them. Then my mother – who had her burnt finger wrapped in a tissue – knocked the top off the grinder while it was going and bits of nut shot all over the window sill and into several of the pot plants. Patrick said there was a strand of clumsiness in all

54

Leadbetter genes which came from some weirdo ancestor and my mother said, 'How interesting, I don't think!'

'Daddy didn't like her either,' Daisy was going on. 'Daddy absolutely couldn't stand her most of the time. Daddy totally *loathed* her.' Her voice was beginning to swoop up.

My mother dabbed at the window sill with a damp cloth, began picking bits of nuts off the leaves of the grape-ivy plant and said that Henry really loved Ginny a tremendous amount, but that they weren't used to being together after all the years apart, not like Daisy was used to being with her and Henry, 'and with Petra', she added hastily, so as to emphasise her usual myth about us being all one family.

'Mind you,' said Patrick, who had refilled his whisky glass, 'both hate and love are inadequate words. I was never too keen on my mother anyway.' He went on to say that he had probably been in love with his Nanny. This is an ancient story oft repeated and my mother has always held the theory that all Patrick's girls and women, including his ex-wife, look a good deal like old Nanny Willis who is still alive up at King's Radlett even now. Even Karen, the Danish girl, whom Patrick fancied, had an undefinable Nanny Willis look about the eyes.

In the kitchen, as we finally got the quiche shifted on to the plate, Patrick was mouldering on about theories of familial relationships, but no one was really listening. I will say about Patrick that you can ignore him, which you never can Henry.

Perhaps Henry, I was thinking, is less like the generous characters in literature and more like those who make things happen – like Sergeant Troy in *Far From the Madding Crowd* who was charismatic and plausible but messed everything up. Or like Edmund in *Lear*, except that there is nothing Machiavellian about Henry because he doesn't think ahead much.

So we ignored Patrick and concentrated on the quiche and there was quiet for a while except that we could hear Henry upstairs singing in the bath, mostly old musical numbers like 'You're just in love'.

55

My mother banged the quiche tray into the sink and began to run water on it. 'You're next in the bathroom,' she said to me. 'What are you wearing for the party by the way?'

I need to explain what I wore on account of a lot needs explaining about that evening and what I wore is part of it. So here goes. When I was in Aspen there were these super boutiques and my father said: 'Choose anything.' How rash, I thought, but didn't disagree with him and he came with me, which was peculiar because he's not a person who takes any interest basically in what people wear, but Laura, my stepmother, was attending some residential school in criminology or whatever.

Since my father was being so recklessly generous, I thought I'd better give him some say in where his money went, so I tried on dozens of outfits to check on his reaction to them. He went over the top for a white silk shirt and black silk baggy pants. It was ever so many dollars and it had a French designer label in it.

'I have got something I might wear,' I said to my mother. Following my policy of boxing clever in the matter of goodies from Colorado, I hadn't shown her the outfit yet.

'A lot of people have got to use the bathroom,' she was saying, although I couldn't see why she was worried once Henry had used it. It was only keeping him out of it that caused trouble and I'd heard his bath water running out. He was still singing up there.

Or there was a dress Ginny bought me – all forties style such as she would have worn in her prime when entertaining troops in theatres of war. She even bought me bright red lipstick and did my hair in electric tongs, raising it in front into what she called a pompadour. Mascara for the eyelashes as well. This was earlier last summer and Henry freaked out when he saw me, since I suppose it all reminded him of wartime when, so the story goes, she wasn't mothering him properly. (We've done a bit of Freud in General Studies psychology option – one question picking up a maximum of thirty marks.) Luckily

56

the forties dress incident was near the end of Ginny's visit . . .
he hardly spoke to her again. I'd never worn it since. Ginny
said his being nasty about her present to me was his father
coming out in him.

But maybe by September he'd got over all that, I was thinking. I heard him singing 'Waltzing Matilda' while changing,
which meant he might have passed through his Ginny-
rejecting phase.

So I was supposed to be using the bathroom, but the mayonnaise – it occurred to me – would just do to decorate the
quiche – to disguise the cracks in it: it was a good consistency. I
did cake-icing one term in Domestic Science and am quite
nifty with a forcing bag and nozzle.

To keep Daisy quiet I'd made her a bag as well and let her
squeeze mayonnaise in blobs between the lattice patterns I was
making, but she'd made a mess of it, smeared my delicate
tracery, so I snatched the bag from her and lifted her down
from the stool. She'd been leaning right across the table and
was about to ruin a cheesecake my mother had made. Daisy
went to the far end of the table, put her chin in her hands,
kicked one leg up and down, beginning to sigh somewhat with
her mouth turned deliberately down.

Then in came Henry, blazingly clean and smelling of
Badedas, casually smart in open-necked white shirt with rolled
up sleeves, but wearing his black city-striped trousers hitched
up with a leather belt. He often wears deliberately unmatching
things and never dresses in a studied way. I vaguely wondered
if he'd think I was aping him if I turned up in black and white as
well, although that wasn't why I finally wore the 1940s flowered
dress with padded shoulders and the incredibly high-heeled
platform shoes which made me almost as tall as him.

He was still exuberant and started straight in with a joke:
'Christ! Is that all you are going to give these people? How
pathetic!' he said, stretching his arms to gesture at the vast
array of food we'd now spread on the table. Everyone laughed,
including my mother, and he kissed Daisy on top of her head

before putting his arms round my mother. 'Happy now?' he said to her.

'Yes, of course,' she said.

In my view she has to be. I mean she has to say she is or everything goes wrong again. It's like he's dragging something out of her. It was like he wanted her to acknowledge that the food she'd prepared (rather *we'd* prepared, but let that pass) was some kind of offering to him exclusively rather than for all the guests who would be coming in an hour or two, and as if she had to offer him that food with a smile or he wouldn't look at it. I think that's how it was. I only know I didn't particularly want to look at her face while she was looking up at him saying she was happy.

Daisy was doing her prelude to a screaming fit, making her chest heave in and out while looking at Henry sideways, while he kept his arms round my mother telling her that as long as she was happy he was happy and so on. That sort of thing. She stayed very still.

I've sometimes thought my mother has or tries to have some of the generosity of spirit Mr Forbes talks about. Maybe hers is more the kind of suffering patient willingness, like Gabriel Oak displayed by waiting all through *Far From the Madding Crowd* for Bathsheba Everdene. Like Edgar made himself into the lowest possible form of humanity to look after his old father and his old uncle or whatever relation Lear and Gloucester were to him.

Then Henry asked Patrick if he'd pour everyone another drink to keep us all up and going. Then he said, 'So who's going to get the September party medal? The Distinguished Order of the Balcony?' which was a reference to another ongoing joke about striking imaginary medals for family events and awarding them to those who contributed most to the proceedings on any special occasion. Like we had the Honourable Cross for the Trip to Rome two years ago, which no one got in the end.

Meanwhile Daisy was making stupid panicky faces. Henry

scooped her up on to his knee. He doesn't always twig when she is only playing silly buggers. He sat down with her opposite to me and held her tight and, with a drink in his free hand, raised his glass and called upon us all to raise our glasses to the success of the evening, raise them in the Danish manner which Karen taught us, saying 'Skol!' 'Skol!' is what you say when you have to look into only one other person's eyes, then drink, then look into their eyes again before lowering your glass.

He raised his to my mother first. I was watching him. The expansive ingredient was pouring out of him, kind of bursting forth and shooting across the laden table, zooming over all the polished glasses and multicoloured food on plates and dishes towards her. I was beside her.

The whole place was buzzing with all this energy. He was on top of the world tonight, wasn't he? As if all the past had been blanked out and any minute he might want to toast me too.

But he wouldn't, would he? I mustn't expect him to. So I kept my head down working at the decoration with the mayonnaise, making patterns, little circular swirling blobs of it. Henry's force of concentration on a person asks for chunks of that person, asks for total dedication from that person. Like asks for the person's soul, doesn't it?

'Now, Petra . . .' someone said and I went on squeezing the nozzle of the forcing bag and said 'Yes?' without looking up.

'Your glass,' I heard my mother say and realised that he really did want to toast me as well.

'OK,' I said. 'Yes, just a minute, yes.'

'Here's looking at you, kid,' I heard Henry say.

I would have reached for my glass. I was thinking about how I'd have to look into his eyes and acknowledge him and look into his eyes again. I was going to reach for my glass any minute. I think I was going to reach for my glass any minute. I mean I may have wanted to hesitate a bit because of not wanting to give him everything or whatever it is he wants from people. But things were going on around me. I mean nothing actual but the feelings were, the vibes. Sometimes I think the pot plants in the kitchen can't know where they are at all with all the changing vibes which have gone on between people in there. And by the time I looked up Henry had his head down on top of Daisy's head and my mother was staring at the ceiling and Patrick was looking at his shoes and I had fucked it up as usual. The mayonnaise was spreading in a wiggly lane all down one side of the quiche and on to a plate of wafers which my mother had just arranged.

'Bit of a mess that, isn't it?' said Henry.

Generosity and expansiveness? Whoever thought those things existed? People don't have those. People have desires and arrogance and needs to be admired. Spirit, generosity and all those words are only words that people use to make them feel better about things generally.

'You don't usually worry about what food looks like,' I said. 'You usually only eat it. Anyway who broke the quiche?'

No one was moving or saying anything; silence was all round, except in my head where my ears were ringing like they do, like they often have.

'Have it your own way, Petra,' said Henry, getting up and pushing Daisy off his knee. 'As usual have it your own way.'

OK, so it was too late to get toasted or to get the Order of the Balcony. So what – I never got the order of anything yet. And I hadn't wanted my own way about anything. OK, so he wanted to make it was like a battle, did he? Make out like I was making trouble, did he? So what was I supposed to do? Act victim? Hang my head and say: oh, sorry, ever so sorry, pardon me for breathing. I will change my ways completely, you are right of course. Willing victim? There is no such thing. Victims can wait to get their own back usually, except for plants who can only wilt and die from witnessing aggression and disappoint the people who are looking after them.

Then I felt my mother staring at me, wishing me to decide it was time I went to use the bathroom, so I flung the forcing bag full of mayonnaise down on the table and left.

Maybe it wasn't exactly like that. Maybe what made it worse

was Henry using that *Casablanca* quote: 'Here's looking at you, kid' which is all the funnier because of Peter Sellers using it when acting Inspector Clouseau in Pink Panther films. Henry used that accent, which actually made me start to laugh, but because of not looking up the laughter began to go sour and turn to tears, which I couldn't show him, which may have been why I kept my face down.

FIVE

He was down there, moving among guests and I was up level with the hangings and the chandelier. I could see my mother too – in purple pleated silk with pearls embroidered on it. She had the Leadbetter diamond earrings on. At parties she tends to look radiant to start with and kisses everyone, even people she hardly knows. Possibly because she can't remember who she usually kisses and with whom she usually shakes hands. But she once said that it must be better to exceed a normal welcome than fall short of it. My mother is supposed to have beautiful full lips and her eyes are grey. My grandmother told me – I can just remember her telling me – that my mother's eyes were the Lazenby eyes, smoky grey as if put in with grubby fingers. She looks grotesque if she adds to all this any eye make-up.

I may not have the Lazenby eyes and lips, but I'm said to have the McLaren neck and, remembering a portrait of my great-grandmother McLaren (now sold), I tried to hold my neck like hers. I had the Ginny dress on, the shiny red belt and high-heeled shoes. I'd tonged my hair into a pageboy and the bright red lipstick separated gungily whenever I opened my mouth. I had bracelets all the way up my arms which were still tanned from Colorado and my hair was still bleached from that sun as well.

Actually it was more like another film. My descent of the stairs would be like in the Hitchcock movie where Laurence Olivier sees Joan Fontaine wearing all the wrong clothes, reminding him of his reputedly beautiful first wife.

The party had been going on for an hour or so. Glittering guests, smells of scent and wine glasses clinking. The shop wares were mostly moved against the walls or put away. Any minute now Henry would look up. He was moving through the mass of people's heads with a bottle raised in either hand, coming from the far end of the shop towards the bottom of the stairs, passing my mother, greeting people, slowing down and, yes, looking up, understanding the film allusion I would guess, understanding other allusions possibly, but flanked by friends.

I remember watching my mother who, having seen me, looked no more at me, but at Henry who was standing stock still beside her with the bottles, one of red and one of white wine, poised above his head like molotov cocktails.

When Henry was two or three he caught tuberculosis which people did apparently in those days, and had to spend six months in an isolation ward. The story is that his mother, Ginny, hardly ever came to see him there or only visited him once. My mother has often said there are things he cannot understand about himself because of this. His father was killed in the war in 1944.

He had to meet my eyes and I had to stop again half-way down the stairs in order to steady myself. I imagined I looked at him much as Cordelia looked at Lear when she spoke the truth about her feelings for him in Act One when he freaked out and the play began.

Quickly say something good about Henry. Quickly say that whoever looks for him looks for a man who, when I fell off Troy once, came rushing out in the car and took me to the hospital for X-rays and bought me a new riding cap and boots. Say that we play games at Christmas at King's Radlett and he leads the games and thinks of new and funnier ones, although he feels uneasy being there. Say that he taught Daisy to read as well as swim and balance on her bicycle and fed her at nights with a bottle when my mother was ill and walked up and down endlessly singing to her night after night.

Say that he said that he had heard that when you fell off a horse the thing to do was to get right back on it and that, although he loathed Troy and was basically shit scared of him, as soon as I was over the bruises, he held Troy's head while I got back on him again. And after that he said why didn't I try going in for gymkhanas? So I told him that we hadn't got a horsebox to take Troy anywhere and he said he'd hire a horsebox, even though the shop had only just opened up and they were making nil income from it.

Well, he didn't hire a horsebox, but he'd offered to. He didn't hire it in the end because I didn't much want to ride in gymkhanas. 'That isn't what riding is about for me,' I said. He was offended and said: 'Catch me offering to hire a horsebox ever again.' Say that he wanted to be my father but couldn't be because of me having one already. Say thank you for having offered to hire a horsebox, Henry, and sorry that it wasn't the right offer to make.

'Hullo beautiful,' someone said when I was mingling with the guests. Say Henry does have some nice friends and this was Jim who is in carpets but of the fitted kind and who comes from the north of England like Henry did originally. Jim is warm and always hugs me when he sees me. He was clutching me while Henry walked away unable to say anything to me of relevance while Jim was holding on to me.

Say Henry has many friends and admirers, another of whom was Ronnie, whom I met that night – not for the first time – but had never really talked to much before. Say that Ronnie may have thought, like Ginny, that I was Henry's daughter since he didn't have any reason to think otherwise, not having known us

64

that long. In fact my blonde hair comes from my father's side, from the Frobishers, who have a family tree on a par with the Leadbetters but maybe less spattered with eccentrics, although I cannot be doing with harking on ancestors.

Ronnie worked on the local paper and did a feature on Henry and my mother for the opening of the balcony. Henry much approved of him and his efforts on behalf of Harrison's. For Henry, people who have energy and verve are usually OK people. It was a shame, I thought, when I heard that Ronnie was leaving soon to get a job in London.

'I might go to London either to work or university,' I said.

In the far corner by the door into the office and the work-room, leaning against the wall, I was having a long conversation with him about how people become journalists, although I'd never thought that much about being one. I'd never thought about being anything specific, but do hope to go to university, maybe in order not to have to decide for several years. 'Pretty good life, journalism,' said Ronnie. 'Hard work and low pay to start with.' He'd been the editor of his student paper while at university and had had a year off, which sounded like a good idea.

Mr Forbes says any kind of degree fits you for all sorts of things. He went to somewhere in Wales or maybe it was Manchester for his, for his degree I mean.

'I shall be glad to leave,' said Ronnie, but then said he'd be sorry to miss the more interesting people here like Henry – or words to that effect. 'He is amazing, isn't he?'

'Definitely,' I said.

It would be a change, I was thinking, to have a bloke whom Henry admired. It would make life a good deal easier. Giles was OK but very much in awe of Henry like most Leadbetters were, and hardly ever came round to the flat. Kevin, whom I'd had in term-time up till recently when he went off to some poly somewhere to do optics, was heavy-handed, knocked things over in the shop, sat watching telly taking up too much room and had somewhat smelly feet. As for Bentley – I'd been mates with him for years, but he's not a boy friend like a boy friend is, being homosexual. He can't darken the doors without Henry walking out. As Bentley has often said, that's a natural reaction from someone with leanings that way himself.

I'm not too sure about those leanings, but I did ask Bentley the other day if he thought Henry might have gone off with another man, and Bentley said that Henry, if at all gay, is a closet gay like most men are, but too inhibited to go all out for it. 'No way is Henry inhibited,' I said. 'You'd be surprised,' said Bentley and went on about seeing blokes in the Southampton sauna baths gazing at other blokes but never daring to do anything until other blokes come on strong with the right signals.

So anyway the gay area of Henry maybe a dead end if that doesn't sound too pornographic and I'll leave it to Patrick to sort that out if it comes to it. He has had a sauna bath with Henry once or twice. But this Ronnie who I'm on about was totally hetero I guess and fanciable too in a navy blue striped suit and waistcoat. People are going in for waistcoats more. Mr Forbes wears a waistcoat some days.

'Definitely, yes, I shall move to London eventually,' I said to Ronnie. I also told him about my holiday and the mountains and the altitude and the possibility of the college you could get to without A Levels. But I soon realised Ronnie wasn't listening to me, but looking me up and down in a welcome fashion. He was older than most blokes I'd had before. London wasn't that far in any case.

He reminded me of Sebastian Coe. I'd given him ten points for style. But he was shortish, so I kicked my shoes off as time went on, which was a huge relief. I guessed he had a smooth spare body, but not too muscled under his pink shirt. I was supposed to be helping with the food which would shortly be served upstairs, but Ronnie was telling me he had a sports car as well as other interesting facts about himself. It sounded all right, being a journalist. Later he let on that he had a girl friend in London. Sod it, I thought.

I told him I could drive a bit, that Henry, being an amazingly nice, kind stepfather, had given me some driving lessons once or twice (once actually) but didn't let on that I wasn't quite old enough to have a provisional licence. From the corner of my eye, I could see my mother ushering people up the stairs towards the buffet meal, and Henry looking as though he wanted to approach Ronnie, maybe wanting to introduce him to someone else by this time. Ronnie had his back to Henry, so he couldn't see Henry hovering.

Ronnie was gazing up at this extra good wallhanging made by my mother and saying how splendid it was. He had had a good few glasses of wine. He was also saying how splendid and beautiful my mother was. I was looking Ronnie in the eyes, trying to recall exactly what Henry does with his eyes when he fancies someone. Maybe it was what was in your head about a person when you looked at them that way. I visualised Ronnie's body and how much I liked his springy thick dark hair, short about his ears, and I tried to show my thoughts in my eyes, but not too earnestly.

We had been sitting on the stairs eating our supper with our forks, Ronnie and me, Ronnie and I that is, and he'd been stroking my ankle between mouthfuls – since I was on a stair or two above him. I mean the stairs up to the top floor where the bedrooms are. He leaned back whispering: 'Which is your room?' His throat looked white. He'd loosened his tie. I had to tell him that I didn't really have a room – not tonight – Henry's friend Jim and his wife Lily were staying in it. I'd be sharing with Daisy tonight and she had already gone to bed.

'You promised me a ride in your car – and a driving lesson, didn't you?'

He seemed to understand. At least he was a bloke who understood a bargain. 'Get your coat,' he said.

We must have been sitting talking on the stairs for longer than I thought and lots of people had already left.

'I should say goodbye,' he said.

Even Henry had walked past us and not commented. And my mother had walked past us, staggered past us rather, rather drunkenly. I didn't see any problem in my leaving now, with them being at the still elated stage of drunkenness. So I fetched a cardigan and my Broncos cap which I thought Ronnie might admire – and I went outside and waited at the bottom of the steps. It was cool out there and fresh and a wind had got up so the trees in the tubs rustled and the creeper swayed against the yard light making shifting shadows and I felt great there with a sense of achievement with the music coming out of the flat still and last visitors sounding cheerful as they said goodbye. I leaned against the bottom railings of the steps saying to myself: all righty then and good old everyone.

Then there was my mother on the top step, swaying slightly and I maybe should have said hullo or are you all right, but didn't and stayed a bit pushed back into the creeper. Both of us like to be on our own between being with a lot of people, but after all, in her state of drunkenness she wouldn't have queried my presence there.

To be truthful, I worry about my mother drinking quite so much. I point out to her newspaper articles about how women's livers are more vulnerable than men's, but then she points to Ginny whose liver must be 80 per cent rotted by now and says daft things like 'What a great way to go!'

She didn't see me, but the kitchen light caught her cheeks making her look quite pale and ill in fact, but I told myself that she did have amazing powers of recovery and couldn't do with people fussing over her. Especially me fussing over her. Perhaps because for every time I fuss over her she feels obliged to fuss over me, and there isn't really room in her life for that.

Then she went inside again and I stood out under the yellowish light again feeling like some old-fashioned street-walking prostitute in a forties movie, telling myself that this was the best moment – in anticipation and warning myself that Ronnie might be disappointing in the end possibly.

Which he was. A bit. In a way. In the end. When we finally

made it. Owing to delays possibly, owing to him not appearing while I waited outside. But there was no way I could have had him in the flat or earlier.

Even if I'd had a room to myself that night, it would have been a dicey process. There are rules, you see, which were in my mind as I waited for him, getting fairly miserable and kicking myself for having expected him to keep to our arrangement. Even quite intelligent people can be dim when you make plans with them. No Order of the Warm September Night for him, I was thinking.

Ever since the time I had Kevin in my bed one night, there had been rules laid down. Ever since that night when my mother and Henry were going to be home late from a party and weren't. Home late I mean. Home early in fact and my mother came to my door and peeped in to say that they were back. Kevin had to lie like dead and I pretended to be asleep. If my mother noticed an extra shape in the bed she never said, but Henry heard Kevin going home and challenged me about it.

Thinking about blokes I've had and things that have happened as a result of it, there's this girl I know. She has a boy friend and always takes him home to bed with her and her parents are agreeable. But then they always know exactly who she's in bed with, which may make a difference.

But for me, after the Kevin episode, Henry said that if I had to have blokes, I must go elsewhere to do it. But go elsewhere and be back by two o'clock. He'd lock the door at two o'clock. That was all just under a year ago when I became sixteen, but several times since then I'd come in at one-fifty-nine and find Henry half-way down the stairs to lock the door. But there were exceptions: once I came in at two-fifteen and found the door unlocked. But the kitchen clock said only one-fifty-five and that clock is never wrong; nor is my watch: it's digital. So I guessed that someone had changed the clock on my behalf – my mother almost certainly. Cunning, I thought, but was grateful. These days – well it doesn't matter anyway, since I haven't anyone and no one to check my return in any case.

The party was more or less over when I went up the steps and through the kitchen and heard voices coming from the lounge and went in there. Or rather slipped in there, not making a thing about my entrance, but just joining them and sitting beside Ronnie, leaning against a floor cushion and trying not to look miffed with him by not folding my arms or anything. He hadn't even fetched his coat. I could tell by the conversation that Henry had waylaid him, wanting to talk to him before he left. I have to say that I don't think at that stage that Henry had deliberately prevented Ronnie from coming to find me. Henry, as I've said, is not that deliberate, not a Machiavellian. But all the same I sat on my hands and scratched the cushions underneath with my nails, pretending it was Henry's face and tried to feel forgiving towards Ronnie.

Our upstairs lounge reminds people of a ship. Henry in fact said he thought in shipboard images when he was designing that room. It's long and looks out on the back yard with extended bay windows jutting out. The boards are pale and sealed with lines of darker stuff – like a ship's deck is. The scattered carpets are the best, most lustrous orientals and the cushions used for extra guests to lie on or lean against – these are made of oriental carpeting as well – off-cuts of it.

As for the party, this was the draggy end of it and the hard stuff had been brought out and there was the usual topic of conversation for that time of night, which was how awful everything was and there was Ronnie trying to tell them it wasn't really awful – not in his view at any rate.

No one in their senses thinks there is much right with the world, so why go on about it, I was thinking as usual, trying not to roll my eyes in boredom, trying not to join in as well. Ronnie was doing his best, though, trotting out all the benefits of scientific advance like the old micro-chip, plus increased concern of people for each other – plus people being more enlightened than they'd been at any time in history. Might as well bash his brains out on a brick wall, I was thinking, but they'd

70

given him a large scotch to keep him going until they decided to trample him and his argument into the ground.

Not that everyone was taking part. As usual only men, please note. My mother, for instance, lay back in a chair, although she was listening, monitoring the argument in case it became personal. She still looked knackered, but not quite as pale as she had outside. But her hair was half coming down. She spends hours getting ready for a party, but then forgets to check her appearance.

The chief protagonists were Henry, Ronnie and Patrick, both the older men getting Ronnie for saying things were any good these days. Except that every now and then Patrick said that he'd felt optimistic when he was Ronnie's age – well, almost optimistic about a very few things.

Jim was still there too, hanging on in there occasionally saying life was a sod and the bottom had properly fallen out of the fitted carpet market now, but he did value friendship which was all that was left to him. And Lily, his wife, who is small and quite lovable, mentioned instances like the scanning of the unborn child in the womb and that.

I poured myself a weakish scotch and tried to feel relaxed and patient, to button my lip and not add to the argument or prolong it. I sat perfectly still, but from time to time I did press my thigh against Ronnie's thigh and in between making points to Henry and to Patrick he did seem to be pressing back.

I remember Patrick saying that the thing he most believed about human nature was that people had a habit of going on doing what they'd started doing on the whole, and that while he had no hope of making a fortune out of selling second-hand books, it was what he was programmed to do now and he'd probably go on doing it.

'Is that really all you believe of people?' Ronnie said.

'That is the only statement I can make at this time,' said Patrick, pouring himself another drink and then sitting back with his feet sticking out in front of him on the floor. He seemed to be admiring his grotty shoes. He never changes or

71

tidies himself up for parties, presumably believing his own individuality might be disturbed. That's all he's got I suppose.

I gave Ronnie the tiniest dig in the ribs with my elbow and he turned and looked at me and took my hand. 'But, given there is a bad recession now, but after it . . .' he was saying. He had hold of my wrist and was touching my forearm and the hairs on this were standing up.

Henry was saying: 'There'll be no end to that. There'll be no jobs. Work which has given people self-respect will end. There'll be no more of it,' and I saw that he was watching Ronnie stroking my arm.

He wouldn't have felt jealous – he's never fancied me – that is self-evident, but he might begin to resent the idea of me having Ronnie – or of anyone having anyone maybe. Or of my breaking the rules. Or of me enjoying myself.

Ronnie let my wrist go, but whether because of Henry watching or because of being worked up about the argument I couldn't tell. I lay back and pushed my Broncos cap on to the back of my head and maybe I rolled my eyes a little or maybe some tiny things I did got up Henry's nose and led to him getting more than usually worked up in argument and ended in the kind of mess where no one gets the order of the anything except the Order of the Best Forgotten possibly.

As for me, by that stage, I was trying to get lift-off from this situation, aiming to beam myself on to Mount Evans among the glittery fragments and the sky which seemed a hundred different kinds of blue like all the blues on a Dulux Matchmaker chart when you are choosing paint.

I suppose one of the reasons for Henry's disappointment in the world today is the people of my generation, and maybe his hopes get raised when he finds someone young and likeable to admire. I guess this was the case with Ronnie. Up till that night, at any rate, when (tough luck, Henry!) Ronnie was letting him down badly, showing himself to be wearing the wrong colours after all, disagreeing with Henry and getting

72

very fervent and worked up about it, going pink with it all and pointing a bony finger saying things like: 'Surely if we know more, as we do about ourselves and our surroundings, it follows, doesn't it, that our condition is infinitely capable of improvement?'

But I wasn't listening that much – I was thinking of how we could get away in time – so I've never been quite sure why Ronnie got so agitated, unless it was that Henry kept flinging facts at him, facts which Ronnie didn't always know about, upon which Henry kept on saying things like: 'But, as a journalist, surely you must know . . .' etc., and later on: 'Don't tell me that, as a journalist . . .!'

Patrick didn't help a lot. He kept on trying to calm Ronnie down by telling him how most of what Henry said was only a subjective view, upon which Henry got even more riled, which caused his voice to go more northern, more like Jim's and got him standing up in the middle of the semi-circle of chairs and cushions, kind of towering and firing from both barrels. It was really getting very personal and my mother had to pour herself another drink. She could have stopped it any time, but oh no, no such luck: too scared that Henry would round on her, I dare say.

Or Ronnie could have stopped it too. If I'd been him, I'd have stood up and yelled at all of them: 'You're full of shit, the lot of you.' But he was ever so well-mannered in the short time that I knew him – viz. that evening and no longer and he had an agile intellect. Mr Forbes is always praising people with agile intellects and telling us that's what we should aim to achieve.

'What would have to happen, Henry,' Ronnie was saying, 'to make you agree that things were in some ways better in the world today?'

'Ah, now he's got you, Henry,' Jim said, lolling back.

No one's ever got Henry. Henry isn't to be got. I've found that out long since in arguments. Maybe he didn't go to university, but however good the point you make, it doesn't get you anywhere. This power he has must have come from having known so many people, through having travelled on business and spent evenings arguing with people as well as smiling on them all over the world.

Patrick looked at Ronnie and held one thumb up: 'What a very good question, mate,' he said. 'Congratulations!'

I looked at my watch. It was one-fifteen.

'A fairly bloody stupid question,' Henry said, looking cornered, which is like Troy looking cornered when you're getting near him in the paddock on a day he's decided he doesn't want to be ridden. 'That question gets us nowhere, nowhere!' Henry said.

Lily was yawning, putting her hand up to her mouth, and my mother was, between drinks, emptying ash trays into the wicker wastepaper basket, but spilling some of it. But she wasn't that far gone and for several minutes had been looking across at me, giving me the old silently communicated orders, saying: get to bed: leave now: you know your presence only aggravates: we're burning, aren't we? don't forget the erstwhile rule about not earholing grown-up conversations.

But I was having none of that. Catch me noticing that, I thought. Can't you see I am with *your* friend tonight? I signalled back.

This argument, I was beginning to think, was the worst there'd been since the one about Northern Ireland with Patrick some months earlier, or the one about the Common Market just before, or the one about private education there'd been with some friends who had crippled themselves financially to send their children to some posh dump or other and who, needless to say, weren't friends any more. Sometimes, I reflected, I could calculate that I have spent nearly all my life sitting on a cushion listening to Henry arguing and I still can't say what his philosophy of life is truly. Except that I could say what it wasn't. Like it isn't politically very left or very right because he can't stand either Thatcherism or Bennism, but doesn't seem that keen on any people in the middle either and would die rather than vote Social Democrat. I suppose it must be rotten feeling passionate but not having anywhere to commit yourself. If only he could have been like your average shopkeeper and monetarist or whatever.

By now it was getting really really bad and vicious with it, with Henry going on at Ronnie, telling Ronnie that as a journalist, which he was, wasn't he, surely it was important that he should be dispassionate and see things as they really were, while Patrick was saying that Ronnie did see things as they seemed to him and was very young still and Ronnie was beginning to say that they were telling him he didn't know how to do his job.

Then Patrick put his great feet in it offering to mediate and Henry said how typically Leadbetter that was, sitting on the sidelines, that was.

I could feel Ronnie getting very tense, like his leg muscles against mine were twanging and his eyes were getting wild like Henry's do and were that night. Not blazing yearning, but blazing-shooting-people-down and away from him. 'Listen to this, Ron,' Henry said. 'Just listen to this. Now this is journalism,' he said and he began on his favourite quote, which was this one by Hunter S. Thompson about the world being weird and cruel and no one, not even the meek, certainly not the meek, being likely to inherit the earth and that you have to live with the idea that there's no chance of finding peace and happiness, but that if you can get your hands on either one of those once in a while, you have to do the best you can between high spots . . .

Now usually when Henry quotes Hunter S. Thompson, people sit and go dead mousey quiet and then say oohs and ahs. Most people say that they think the quote is very deep.

And most people did go quiet at that, except that I remember hearing Patrick sighing like he was sighing about having to hear that quote again after hearing it a zillion times before.

Then Ronnie said: 'And you think that says it all, do you?'

And Patrick giggled a bit and my mother looked into her

glass and Patrick said that Ronnie was right and no one statement could ever say it all, could it?

All that time I hadn't said a thing, had I? And of all the things I could have said, the points I could have made about improvements in the world today like, say, at the very least about the betterment in women's rights and all that stuff, I had to say the worst thing possible. Maybe it was something in me wanted to diffuse things like my mother can occasionally diffuse things if she has her right head on.

Anyway it doesn't matter why I said what I said, but what I said was: 'Hunter S. Thompson lives in Aspen, I think someone said, but I didn't see him there.'

Then Henry said: 'Oh very relevant! So, Hunter S. Thompson lives in Aspen, does he?' and he imitated my voice as if I'd been putting on an American accent.

'Now, now,' Lily said. 'Now, Henry Harrison, don't be like that. I expect Petra had a lovely time in Colorado, didn't she?'

I didn't look at her, although I'd have liked to have thanked her for being on my side and meant to thank her the next morning, except that everything was so confused because of what happened later and various other carelessnesses of mine which led to everything else and probably to the end of everything one way and another. Anyway at that moment I couldn't look up at Lily and be grateful, because I'd got my head down, feeling I might cry if anyone looked into my face.

'I may have seen him, but I don't know what Hunter S. Thompson looks like anyway,' I said. 'I can see why he lives there though.'

'Oh I'm sure,' said Henry, 'that everything was perfect in Colorado, absolutely perfect, wasn't it? Oh why oh why did we have to come back to boring old home then? What a pity! What a come-down when everyone in Colorado knows exactly what should be done about the world, don't they?'

'I never said that. Never said anything like that,' I said. 'I bloody hardly ever talked about it, did I?'

'No, of course you didn't. Your pleasures are too private and have to be kept to yourself, not shared.'

'Oh come on, darling!' my mother said to Henry, leaning forwards to touch his arm and he moved his arm away from her and she looked at the ceiling, pretending nothing had happened.

'That's not the way,' said Jim. 'Oh come on, no, that isn't the way.'

In fact everyone kept saying 'come on' to each other and Ronnie began apologising for the fact that his views had upset people and Henry said to Ronnie that of course Ronnie knew better than him anyway, what with his university career and trained intellect. Which is what Henry hates in people on account of not having had that himself. He had got up by then and gone to the far end of the room by the window bay and stood there by the white curtains, but it was as if his back was shimmering and sharp and sending pointed missiles out at everyone.

'Perhaps I ought to go,' said Ronnie, getting to his feet.

'Of course,' said Henry from the far end of the room, not turning round.

Lily and my mother were tidying up again. I was helping them, but watching Ronnie and looking at my watch which said one-twenty-five. I remember Patrick was just sitting there still drinking and people were having to step over his legs.

Ronnie fetched his coat and was standing with it over his arm looking as if he wondered if he should approach Henry or not. 'Well . . . goodbye . . .' he was saying with one hand held out.

'Say goodbye to your guest, Henry,' said Patrick, truculent. 'Breaking a few tabus here, aren't we, Henry? After all he is your guest. You're awfully hard on people sometimes, Henry.'

'You're awfully hard on people sometimes, Henry!' – that was Henry himself imitating Patrick.

Patrick swilled the contents of his glass; 'I see it's better dead than Leadbetter night again,' he said.

77

Jim laughed, bending down and patting Patrick on the shoulder. 'You're as bad as him if you ask me,' he said.

No one did approach Henry in the end. Everyone went out of the room and left him there.

'I could talk to you lot all night if you'd only not get angry with each other,' Jim was saying.

Henry shouted from the lounge: 'I'm sorry the floor show is over now.'

Lily called back: 'Come on, Henry Harrison.' Lily has known Henry for years, ever since he and Jim were window-dressers together in a department store in Manchester or maybe it was Liverpool. Both she and Jim are used to Henry's flashpoints and would not be that disturbed by it all. In fact they have stayed friends and were the first people my mother rang to say that Henry hadn't come home on the appointed day.

Ronnie was standing by the door into the lounge with his coat on now and his university scarf round his neck. I think the university was Exeter.

It's all been very difficult to explain, this. My mother was leaning against the wall in the corridor with her arms folded across her chest and looking like she only wanted everyone out of the way. Ronnie was hovering, obviously wanting to shake hands with her, saying thanks very much and so on and he hoped, etc. . . . She must have been really far gone since she didn't seem to notice his extended hand. In fact she just walked past him and back into the lounge.

I should have explained to him later that it's Henry makes her like that, but didn't what with everything.

Anyway it was while she was in the lounge that I followed Ronnie out along the corridor and down through the shop, using the inside key which was on a hook in the corridor that night, knowing that someone would go down and remove it when they cleared the shop last thing, which, however many flashpoints there have been, however many orders for good behaviour haven't been awarded, is unfailingly completed.

SIX

Henry tells this story of a man who went seeking after the meaning of the universe and walked and walked through Asia and the Himalayas or wherever it is you find gurus and that. He climbed mountains and went through valleys and through villages asking where the wise man was who could tell him the meaning of life or the meaning of the meaning. Further and further he struggled, knackered to the core until eventually they said the man who had the truth about life and everything was up there in that grotto in that wood on that mountainside and he went there. And said to the wise old man: 'What is the meaning of life and the rest of it, old man?' and the wise man thought a bit and held his hand out, palm down and said: 'Life is like a fish.' And the man who travelled all that way, said: 'What? A fish?' and was terrifically disappointed.

'All right,' said the wise man, 'if you don't like it, then life is not like a fish.' And that is the end of the story which I don't tell as well as Henry does, but I tried telling it to Ronnie that night in the car. He didn't even laugh, but kept smoking and throwing barely-smoked fag ends out of his window and leaving the window wound down. My hair was blown about and I was freezing.

As he drove, his woollen university striped scarf blew out behind him. His mouth was set a bit open so it seemed; his teeth were very white. There was a moon showing up the chalky rounded hills around us as we crossed under the M3 going under it and north and still on north. He'd hardly said anything much, but turned his radio up so there was the sound of late night Radio Two and a cheerful disc jockey chuntering on while I was wondering what the hell Ronnie was about, realising I knew nothing about him except what I've said so far and that it didn't look like I was going to get the offer to drive.

I knew I wanted him but had got somewhat confused about that by now, but was trying at some stage to explain about Henry and his problems to do with having been in hospital at an early age, so being fair to Henry, telling Ronnie that he gets these irrational patches partly on account of he doesn't feel he's doing anyone any good or improving the life-style of anyone except rich people who can buy things in our shop. I also told him that scenes like the one he'd just been in weren't that unusual and that Henry would probably want to be mates with him again eventually.

The sports car was dead draughty, the temperature having plummeted quite suddenly. Though the sky looked about the same with a few stars and the clouds were moving speedily and the moon dodging in and out of them.

'Anyway, I bet you don't really believe life is getting better rather than worse,' I said, 'the quality of life, I mean, with the holocaust and everything.'

It crossed my mind that it was way after two o'clock by now and we had driven so far that I was never going to be let in to the flat again, so he had me on his hands for the night. Presumably he had a room somewhere.

'Though the quality of life itself isn't that awful until the holocaust,' I said so as not to seem too like Henry in my views of life. 'Haven't you a flat in town or anything?'

I'd never known a bloke so thrown by an argument. Except for Henry himself that is. But then most blokes I've known have been younger and not got Ronnie's brains and success behind them. Even Mr Forbes, who gets hysterical about ideas and abstractions, never goes over the top – not in class at any rate.

I couldn't think straight what with the speed, the cold air whizzing around and the terrific volume of music from the radio. We seemed to have got into high wooded country on narrow roads in among low trees where there were endless junctions and we might easily be getting lost. At corners he jerked the brakes till they squealed and then revved the engine up like he couldn't make up his mind which way he was heading.

Sex first time with anyone is always interesting but never that terrific, and no way did it look like I'd have it more than once with Ronnie. His ears when he first got his head against mine were like ice lollies. When he stopped the car by swerving off into the woods I could see the tops of bracken were still green as they leaned one way in the wind.

Sitting in the car I was even blowing my hands to get them warm. He'd gone to have a pee behind a tree, but hadn't said 'Excuse me'. Maybe there were other men besides Henry who lost all hold on normal mannered behaviour when their ideas were challenged.

It's a weird place, that wooded country where none of the trees are very tall, and I'll say it's windswept, not half windswept. My new friend Liz, with whom I spend a good deal of time these days, comes from there originally. She says that most folk there are from didicoy or gypsy families and talk unlike people from round here. In the past they were nearly always woodcutters or charcoal burners if they weren't gypsies. We must have nearly got into Berkshire.

When he got back into the car he began to kiss me and go further. The moonlight came and went with the moving of the trees and clouds and sometimes gave me glimpses of his eyes which looked ferocious like Henry's had. He wasn't forcing me. I was still keen, but remember thinking that the touch of

81

violence that he used with me was his way of getting back at Henry.

'I'm sorry,' he said afterwards. 'That was not my best.'

'It was pretty good,' I said, which was not entirely a lie.

Perhaps what was missing was the cosy bit where, when you've had a bloke for the first time, you tend to reminisce about past times with other people and reveal pieces of your past to each other and hopes if any. I never got to drive his car which was a pretty old one with a hood, maybe an MG.

Otherwise he hadn't forgotten himself entirely, having made the usual enquiries about the pill, etc., which made me think that being really mad and irresponsible is rare and people usually keep some kind of control. His enquiry reminded me of the pill which I was due to re-start that day, but hadn't started. All of which made me plan to get home pretty fast and take the first one of the month.

I'm trying to remember what we talked about on the way home. We did talk, I am sure, possibly about his girl friend who was at London University reading something to do with the environment. He may have said the name of the paper he was going to work for, but I forgot it, though I've often looked in the *Guardian*, which is our newspaper, to see if his name crops up anywhere, likewise in the *Observer* on Sundays and in Liz's *Daily Mail* and Jane's *Daily Telegraph*.

Kindly he lent me his mac and scarf on the way back. Oh yes – he did say: 'Sorry I can't take you anywhere tonight. I've given up my flat and am staying with an aunt.' He was leaving in the morning.

My dress was torn under the arm but I didn't mind about that. I haven't worn it since. I suppose if ever Ginny came to stay again I'd mend it and wear it since I wouldn't want to hurt her feelings.

Funny to think that if Henry never returned we might never see Ginny again except that she is Daisy's grandmother whatever Daisy says. Or she might come to a funeral, which I shouldn't think about.

Whenever I think of 'life is like a fish' these days it reminds me of Ronnie, so I've rather gone off that story.

I remember standing there when he dropped me, standing across from the shop near the bottom of the park with my heels sinking into the turf which had been softened by this rain that had begun to drive down from town.

With any luck they'd have gone to bed, all of them so drunk they might just have forgotten about the back door for once. Or even luckier – my mother might have stayed awake until Henry had gone to sleep, in which case she'd be bound to make sure it was unbolted for me; that surely wasn't something she'd forget to do. It's the kitchen door I'm speaking of; no way would anyone wish anyone to leave the shop unlocked.

So I went into the yard and could see that all the house lights were off. The door was bolted. Sod my mother, I was thinking, though I do not blame her in the long run for such things. Likewise the back windows into the downstairs workroom were well bolted. Likewise the door into the bike-shed where I have been known to spend nights in warmer times.

So I went back across the road to get a good look into the shop, clutching my arms, teeth chattering, hair wet and hanging down damp on my shoulders. It wasn't until the other day that I had it cut. The shop had its lights turned down, as it always does at night, leaving just enough light to show passing policemen that all is well inside.

Ronnie had offered me his mac to keep until the next day, but I didn't feel like being obliged to him and having to wait around expecting him to fetch it from our place or anything. So I needn't have felt so cold and miserable, but did.

There *was* someone in the shop, so I could have banged on the door or window, couldn't I? It was just that – well it isn't easy to explain or tell about – it was just that there was the shop all put back to rights and there were my mother and Henry up there on the balcony. Not making love or anything. Just lounging there on the carpets – her propped on cushions with her eyes shut and him lying with his head in her lap and her hand

83

was on his head like it was protecting him. Once or twice she seemed to open her eyes and look down on him and stroke his head. It was a bit like one of those old paintings people did of Jesus having been taken from the cross – the way that Henry lay, so flopped and relaxed. Almost as if it was he who had been sinned against.

The rain was streaking down across his name on the door where it's emblazoned in gold leaf, where my mother's name is emblazoned as well, where the rain was running down over the golden Harrisons.

Life is a bloody fish, I remember thinking, waking up at Bentley's on Bentley's sofa with his old ex-army greatcoat over me, thinking that I must get home, then going home and throwing sticks at Daisy's window at the back, Daisy coming down in her nightie asking me if she was to say I'd been there all night, me saying: 'No, don't bother.'

Remember getting into the bunk I was using in her room because of Jim and Lily being in my room. Remember going to sleep again because I couldn't get into that room until they woke. Remember going into the passage to see if I could hear them stirring. It was dead cold and the heating wasn't on, suddenly winter which makes a difference to everything with people having to stay inside and look at each other.

So I was waiting, but when I got into my room I found I couldn't find my pills in the drawer and had forgotten that I had no new pack. Being Sunday and no chemists open except for emergency prescriptions, I'd have to wait until Henry got up, then I'd pinch one of my mother's – same brand as mine.

Jim and Lily were cheerful in the kitchen, helping my mother cook breakfast. I didn't feel like eating anything. Then everyone was going out to lunch in some pub they fancied somewhere, one that had a kiddies' room so that Daisy could go. Henry got up in time to do that. Meanwhile I went back to bed and pretended to be asleep so that there was no chance anyone would expect me to go as well.

Alone at last: my mother's room: the double bed in chaos and party clothes spread everywhere. The drawer she always keeps the pills in, where she also keeps some less valuable jewellery and tights and that. So many other pills, though, beside the flat pack: pills she takes for everything from nerves through to headaches, backaches, apathy. You name it, she takes pills for it, vitamins, the lot, like she believes in anything to keep her going, I suppose. And all these days passing now when she is straining, I guess, against giving in, you can catch her popping a pill into her mouth between cigarettes and sips of gin. Oh mother, mother, how could you! Take it with more bitter lemon, for Christ's sake.

I was telling Liz about the pills the other day. We were playing space invaders in this pub at the time. She said her mother does the same and every night drinks like alcohol would run out in the morning. Playing space invaders costs a bit but you don't drink while you are playing it. I told my mother the other day she should try playing space invaders since it takes your mind completely off your hangups. I even suggested she should get one installed at home because the saving on drink would pay for it. But she said she'd never get the hang of it, that her mind was too worn down with other concerns to absorb new techniques of an electronic nature. 'You mean,' I said, 'that you don't think you could ever get your space invaders head on?'

Making her laugh for a milli-second, but then she looked tearful because jokes about which head she has on are jokes that Henry makes best.

In my mother's drawer back last autumn there was just one packet of pills and that had only one pill left in it. I stood in their bedroom which was gloomy because of the greyness of the day and the bluish colour scheme; I drew the curtains right back and searched again. No sign of any other packet of appropriate pills anywhere in any drawer.

Never mind, I thought. Surely at the end of a cycle or the beginning of one, the ovaries are not suddenly going to burst into egg-releasing action on account of one pill missed. Surely not mine and even more surely not her ageing ovaries.

I imagined eggs popping out of ovaries like in space invaders the invaders pop out of space on the screen and rain down missiles. When they meet a lively sperm and knit with it, the screen would light up: 'Well done, earthling' or in my case or in my mother's case because of her age: 'Tough luck, earthling.'

Which would be the most tough-luck-earthling pregnancy? Mine by Ronnie or my mother's by Henry? Could she survive another pregnancy? Could any of us survive another pregnancy of hers? Could I survive another Daisy and Henry's pride in her and Henry's blow by blow account of the birth which, typically, he would claim he had accomplished practically unaided?

Tough luck everyone, it would be. Although my mother would not complain about a missing pill. She'd raise her eyebrows, put her hand up to the back of her neck and tell herself she hadn't got her pill head on that day, assume she must have taken the pill already and forgotten doing it. Then take a pill for worrying about being absent-minded.

No, Henry didn't really say he'd done it unassisted. He went on for months about it being the most moving experience in his life and anyone who had seen someone giving birth would always be totally committed to that person and the person given birth to for ever and ever. So, Henry? A gentle reminder, Henry. That's all that this is, Henry. Henry Harrison, space invader, this is your life. Though I know you don't like being reminded of things you said in the past. OK, Henry Harrison, life is a fish, but is it a sprat or a shark, I ask myself?

That Sunday I rang up Jane, but she was out. I rang up Jenny, who is the girl who is allowed to have her bloke in bed in the family home, but she was out as well. I didn't know Liz then, but she doesn't take the pill because she doesn't get screwed, she says, and reckons the bloke should be responsible. Liz says her mother is nutty but not entirely without brains and goes, in her saner moments, to some feminist organisation which preaches all this and Liz agrees with it. I haven't really argued this out with Liz yet. It is what Mr Forbes would call a very tenable theory, I suppose.

A third extensive search through my mother's drawers and even Henry's drawers revealed there were no pills anywhere. Nor any other form of contraceptive. Suppose they didn't make love tonight, I considered. After all she was, the evidence suggested, right at the end of her cycle when the urge on the woman's part is reputedly low.

Look at it another way: be intellectually agile on the matter, I said to myself. In the event that they did make love and she did conceive, who would most easily procure an abortion? She or I? Surely her age would encourage any doctor to recommend one. But what would Henry say if my mother had to have one? What would we feel if this new fusion of his flesh and blood and her flesh and blood had to be sucked out and removed and chucked into a pedal bin? While he wouldn't need to know if I had an abortion, would he?

After all these calculations, quite exhausted by these calculations, I went back round to Bentley's since he'd told me that morning he had some good stuff to smoke. On the way I reflected: if my mother had an abortion recommended by a doctor, it would be on the National Health, wouldn't it?

From a call box outside Bentley's, I rang up Jane again. She was still out. It was freezing cold. I went back into the park and ran chased by the black dog. Maybe it has no real home. It's always fastening on to people.

Unable to get warm, I returned to Bentley's to think further. He has an electric fire into which you have to put money. But he had no cash, so I lent him a pound's worth of 10p pieces and sat by the fire and smoked with him.

He has a map of Britain on the wall of his bedsit. He was always good at geography: it was his only O Level – or maybe CSE – I can't remember which. He'd marked the map to show where the fallout would reach if H bombs fell on London, Birmingham, Manchester, Bristol, Glasgow, etc. Bentley claims he's never bothered to think about his future life, because he is fairly sure he hasn't one.

Even if my mother couldn't get an abortion on the National Health, she and Henry could afford one of the other kind easily enough. If I hurried home, I was thinking, gazing at the map, I could get there and take the pill before they got back from lunch at the pub. I was gazing at the map and thinking how my problem might be not one future life but another as well.

Bentley said: 'Whatever's bugging you, forget it. Now is a time we can do exactly what we like because of not living to see the consequences.'

'Long-term I agree with you,' I said, 'but this isn't that long-term a kind of thing to have on your mind.' But I stayed. I'd already invested in the heat of his room which was giving me, as was the smoking, immediate benefits.

Liz, when she's playing space invaders, talks jive talk, calling out: 'Shee-it man!' when she loses. She does accents and imitations pretty OK. It turns out we have another taste in common, that of Bob Marley. So, having a bit of spare cash today, which is ten days after Henry's disappearance – rather, seven days after the day he failed to return from British Interiors – or D Day plus ten, as they say in war movie titles, I bought us both Bob Marley double albums. Even my mother is in favour of Bob Marley, saying the Wailers have a nice calming sound, calming and repetitive. Anything to keep her off the pills and gin, I say.

SEVEN

So that's September recalled and what led up to later events. Meanwhile Patrick has been sussing out how to go about private investigation. He says that's the only thing to do if my mother won't go to the police or even talk about going to the police, or even talk about Henry at all, except on the phone to other people.

People saw Henry at the exhibition. People didn't see him with anyone particular – or so I gather from what my mother says at her end of the phone.

British Interiors is held in Birmingham biennially and it may be of interest that it was there, I think, that he first met my mother. Details have never been revealed to me, but I reckon Daisy must have been conceived there. At the time he was married to a woman called Vivienne.

'Do you think he could have gone back to his first wife?' Jane said yesterday.

'He couldn't stand her, could he? He was always saying so, wasn't he?'

'That may have been a façade,' said Jane. She's been on about façades a lot recently. She works with a woman who is having a menopausal nervous breakdown and keeps crying, saying everything is a façade and no one speaks the truth to anyone.

My mother has not reached the menopause – which I deduce from my observations that she still takes the pill, etc. Nor, now I come to think about it, has she Vivienne's initials on the list of those suspected of harbouring Henry.

'You never really know for sure about the real feelings and opinions of people even when you live close to them,' Jane said.

This lunchtime I was buying her cocktails and sandwiches because I'd found a tenner lying around in the kitchen on the dresser this morning. I put down the sandwich and thought about Vivienne. After all he stuck living with Vivienne for ten years, which was longer than he seems to have stuck living with us.

'People make other people's lives a misery without intending to, don't they, I think,' said Jane.

I looked across at the bar where people stood in posh winter coats because of this east wind. It's been like that for a few days now and when it's like that I shrivel and don't feel like doing anything. But there was this woman at the bar who reminded me a bit of Vivienne. This woman wore a beige coat with a long fur collar and was obviously well satisfied with the way she looked. I only saw Vivienne twice. The first time she was with Henry after he had begun knocking around with my mother after they met at British Interiors.

'I think you really deep down want him back,' said Jane.

'Yes, possibly,' I said, leaving it at that because I'm not really sure whether really really deep down inside people there is anything.

The first time I saw Vivienne with Henry, I was with my mother and my mother seemed not to look at him, but I could feel her hand which was holding mine getting sticky with guilt. I had been about to say: 'Isn't that the man who . . .?' but realised that she didn't know I'd seen her with him across the river. They, Vivienne and Henry, were walking along a pavement in Winchester and he was in the white raincoat that he went on wearing for years and still has. He once said she used to choose his clothes for him and, since he still has some of the clothes she chose, he can't have quarrelled with her taste.

'You see, you are upset,' said Jane. 'You haven't finished your sandwich.' That was one thing she was right about, the sandwich, I mean.

Henry actually met Vivienne at British Interiors too. He would say that both the worst thing (Vivienne) and the best thing (my mother) had happened to him there. Although he wasn't always nasty about her – to be fair. The other time I saw her was when she came into the shop a few years later for some books of hers he'd taken by mistake at the time of the separation. I remember watching him hand them to her smiling like they were fairly friendly old acquaintances.

'If it would help,' said Jane, 'I'd come with you to Winchester. It's my half day and I'd like to go to Debenhams.'

'OK,' I said. I hadn't any classes that it mattered about.

'There's a bus at two-fifty,' said Jane. 'Leave no stone unturned I always say.'

While Vivienne might have gone to British Interiors, it's unlikely she'd have been at the carpet fair last September. And, although it seems from the hieroglyphics in my mother's diary that it's been the same unknown person she's suspected ever since, Henry's unpredictability must be considered. And so, although it seemed a bit daft going to Winchester, I went and on the way we talked a lot about the dreams we had been having. Nothing to do with Henry at all really. Jane had been having this anxiety dream about Geoff being kicked in the crutch at a rugby match. 'It's ever such a recurring one,' she said.

My recurring dream, I was telling her, is about getting dragged by some strong fast horse along a rough ground like a race track, rather like in the *Ben Hur* chariot race. I cannot see the horse but can hear its hooves and dust is flying in my eyes. People are cheering and the sharp metal edge of the spectator

91

stand is getting nearer with every lap of the track I take.

'Henry dreams about his first wife still,' I said. 'He dreams she's standing on a pier at some seaside pointing out to sea and telling him to dive in and rescue someone.'

'He must have terrible feelings of inadequacy towards her,' Jane said. The bus was grinding up this steep hill and the countryside around looked starved and grey. 'And does your mother dream about your father do you think?' she said.

'She hasn't said she does. She had one about being dragged like me, but by two horses and in different directions. That's the only dream she's ever mentioned that I can remember.'

But mostly we talked about Jane and Geoff and how she'd been to dinner with his parents and they'd talked about clothes afterwards. Geoff's mother had taken her upstairs to show her all her evening dresses. Jane wondered if this was significant, like did the mother see her as a future daughter-in-law or anything? 'I mean it's very intimate showing people all your clothes like that.'

I said that it sounded like she might *want* to be considered as a daughter-in-law from the way she was speaking of it. Then she turned to talking about the marvellous sex life she had with Geoff, but paused and said: 'Oh, Petra, I am sorry to be going on about it when you haven't anyone, you know, I mean . . .'

'I could have someone, couldn't I?'

'I think you're very wise to leave it, you know, after everything . . .'

'Oh well,' I said. We'd got to Winchester.

I was half thinking that I might quite like to hang around in Winchester till evening, to avoid Patrick's company and questioning. Although in some ways he is easier to have around than Henry. But he sits in the chair which Henry used to sit in which happens to be the best one for watching TV from, and, because my mother drinks, he drinks too, using the excuse that it's bad for people to drink alone. He's got through nearly one whole bottle of Henry's scotch and gets to talking about his ideas, like this cock-up theory of history which he has, using as a prime example this subject he was doing for his PhD which was the Austro-Prussian War, which was more or less started by mistake.

Henry used to shut him up about this, saying that the cock-up theory only went so far and he would argue more for a conspiracy theory or even that there had to be a prime mover somewhere, making things happen. Although Henry is in no way a Christian and certainly not a practising one.

Apparently in this Austro-Prussian War, neither side wanted to fight, but each thought the other side was mobilising and began to think it might be a good idea to attack – before the other side finished mobilising. Something like that, anyway. I did History O Level, but I never heard of that war.

My mother doesn't really listen to Patrick and keeps watching TV and not commenting. Sometimes we play three-handed bridge, which isn't a bad game but one which Henry would never play for long. It's like with Henry away that everyone is doing things they couldn't easily do when he was there, but no one feels very happy doing them. Except Patrick possibly. Mind you, you have to concentrate nonstop in three-handed because of there being no dummy, so my mother has to get her head together for it and gets riled when Patrick wins and he vice versa. Perhaps they are re-living old childhood patterns.

Last night Patrick went on and on about the cock-up theory and said it applied to nearly everything in life, his own marriage for instance: how his ex-wife drove him into being unfaithful. I'd always thought she was unfaithful to him, but he explained last night how she suspected him and suspected him until eventually he got a trapped feeling and *was* unfaithful. Which meant she, in the end, started been unfaithful as well in order to get even with him. 'I drove her to it, you see,' he said.

'You really don't think there is a prime mover in any way at all?' I said.

'God knows,' he said and began laughing like a drain at his own joke, so I gave up.

'All I know,' my mother said, 'is that if there is a prime mover he is not on my side.' She looked fairly upset and went to bed soon after saying that, which was the nearest she has got to mentioning that anything is wrong at all.

The prime mover versus cock-up argument used to be quite interesting with Henry there, although I can't believe he really believed in any kind of ordered universe. I reckon his life would be total chaos if my mother didn't organise it for him. And Vivienne seems to have organised it even more, which he resented like mad. So there I was today wandering around in Winchester and getting more and more doubtful that he could possibly have got it together with her again.

I knew the house they lived in by the fir tree in a tub. It was a tree he'd planted. He used to say he'd planted it to signify that he'd made it to this house, a house he at last owned for himself. He said we Leadbetters would never understand the pride of owning a house and planting a tree because we had all the trees we wanted and could gallop through trees till kingdom come and never know what it was to go out and buy and plant one single tree outside your own house.

That little house has four windows and a door, like a doll's house Daisy has. The paint is bright and neat and today I was sure there wasn't anyone there. The east wind blew down the Romsey Road where the house is, and I felt conspicuous. It was a narrow road and when trucks passed they blotted out the house completely.

He also said that the house was a dead house with no family, no clutter and every time he used an ash tray, Vivienne emptied it straight away. 'I let her down,' he used to say. 'I used the ash trays.' But the odd thing was I knew he'd kept the key of the house in a drawer in the office desk at home. The key is still there. So is a photo of Vivienne. I checked that only a few nights ago.

With Vivienne meals were always on time, too many meals, he said, because she felt she must provide him with meals on time. Because of not loving him perhaps, he said. To compensate, he said. And she darned his socks which my mother has never done. They didn't have kids: I think they chose not to have kids, although he must have wanted some seeing that he is so crazy about Daisy.

In that house, Henry also said, there were endless clocks ticking, and the one thing among all other things he can't stand are noisy clocks. Time bothers him or bothered him. Although he wasn't often late for things, but got in a state about being late for them. In case he was late for them, I mean. He should be in a state now, shouldn't he? I wonder what anxiety dreams he's having about my mother.

I usually am not bothered about going up to doors and ringing bells. Partly it was being so cold made me not want to go and ring that bell. What would I have said if he had been there anyway? And if he'd seen me coming, would he have even answered the door? I decided that I'd pretend to Jane that I'd rung the bell and drawn a blank and wondered what to do until it was time to meet her.

I suppose that people who go into cathedrals don't need to spend a lot of time worrying about the prime mover versus the cock-up conspiracy, and the best of luck to them I'd say. But I will say that cathedrals are better than pedestrian precincts like the one I'd spent some time standing in hoping to see Jane again. Yes, it's probably a good thing that they have cathedrals on the whole. The music tends to be rather Radio Three, but OK if you like that sort of thing. It gives you a clean feeling.

I recognised Vivienne just inside the door. I wasn't surprised to see her since I'd noticed a poster about a flower festival which was starting the next day. I haven't said she was a flower arranger by profession and writes articles and teaches it all over the country, have I? Anyway, she was standing there near the door of the cathedral with piles of flowers in cartons and buckets, ready to be arranged on this wooden pedestal. She was holding up spring greenery, daffodils, white narcissi and other flowers, holding them up as if speculating about their shape and suitability. In the distance was organ music and a man speaking the words of a service in a singsong fashion.

She was standing by this massive stone pillar which had a spotlight fixed to it. I recognised her by the glasses, same as in the photograph, swept up spectacles jewelled at the corners of the lenses – and her blonde waved hair. She had a smoother complexion than I had expected somehow.

I watched her for a bit, then wandered off along a passage near this closed off bit where the choir were singing. I went along beside it towards the far end of the building where there were memorial stones put up to remind people of quite interesting people from the past who had achieved a lot. A boy was singing solo in a clear high voice. The sound went up, right into the dark ceiling spaces miles above my head.

Which reminded me of Giles who was in a church choir at prep school. I used to tease him, tell him it was rubbish, but he never changed his mind about it being a good thing to do. It was probably that experience that caused him to decide to be a clergyman; which partly led last year to our agreeing to end having sex together, though I was quite glad of the excuse in some ways. So Giles got into the habit of being in church whereas I have only been in a few of them, like for grandparents' funerals and so on and for my christening I presume. My parents couldn't agree about my name so they gave me one each. My father's choice was Olivia, so my mother won, it could be said. Although he calls me by that name still sometimes.

The cathedral seemed dustier than churches that you see on television, not so well lit and the only colour seemed to be the choirboys' robes, bright red with super white ruffles. It reminded me of that film where a nun prostrates herself on the altar steps, but it looked like you would get dirty if you did that, though I'm sure people working in cathedrals try and keep them clean.

So I was in this dark passage now and there was no one here apart from me. Because of the music I couldn't even hear the sound of my trainers on the stone. I read this plaque about a man who had gone down under the flooded foundations in a diving suit – years and years before they had frogmen that was – when they thought the cathedral would be undermined by water. Poor bloke, I thought, at least people don't have to do things like that now. And Henry's always saying that the quality of life gets worse.

Then the music stopped and I turned the corner to go back to where Vivienne stood. Her hair was more white than blonde I noticed as I watched her across this enormous expanse of stone floor, thinking what a lot of space there was in this cathedral, though I could imagine once that it used to be crowded, packed with people in the days when it was popular.

My mother, in addition to rejecting other values with which she was indoctrinated, has never bothered much about formal Christianity, except she claims to have kept roughly to the ethic, by which she means, I presume, turning the other cheek and being humble – in regard to Henry anyway.

Mr Forbes goes to church: surprising, that. He once said it wasn't that he believed in everything that went on there, but because he'd had his kid christened and felt a sort of obligation to the vicar. The wine is good at communion, he said. 'Christianity is responsible for all the trouble in Northern Ireland,' I said once, but he said that people who didn't believe in anything were more likely to go mad than other people.

Prayers were going on again and there was this whispering behind me. I turned and saw a little man in a macintosh mouthing the prayers with his eyes shut like he was in pain or agony or something. It gave me shivers up the spine. I had to move. I was thinking how if my mother was in her right mind, when I went home we'd have an interesting argument. I'd tell her I'd been to Winchester Cathedral and there was this man and wasn't Christianity a waste of time and hadn't it caused a lot of trouble in the world. And she would say: but Christianity is there and we can't change history can we? And I'd say yes but it was terrible and it fooled people like Mr Forbes and she'd say

97

that it maybe had done good as well as evil and that was something, wasn't it?

It was like the man I'd seen praying was having someone saying to him: 'There's no answer to that; there's no answer to that' over and over again in his head. And I was thinking how it had been silly coming here and had depressed me and how I could have stayed at home and done my *Lear* essay on pernicious daughters. Mr Forbes said the other day that we might consider that it was being disappointed in his daughters and the crumbling structure of his life generally had sent Lear mad.

Then the organ blasted out again in a springy tune, like trumpets with strong rhythm. The choir came out, processing, little boys in front and larger ones behind, then some men, one of them carrying a highly polished silver cross which looked extremely valuable. After that some more people followed, passing me while the music blared out as full and stomach-churning as any quadrophonic sound. Then I was watching Vivienne again, making the foundations of her arrangement which seemed to take on a fan-like shape with a pale look to it: lime green tracery spread out against a dark stone pillar, frilly edges to the leaves. I watched her picking up a daffodil, stroking its stalk as if persuading it to curve. Like Henry used to say she did. Like Henry used to say she wanted him to fit into a shape he didn't have. I've never heard that she married again.

He's always talking about what went wrong with him and Vivienne. My mother never really talks about what went wrong with her and my father. It's like a part of her life she wants to cancel out, pretend it didn't happen. Nor does my father ever mention it, things that we did while he was still around. Not that we did much all together like some families do.

Vivienne stuck the daffodil into the container in the shape she'd bent it to, then walked back a good few steps on her little low heels and looked at the effect. Then she saw me standing there and came across saying: 'Are you who I think you are?'

Perhaps all sorts of people seem nice if you only talk to them for a few minutes, but it was hard to imagine Vivienne saying all the rotten things to Henry that he claims she did: about him being an inadequate non-home-loving husband, oversexed and the rest of it.

She stood under her spotlight and the corners of her glasses sparkled, although her style in general was dead plain and lady-like. I was amazed that she'd recognised me since she'd only seen me once before properly – that time in the shop.

I couldn't tell her why I'd come, so made up a story about doing a project for sociology. She went on stroking another daffodil, trying to beguile this one into an arc like the other. Then she shoved a length of fine wire up its stalk: 'Is that to make it taller?' I asked.

Vivienne smiled and said 'Yes'. She had very good teeth, much better than my mother's – possibly because of not having had children, so that all the nourishing meals that Henry told us about had gone into her tooth enamel. Having good nourishing meals forced on him was another thing he beefed about.

Several other women had set up pedestals and were arranging flowers as well. One woman nearby had silver leaves and what looked like silver-painted twigs mixed in with deep red tulips.

'I like your arrangement better than that one over there,' I said to Vivienne, feeling that I needed to keep the conversation going.

'That one is for St Matthew,' said Vivienne. 'It represents money, commerce, which is why perhaps it has more dead material than mine. Mine is called St Luke, the healing quality of spring. At least that is the way I think of St Luke.'

Vivienne's voice is light, something like Jane's voice, but with hardly any accent although she comes from the north like Henry does. Her voice is more like a telephone operator's voice or a schoolteacher's voice. I kept thinking that if she was harbouring Henry she wouldn't be so calm, wouldn't go on talking in that dead calm way about the differences between St

99

Matthew and St Luke as though it was the sort of thing people spent a lot of time worrying about or arguing about.

'I suppose you had to read it to find out about it, read St Luke I mean,' I said. I needed to leave now. I also needed a cigarette.

'Well, it wasn't as if it was for the first time,' said Vivienne, in a tone which suggested that Bible-reading was something she did for a pastime like knitting or watching television. She was wearing a neat grey suit and a navy polo-necked sweater. In some ways she reminded me of Mrs Thatcher in style, although she wasn't so aggressive with it to my way of thinking. No, I can't smoke here probably, I was also thinking, as she clipped the stalk of a narcissus with her yellow-ended scissors so sharply that the tip of the juicy stalk shot beyond the newspaper spread at her feet.

More people kept coming in through the main door, which sent wind scudding across the floor. I was freezing, but rooted to the spot with my hands wedged in the pockets of my tracksuit top and wishing I'd come out in my duffle coat. I thought of Jane who'd soon be waiting for me in the café where we'd said we'd meet. Here the wind belted through the huge doorway, so I moved my feet up and down. Maybe people who go to cathedrals intentionally are prepared to put up with sub-zero temperatures.

Vivienne looked at me with her head on one side as if about to ask me what it was I'd really come about, then said: 'You ought to come to the opening festival. We're having a procession and some of the local schools are joining in. Then in Lent . . .' She went on talking about dates and saints' days and all sorts of times which mean things in the Christian world and someone crossed the floor towards the vast cathedral double doors and clanged them shut. Most doors when they slam make the whole building shudder; this one made a heavy noise, but no way could you feel it through your feet or any of your body. The flowers on the pedestal nodded because of the sudden change of draught. While Vivienne went on smiling,

100

always peaceful with the same fixed smile. Everything about her made me realise that she was hooked on church like some people are hooked on pubs or darts matches or cricket or rugby football or space invaders and fruit machines and that church was probably the thing she had been driven to like Patrick's wife was driven to being unfaithful. But what a thing to be driven to in Vivienne's case.

'And how is Henry?' she said suddenly.

I had been here before, I remembered, with my mother that time we saw Henry and Vivienne. After we'd seen them my mother suddenly took to trying to make the day into an educational outing for me, making me read the memorials and that, telling me how I had been christened but only out of social necessity to celebrate my birth and because my father wanted it. That time we visited here was the time we went home and my father asked me all about what we'd done as if he suspected something. I remember thinking I could have shopped my mother about Henry then, could have made up something about meeting this man in Winchester, but decided it was too definite a lie. I could have shopped her other times, like at King's Radlett when they thought I was at school, the time I saw them walking behind the willows; more than once I'd seen them sauntering behind the willows hand in hand.

Not long after all that my mother, with a highly nervous expression on her face, told me about Daisy being on the way and Henry arriving in our lives as if it was all a promise of joy to come. She was right about Daisy coming.

This evening in the early evening Daisy was calling out. I ran upstairs to my mother's room where Daisy was looking very tiny in the huge bed which she shares with my mother these nights. I picked her up in her cream viyella nightie and her hair hung down over my arm. She said she was cold, so I took her into the lounge where the gas fire was on. Then I fetched the huge blue-flowered double duvet and spread that out and

101

cocooned her in it. My mother had gone out for the first time since Henry left: she'd gone out with Patrick for a drink.

Daisy cheered up after a bit and made the hell of a mess humping the duvet up and pretending it was an igloo and she an Eskimo. She got to be something of a nuisance asking me to play with her in there and to be the Eskimo wife or husband, whichever I chose, as long as I would be one of them.

'I'll be the husband,' I said, 'out killing seals, but not all that far away.'

'You'll be away for weeks and weeks and weeks,' said Daisy.

Sometimes she says exactly how long Henry has been away for and begins to sigh and we're running out of ideas to distract her with. But luckily tonight she got worked up because we had an argument about which pole these Eskimos were at. I said the south pole and she screamed: 'There aren't any Eskimos at the south pole. Only teams of research experts.'

I really had a tussle with her, rolling on the floor, no holds barred, which took her mind off things. I'd only just quietened her by the time my mother came in.

My mother was slurring her words and unsuccessfully trying to make the ends of them sound neat and asking me if anyone had rung. She'd dressed up in her black velvet skirt and silk Indian top and was sitting by the fire, rather swaying by the fire, playing with her long string of beads. I wanted to ask her if she and Patrick had decided anything, but she got up and began rearranging things on the mantelpiece and went to bed herself soon after that.

It was time to check the diary again, so I took my torch down to the workroom. The key to the locked drawer is always in her handbag somewhere. I re-examined the hieroglyphics which take the form of small red triangles. They first occurred at the time of the carpet fair, then reappeared on various days last autumn. Then there's a gap until this year's diary: here – a larger triangle for the day he left for British Interiors.

Famous infamous British Interiors where Daisy was conceived six years ago. She is definitely Henry's, by the way. They

102

had to adopt her legally after they were married. Maybe my father and mother couldn't have any more children between them. Nor has my father any by Laura in Colorado. Maybe his sperm has gone off or whatever, though he's not the kind of man to wear tight jeans which Jane says causes that kind of deterioration. And maybe Henry only married my mother because of Daisy and now he reckons he has done his duty by the two of them and left.

None of this which I am telling is for Patrick yet, or for any investigator he might get. I've told him nothing and it's up to my mother if she wants to tell him about the significance of the red triangles. But I have been telling Liz how it began last autumn, the countdown to it all, the night of the long whatsits, Ronnie and the rest of it.

'Sex *is* the strongest passion known to human beings, isn't it?' said Liz, reminding me of how Forbes said that was a quote of Hardy's somewhere. 'If you like that sort of thing,' she said.

EIGHT

Since the fruitless trip to Winchester I have begun two essays, the 'pernicious daughters' one, plus another left over from last autumn: 'Compare and contrast the characters of Shepherd Oak and Sergeant Troy.' Perhaps if I can finish at least one of these I will be rewarded with a warm beam of totally unsarcastic approval by Mr Forbes. Which, in turn, could well keep the wolf from the door and me out of the Colorado college.

Funnily enough my father didn't mention the college once in the letter I had from him today. It was full of the snow and the skiing and the beauty of it all. He always thinks wherever he is is the best place to be as if he had discovered it. I suppose people have to think where they are is pretty OK or they wouldn't hang around there.

Mind you, in Colorado they have the best road system of any of the states on account of the government dumps nuclear waste there and builds good safe roads to transport it. Sometimes that made me uneasy, thinking about the waste being transported and sitting around underground. I had to remind myself of that up on Mount Evans that time.

Echo Lake, Soda Creek, Squaw Pass and Idaho Springs – oh yearn yearn yearn, I sometimes think. But the winter must be deathly except for the skiing and you can't ski every day, can you, if there's college and Laura breathing down your neck with her peculiar brand of reproving earnestness.

Oddly enough I first read *Far From the Madding Crowd* up near Squaw Pass and was ever so impressed with Sergeant Troy where he waves his cavalry sword in the hollow in the ferns and slices off a lock of Bathsheba's hair, which he then tucks inside his uniform jacket, unbuttoning it to do so. Which is about as far as anyone disrobes in Hardy and carries this terrific subtext of sex.

Thinking about Troy I should make it clear that I didn't call my horse after the bastard-query-non-bastard Troy. My horse was already called that when my mother bought him for me at an auction. Probably by mistake – a case of having the wrong head on like the time she slipped up meaning to bid for lot 176 which was a Victorian patchwork quilt and getting instead lot 177 which was a collection of flea-ridden bedclothes and a manky mattress.

Possibly she had intended to buy a fleet-of-foot little chestnut pony with a pedigree. Troy was actually trained to be a trotting horse, but couldn't be trusted to trot properly. I heard much later that he'd nearly killed a bloke by bolting and overturning the carriage.

But, looking at the Troy/Bathsheba passage again today reminded me of where I first read it and of how we fished in Echo Lake but never caught anything. I decided that holiday that America had confirmed my father's optimism. Not only because of always expecting to catch fish and never catching them, but on account of his view of human nature. He and Laura had taken to rehabilitating ex-convicts as a kind of hobby and they had with them this girl called Tammy who was fresh out of the state corrective institute or whatever it was called. She was a kind of houseguest, and while my father and I were fishing, Laura was encouraging Tammy to take up painting.

Liz reminds me a bit of Tammy, who was tough and wisecracking, but burly with it. When I got bored of fishing and reading I would go and watch her working away with this set of oils they had bought for her. She used to paint the crags and gritty landscape which was the view uphill from outside the camper which was parked just above the tree line. While I sat she'd tell me about the jobs she'd done and about her bloke who was still inside and whom she missed a lot and cried about at night.

Laura kept saying why not paint the greener landscape downhill from the camper, the spruces and the paler aspen trees, but Tammy went on sketching sharp stones in bright sun and deep shadows pretty skilfully, telling me the while that she'd do anything right up to putting herself at risk of execution by committing first-degree homicide to get her bloke back beside her. Although she was basically a safe-breaker.

After she'd left, I told my father that I reckoned he and Laura were wasting their time. Tammy would go on being a criminal as long as it suited her and whatever anyone did for her. I had a row with him and made him angry for the only time in my three weeks' visit. He told me that maybe I was right and human nature didn't change and hadn't changed and I was a walking example of it. I talked like my mother used to talk and it was as if once pessimism got into the blood, the line would never be free of it.

'Balls and bullshit,' I said, which shocked him and he turned quite pale under his suntan and must have assumed I'd learned that from Henry. Well, I did of course, but it never sounds bad when Henry uses it.

My father is a fattish man of fifty now and usually dead calm and implacable like Echo Lake looks. But that day it was as if he was ready to weep as he looked down on the spruces and aspens. 'It's a creeping disease,' he said, 'a curse almost.'

It all put me off the place rather and still does in retrospect. I thought he was going to start wiping his eyes on the corner of his summer shirt and I'm sure I saw a tear drop on to the toe of his sandals. And it reminded me of how I nearly killed him once.

106

Maybe the only thing he and I ever could have in common was the need for high places. He likes to look, for instance, from high cliffs out to sea. We went to Portland Bill once and he climbed a little way down the cliff. At the top where I was standing there was this loose chunk of Portland stone that someone had quarried and forgotten.

Below me was the sheer drop to the ocean with the milling, swirling Portland Race and beyond it warships: submarines, destroyers, at which my father would be looking with binoculars. He was always looking at things through binoculars. My mother used to say this was symptomatic of his distant view of people, accusing him of staying too far away from life. He pretended he needed the binoculars for bird-watching, but really didn't know a lot about birds. Earlier that day he had pointed out an arctic tern, which was obviously an ordinary heron gull.

That time at Portland I found it, I remember, a frightening place. Perhaps because of the prison that had been there once. The prisoners worked in the quarries, hacking stone for the eighteenth-century builders. Pieces of Portland stone surround the windows of King's Radlett Manor.

That loose stone on top of the cliff: it was enormous, but I could roll it or tumble it slowly along the ground. But I liked it: it was clean and smooth and there were facets someone had chiselled on it.

The Bill is like the starkest island with patches of grass and ragwort growing and the lighthouse at the end of it is now a bird-watching tower. My mother hated going there. It wasn't very warm that day and she sat in the car saying that it was daft conservationists thinking they could turn the clock back and make it into an idyllic place.

We'd only gone there because she had been telling him he didn't take an interest in me or teach me anything. So he said all right we would go bird-watching. I must have been about eight, so the marriage didn't have long to go and Henry was already on the horizon. Like Henry was looming up there out to sea, as it were, beyond the Bill swimming towards us.

As I managed to shift the stone by lifting one side of it, letting it fall and turn again, causing it to move its own length at each tumble, I was thinking more of the poor prisoner whose job it might have been to chisel the stone and how he would have worn old-fashioned convict's clothing with arrows on it. It moved more easily and began to have its own momentum.

Inland from me and across a wide expanse of grass and scattered boulders sat my mother smoking in the car. Portland Bill is an unlucky place. Not long ago winter storms swept over the narrow causeway which joins it to the mainland. The pebbles carried by a spring tide plus a gale swarmed in over houses. On television they showed a family standing outside what had once been a home, but now was nothing but a pile of rubble buried deep in shingle, like the shingle had been hurled at it.

That day we'd done the bird-watching bit and I had tried to show some interest, but you could see birds anywhere any time and I knew most birds. Living in the country I had all the birds I needed in my life already. So my father wandered off down the cliff and my mother sat in the car, smoking, so the car would stink all the way home and there'd almost certainly be an argument about having the windows shut or open.

I don't know why my mother came. It was always miserable with the two of them and only bearable with only one of them, but they both seemed keen to see me having a hobby, although I already had riding. Most people say their parents want them to have a hobby, presumably to keep them out of the way or to give the parents the satisfaction of having children who concentrate well on things and therefore get on better at school.

The stone I was playing with was moving well now. It was more of a boulder really. I pushed it, tumbled it and rolled it across the tufty grass under the grey sky towards the edge of the cliff.

Come to think of it, it was probably the last time we went anywhere as a family. After that our family was like the one

108

outside the pebble-bashed house. Not a very strong home you might say, not a stormproof family you could say. Certainly not with the irresistibly lovely Henry swimming in with a bow wave long enough and deep enough to sink a thousand families.

I gave the stone one final heave. The cliff was not entirely sheer and the stone rolled first for a way taking the near short slope and bouncing as it hit another boulder. Then it shot into the air, spinning as if catapulted and then plummeted.

I was very disappointed that I couldn't see it hit the sea or the rocks far below. That near slope was a little steep for me to reach the edge and peer down. Seagulls were rising in a mass of white wings and cries and the noise they made drowned any sound of splash which my boulder might have made. But there was another sound: a shout, and soon my father hauled himself up, his face appearing over the edge, red from effort, anger and possibly fear. 'Did you do that?'

'Did I do what? No, I've been looking for more birds.'

He stumped towards the car, his binoculars hanging on the chest of his sweater. He ignored me.

I ran after him: 'I think I may have seen an arctic tern. You were right about the arctic tern,' I called after him and all the way home I was making up this arctic tern I'd seen, while he was looking at me in the mirror every now and then, looking wildly at me as if to see if he could guess if I was lying or not.

'I did see,' I said about half-way home, 'I did see a warning notice somewhere on the cliff, about falling rocks and how you weren't supposed to climb down the cliff.' That was true.

My father began to be a successful businessman when he was in the motor business. His cars were always heavy cars, swaying cars and I felt sick in them, especially with my mother smoking and the windows closed. To be a child in the back of a car with people hating each other in the front is never tolerable. He may have known about Henry then or suspected about Henry then. But with him also suspecting me for attempted murder, the journey was even less tolerable.

When he left us or agreed to leave us or whatever the

arrangement was, he sold his business and went to college to study business studies, but gave my mother some of the profits from the sale, with which she started Harrison's, her share of it. Maybe there's a sense in which Harrison's should be called partly Frobisher's.

Portland Bill is not a place to which I would return. In Colorado I was reminded of it, partly because of my father standing looking down towards the aspens nearly crying with rage and disappointment that I spoke and thought the way my mother spoke and thought. One of his dogs, one of his German shepherds, ambled over and began to lick his feet and his sandals where tears may have fallen. Also licked his hand. Then I went back to reading *Far From the Madding Crowd* again, the bit where Sergeant Troy swims off to get away from everything.

Terence Stamp played Sergeant Troy in the film. Last autumn, just as we'd begun to study the book, the movie was on TV. 'Now, you've seen the film,' Mr Forbes said to everyone, 'forget it and concentrate on the book.'

Alan Bates played Shepherd Oak. I watched it with my mother. She said she didn't fancy Alan Bates, but preferred Peter Finch who played Farmer Boldwood whom Bathsheba didn't want to marry. 'Fancy not wanting to fly into the arms of Peter Finch,' said my mother. 'What a pity he is dead, Peter Finch I mean.'

'Speaking of Sergeant Troy,' I said when the film was over, 'I'm thinking of selling Troy.'

'Why?' she said.

But I couldn't tell her why because Henry came in at that moment.

Mr Forbes said we should remember that in Hardy, people's fates are often sealed by tiny coincidences to do with time and silly mistakes. Timing never works out right for people in Hardy, Mr Forbes said. Like in Hardy, the girl who was pregnant by Sergeant Troy was going to marry him, but went to the wrong church in Casterbridge, and by the time she'd turned up at the right one, naughty Troy had changed his mind. Julie Christie played Bathsheba Everdene, whom Troy did marry. She was great in the part.

Timing for me went on being wrong until it began to get too late to tell my mother anything. But I put an advertisement in the local paper offering Troy for sale and gave Jane's telephone number. Jane would ring me the moment anyone was interested. However, the timing for selling a horse with winter coming on was also wrong, what with the cost of feed and everything.

Our telephone rang in the middle of one afternoon and there was no one on the line. Then it rang the same time next afternoon and there was no one on the line again. It also rang very late at night sometimes and stopped after a few rings. Always three rings, I remember, like a signal.

One night in November I heard Henry go and use the phone in the small hours after it had rung three times. Then I heard my mother and him arguing, but stuffed my ears. Then she began crying in the loo late at night, sickening long-drawn-out sobs, so I stuffed my ears. There was no way I could tell her why I was selling Troy now, was there?

I was reminded how years before at Rad Cottage when my mother first knew Henry, the telephone used to ring with signals like these signals and she would always rush to use the phone a few minutes later, making up excuses and shutting all the doors between me and her.

It seems like all through last November my mother kept on watching Henry. And Henry kept on watching me. He'd noticed what she hadn't noticed about me. He must have heard me being sick one morning, then another morning, then a third. He became very silent watching me and she became very anxious because of his silence.

Mind you, all this agony, this trauma and this tension could have been resolved a lot more quickly if all these years I'd been allowed to work in the shop and earn more money than I could out at King's Radlett. But, as usual (sigh!) there was a rule, a Henry rule, which my mother excused by saying it was to do with insurance (sigh!), but a rule which, as it will be seen, she didn't exactly stick to (oh no! sigh again).

The click of the put-down telephone occurred whenever Henry didn't answer it himself. I heard him speaking guardedly one afternoon. The calls came usually at the time when my mother would be fetching Daisy from school. Whoever it was must have known about her habits. And in retrospect this must be linked with what I'm coming to think of as the red triangle lady.

The calls were never from Jane to say I had a potential buyer for Troy, so I put another ad in the paper reducing his price to £150, which was exactly what I needed (though he was worth much more).

In the wettest autumn on record for years I went into the workroom behind the shop one afternoon to find my mother on her own and I could see she had been crying into the wallhanging she was making. Damp blobs could be seen on the soft green cotton and the white cotton and cream cotton she was using for appliqués and inserts. The virginia creeper which had reflected warm light into the kitchen in September hung in swathes over the long picture windows. Its leaves were falling off and sticking with the damp to the cobbles of the yard.

My mother pretended she was out of condition because of not getting enough exercise. But she wouldn't go out anywhere. Henry went off and bought an exercise bicycle which he put in the centre of the workroom between their two benches: his where he designs things and which is covered with papers and hers which is always strewn with materials.

The exercise bicycle is like one of Hardy's unfulfilled intentions. Mr Forbes was always telling us about these: things being planned and going wrong, but as often in nature as in human life. It's covered in a dust sheet now.

When Henry used the bike he used to pretend he was riding in the Tour de France and always winning the day's run and wearing the yellow jersey. He had the pedal pressure turned right down, however. When I used it I switched the pressure to its toughest and hoped to strain my stomach muscles. My mother hardly ever got on to it. This worried Henry, you could see. Sometimes she'd pretend she'd had a ride on it and make up places she'd imagined she'd been biking to.

The tubs in the yard had late summer flowers in them, collapsed and dead. She hadn't bothered to cut them back or pull them out and plant bulbs for this spring. But someone must have done this, since there are daffodils out there now. I think it may have been Stella, the woman who helps in the shop and sometimes in the house and garden.

Then there was the afternoon when I found my mother in the shop looking pretty collapsed and nearly dead: 'Are you OK?' I said.

'Just hang on in here for a minute, will you?' she said and went upstairs, so I stayed and kept the shop open until Stella came, then found my mother fast asleep upstairs. I think she must have been taking some of her tranquillisers or whatever, maybe to stop herself crying or whatever. There are red triangles marked on a good many of the days of last November with 't' beside them, meaning telephone I guess. Not a very subtle code once you get the hang of it.

'Are you OK?' I said again.

'Ask Stella to fetch Daisy in the car, will you?' she murmured.

This I did. Which meant me hanging on in the shop again since Henry wouldn't be home till six or so. I can't remember where he was or where he said he was that day. And I know my mother wouldn't have asked me to mind the shop unless he was well out of the way.

Then Bentley was passing the shop and looked in, saw me there and I gave him the thumbs up which meant 'OK all clear' since he hardly dares even look through the glass when Henry's there.

There's this onyx chess set which is pretty pricey, but Bent-

113

ley plays a mean game of chess, so I put it on the table where the till is – just by the jewellery counter and we played for a bit.

'Where's your Mum?' he said while we were playing.

'Totally spaced out,' I said.

Then some fat woman in a plastic mac came in to look for early Christmas cards and was moseying through our up-market reproductions-of-great-masters cards in a picky fashion. But I was keeping an eye on her as well. I was watching that woman nearly all the time I'm pretty sure. I only left Bentley down there for a second while I went to check that my mother was still breathing. Luckily this didn't take long, since she opened her eyes and asked me if everything was OK and I said yes and she said: 'I'll be down in a minute or two.'

One of the things of which I was accused by Henry later that day was not looking after my mother. He goes over the top whenever she is ill and needs to blame people for it I suppose. But she wasn't ill that day – just drugged. She went on dozing till he was due home, then may have taken another of those red ones she takes to raise her awareness and maybe even had a drink of gin and bitter lemon with it. Which is I suppose the kind of mistake people make when they are as surrounded with pills and booze as she is.

I'd just taken the first of Bentley's bishops I remember, when I realised that the fat woman had left without buying anything. But she didn't leave empty-handed, having taken a glass candlestick, one of a pair. If she'd taken both candle-sticks, maybe Stella wouldn't have noticed it. It would have to be Stella who noticed it. Stella who, doting on Henry as she does, could be depended on to report as well that Bentley had been in the shop with me that afternoon.

It was dark when Henry came in. The shop was closed, but they called for me and there was Stella holding the remaining candlestick. These candlesticks were left over from the time when Henry thought we should get into glass in a big way and contacted this man from Birmingham who blew glass in an artistic way and got streaks of rainbow colours in it.

114

Henry still had his huge dark blue winter overcoat on. I stood at the bottom of the spiral stairs and waited for the storm to break, trying to keep looking at him for as long as possible and working like mad not to let my eyes shrink back into my head or fill with tears.

He took the candlestick from Stella and held it up as if he was about to throw it through the shop window or about to throw it at me. My mother stood near his arm as if to stop him throwing it anywhere. Whatever she had taken had got her to her feet again – just.

He said he didn't want to speak about it, but it was definite that I must never work in the shop any more. He seemed to be saying that to my mother as well – giving her the order to keep me out of the shop as if we were all his servants. She kept on half sitting on the stool by the cash desk, but kept on trying to stand up. Stella was hugging herself with Schadenfreude, but trying to look sorry for everyone.

When the main shop lights are turned off at closing time the hangings overhead are like clouds above you, moving like clouds coming in over your head as they are sometimes shown in speeded-up film of weather manifestations, clouds hurling themselves across the sky with all the fullness of them swirling low and nowhere you can go to get away from them.

Then Stella left and Henry really let fly at me. I remember my mother was trying to look as if she was standing but was actually sitting on the edge of the stool.

'I'll pay for the candlestick,' I said.

My mother on the stool was exactly half-way between us. And shaking like I was.

'I'll pay for both the candlesticks,' I said, 'because I realise one isn't much good without the other.'

He raged for nearly half an hour. The turbulence blanked everything around: it was less like weather turbulence than blast waves of a bomb maybe. I'd never cared for him, he said – rage – swirl, his head thrown back. He'd tried. He'd

115

really tried. He stubbed a half-smoked ciggie out in an ash tray. He'd worked his hat off, hadn't he? Hands clenched, unclenched. He'd worked his balls off, hadn't he, hands raised imploringly towards the hangings. My mother had tried too and how had I repaid that effort, head back, head down, and I knew that any minute now I'd start to cry and it makes him worse when people cry. My mother lit another cigarette and left the packet on the cash desk so that I could take one. He saw this and I thought he would explode and I remembered the story that I'd heard once – how years ago in Hollywood a movie star was shot by his stepdaughter, shot dead.

He said I didn't understand about money or the value of things and used the whole place as if it were my own, the heating and the lighting, leaving the gas fire on all day upstairs when I should be at school in any case.

'In the sixth form you don't have to be there all day anyway,' I said.

But he just repeated that I didn't know anything about paying for things.

'I pay for Troy,' I said.

My mother kept having these twitching spasms. She was holding herself with her arms wrapped round herself as if to control the spasms.

'Your mother and I pay for everything,' he said.

And I couldn't tell him that I knew my father paid for quite a bit of my upkeep. I've seen the original letter of agreement between solicitors and I check the bank statement each month and know the money still comes in by banker's order. But I couldn't point that out because it would have only made Henry worse and it is kind of out of court to do so, i.e. below the belt, i.e. deserving of a penalty, i.e. a goal kick for him.

But thinking about all this and the unfairness of his accusations caused the held-in tears to spurt and my mother passed a Kleenex to me. I sniffed and wanted to say that we all paid for everything. The shop is owned by both of them in any case.

He went through everything again and all his life and all the

116

things he'd done or tried to do. In a way I knew he couldn't help himself by that stage; and there was no way I could do or say anything except sit there or stand there because that's what I'd always done and though it had been hell, at least he hadn't kicked me out or left himself.

He even said I didn't love my mother like I should because I didn't share things with her.

So I cried and soaked the Kleenex through and through. The turmoil was inside my head as well by now, gale force, cyclonic, and I wished it would force boulders from somewhere to fall out of the hangings on to all of us.

My mother just sat there.

But she couldn't do anything because it would have been out of court for her to speak on my side. And he makes the rules.

I remember how it was raining and lashing and bashing on the windows and I hoped that people out there would be blinded by the rain and not see us all being like we were; which I shouldn't really mind about, except that you try outside the home to give the impression that you are basically happy at home and proud of it all, however much you grumble about it.

I wanted to go deaf so as not to hear him or to go blind so as not to see him. I wanted a boulder to fall on my mother too for letting him. It's violence, isn't it? And it comes from both of them. It's like Mr Forbes said about Hardy and the sexual appetite, but all gone wrong, turned inside out. The three of us, sharp blades twisting in our guts.

Then that night in my attic bedroom where there are strange angles in the roof and corners full of shadows, they were arguing next door, being noisy about it, which is worse than when they're noisy about making love, me always hating listening to either of those activities. So I turned the stereo on and locked the door, so when she came to tell me to turn it down again I didn't hear her, but saw the handle moving, but didn't open it.

Until later when she came in and we sort of hugged each

117

other I suppose, although being near her made the chasm between us loom larger. It felt like there were canyons between us. Not the Grand Canyon which I've never seen on account of it being in Arizona. There was no way I was going to be able to tell her anything now.

NINE

In the classroom I was sitting by the window looking out across the playing-fields which looked as Novemberish as anything could – windswept and colourless except for piles of rich brown leaves against the boundary fence. Grass fades in winter, sometimes hardly looking green at all. Maybe we only think it is green.

Mr Forbes had been reading out where the unmarried Fanny Robin, heavily pregnant, drags herself to Casterbridge where she will give birth and die. I was thinking to myself how apt as the feeling of faintness swept up through me again.

'Can anyone,' said Mr Forbes, 'can anyone suggest what was the significance of the dog which helps poor Fanny to the almshouse in the end?'

No one answered. He wrinkled his nose and ran his fingers through his hair as usual. He looked half dead too and as if he had a cold. His hair, which usually has lustre, lacked this. Jane said he had been into Pevensey's for shampoo and conditioner recently, but it didn't look like he had used either. 'Can anyone?' he said again, looking at me hopefully.

'How pregnant was she?' said Tracey.

'It doesn't say,' said Mr Forbes, taking a Kleenex out of his

119

pocket and dabbing his nose. 'We must assume towards full term, although Hardy doesn't go into details of that kind for reasons of propriety perhaps.'

'If she was too far gone,' said Tracey, 'a dog wouldn't be no good. She'd have to have a horse to lean on, wouldn't she?'

Some giggles came from the girls near Tracey, but the boys looked bored and scraped their chairs and crossed their feet. I was feeling even sicker and fiddling in the pocket of my jeans for a Settler.

'All right then. We are less concerned with fact,' said Mr Forbes, 'than with symbolism here. Let's not consider if it's possible for a dog to support a pregnant woman and later drag a pregnant woman, but ask ourselves why Hardy chose an animal at all . . .'

I had the Settler in my mouth, but it didn't make much difference to the ringing in my ears and general lassitude and yuckiness. 'You usually say,' I said, 'that in good literature it has to work – I mean that people have got to be able to believe in it – that facts must work.'

He looked crestfallen, really very disappointed, but at least I'd spoken, hadn't I? He put his hands in his pockets and wandered to the window looking out as I had looked out just before at the totally faded autumn glory. When he gets really fed up with our lot he says he wishes he'd taken a much nicer job he was offered once. I was looking at the text. I'd reckoned Fanny Robin would have had to bend quite a way to lean on any dog, even say a mastiff, and could a very pregnant women bend that far? Hardy, as far as I knew, didn't have any kids.

'It's funny, isn't it,' said Susan, who sat next to Tracey, 'that Fanny Robin is pregnant by Sergeant Troy, but Bathsheba who is married to him, isn't. And they didn't have no contraceptives then.'

'That is totally irrelevant,' said Mr Forbes. But at his desk he banged his copy of the book down and said that this was the last time he'd bother trying to get us to use our brains about anything, let alone encourage us to try and unravel the strands of Hardy's pessimistic view about human character and nature and everything.

'It was a big dog,' I said. I'd found it in the text. 'The rest is easy. It's easy anyway about the symbolism. The dog is on account of men are lousy and it's animals are kind, he's saying. Or something like that – I don't know . . .'

At least that cheered him up a bit. A smile grew on his face like the smile that Hardy describes on the face of Gabriel Oak right on the first page of the book where he says it is like extending beams or rays of sunshine.

'It's spring again! It must be spring again!' said Mr Forbes. 'The clouds are parting. Yes! Good dog! Good dog! Indifferent man!'

Forbes' wife was pregnant at that time. I'd seen her waddling in town, enormous with her stomach up front. Jane said it looked like twins although Mrs Forbes was only six months' gone. Jane lives near the Forbeses as well as seeing him in Pevensey's. But whenever I saw Mrs Forbes in town in those days I felt sicker than ever.

'I think it's all daft anyway,' said Susan. Tracey said that people weren't all bad in Hardy though. What about Gabriel Oak?

'Exactly,' said Mr Forbes, smiling at her. Tracey had just started the phase of having her hair frizzed or maybe plaiting it at night so that it stuck out all over her head.

'Gabriel Oak?' I said. 'Well – he's impossible to believe in for a start.'

This seemed to make Forbes go all miserable again. I was supposed to be seeing him afterwards about an essay that I hadn't done, but didn't bother, feeling as I did.

'Really you must eat,' said Jane that lunchtime. 'Really you must eat, Petra, you see. It won't get rid of it, not eating won't.' Jane had told me where to go to get the test done.

'The foetus, you see, Petra, takes everything it can. It is such a little greedy-guts. You haven't told your mother yet?'

'No,' I had to admit.

'What about your father? Couldn't you get some money from him? Honestly, you've got dozens of such rich relations, haven't you?'

'My father would wonder why I couldn't tell my mother.'

'Why can't you?'

We were in a Wimpy bar that lunchtime which was stuffy with a smell of frying onions permeating everywhere.

'You're sure that in your heart of hearts you don't want to keep it, are you, Petra?'

I shook my head. Then nodded, meaning no way did I want to keep it. As I'd told the counsellor at the clinic already, there was nothing in favour of keeping it: I had a cruel stepfather: I had a great career in front of me. This visit to the counsellor had cost me £25 plus day return to Waterloo and I was broke.

Up on the beacon that afternoon, with the rain slanting from west to east across my face, I galloped Troy to a standstill, knowing there was less and less chance of selling him in time. Then in the potato field – where I'd already earned £30 in the last few weeks, I followed Gerald as he drove the tractor across gungey ground, me following in my wellingtons, bending down to pick potatoes from the matted, ruddy, rutted soil. Also lifting sacks off the back of the tractor when they were filled, lifting whole sacks off by myself.

Finally, as it got dark I went to the municipal pool. By chance Henry was there with Daisy. In the echoing acoustic of the pool, the chlorinated water made me feel sick again and I sat on the edge with my head between my knees. But Henry was watching me so I dived in again.

I swam under the high glass roof and this thing swam inside me, fishlike with flippers and a pinpoint head. I'd drawn diagrams of this kind of thing in Biology O Level, so I knew what it looked like. Life really was a fish I was thinking as I swam round in a circle, then headed back towards the diving end, climbed out of the pool to take the steps to the highest board of all. I dived again with Henry watching me from the far end.

The fish and the frogs whose behaviour cause the fish, I was thinking down there in the murk where I try to keep my eyes open even when they sting like hell. The frogs in *Life on Earth*: I'm always thinking of them and that bit in *Lear* where someone says: 'Let copulation thrive!' I came up struggling through the blinding blue, kicking my legs as hard as possible. I needed £150 and I had £40. I hauled myself out again, crawled across the white slippery tiles, giddy, not being able to look up to see if Henry was still there.

He and Daisy were waiting for me when I'd changed. I drove home with them. Not much was said. There was fish and chips for supper and I couldn't refuse the chips with Henry watching me. Daisy was saying that the mother of Rosie, her best friend next door, had had a baby sister for Rosie, which was nice for Rosie, wasn't it nice for Rosie?

'Isn't Mr Forbes' wife having another baby?' asked my mother.

'Not for several months,' I said.

'I saw her in town,' said my mother. 'She looked huge.'

'Jane says it's probably twins,' I said.

Henry left the table without saying anything. My mother began to blink and clear the dishes over-hastily.

'Actually . . . ,' I said. I really think I was about to tell her, but the upstairs telephone was ringing and she was standing dead still listening to Henry answering it in the corridor just outside the kitchen door.

Say this for Henry: the phone call wasn't anything. No red triangles form themselves into a question mark about that call. At this time Henry was expanding, as it were, honing up his old generosity of spirit – at least towards my mother anyway, encouraging her to buy new clothes.

Mind you, she's always buying zillions of clothes without encouragement and tends to be dishonest when it comes to admitting how much new garments cost, perhaps because she feels, for a self-effacing person she over-spends on her appearance.

That time in November it was Henry, however, who went barmy spending money on her, getting her a new fur coat. She was trying it on the day before they were going to London for a carpet sale.

Yes, my mother is certainly dishonest. She must stand accused of that. She must, for instance, either have been dishonest with my father or dishonest with Henry. She must have been fooling one of them about the kind of person she was. She was different with my father, totally different, always moaning, carrying on and beating Noggin the spaniel, whereas now she's calm and bottled up and uptight. Maybe she needs a dog to belt.

Another thing: she used to complain that my father always took his shoes off and left them downstairs, although he likewise used to accuse her of untidiness. I remember her throwing his shoes at him all the way upstairs before taking me to school. She took to using language which offended him, like my language now offends him. But that was when she was already going around with Henry and signals were coming in the middle of the night.

This coat, this new fur coat, was voluminous and silky, palish fur – I'm not sure what fur exactly. Henry made her walk up and down like a model in front of the full-length mirror just inside the shop. It's a mirror we use for watching customers from upstairs. She was swaggering and she knew I was watching and stopped swaggering.

The coat must have cost him a bomb – at least three times the sum I needed. Henry went into the office to the safe and fetched out her diamond earrings. *The* diamond earrings, I should say: Leadbetter diamonds, and he was fastening them to her ears. Stella was there and looked at her looking up at him. Everyone was looking at her looking up at him. And my mother's look at him was like she was saying: never mind who's watching me, I must look up at him like I am crazy over him. Like even if I know he's a lousy bastard in lots of ways, I am still crazy over him. Like her life depended on convincing him. It all reminded me of Tammy, the ex-convict from Colorado telling me she'd commit first-degree homicide for her bloke.

But my mother didn't wear the earrings the day they went to London which was a Tuesday and not only wet but cold, the wind belting rain from the east down across the park, so that when people came into the shop you wanted to rush and bang the door after them. I watched Stella for a bit and then went to an English class.

Where I heard Forbes' voice distantly giving us an essay topic, going on about the time when Sergeant Troy goes to the graveyard where Fanny Robin and her baby are buried, saying, Forbes was, that this illustrated that, although Troy did have some regrets, it could be argued that there was a moral message here: once done it's done: what's done is done, no going back. 'One life, one death,' he said and then said:

'Petra, are you all right? Petra, are you with us still?'

More voices echoed as I stumbled out of the classroom towards the loos with people coming after me, but managed to get away from everyone in the end and throw up in the bike-shed. As I cycled home there was this light in the sky above the wood, pinkish like a Turner sky – all watery, like my legs felt and my stomach felt.

There were still customers around so I went upstairs, stretched in front of the gas fire on the rug, eating dry biscuits, hearing the shop bell going and the telephone from time to time. Daisy would be going home with Rosie that day. I tried to work but couldn't, so I set the alarm on my digital watch to five o'clock and lay by the fire. I dozed and had the recurring dream that I was being dragged, but not by a horse this time: it was more like a huge fat bird, straining and pumping its wings up and down to create the locomotion.

I can open the door into the balcony almost without sound. At five I saw that Stella was alone by now. For a time I sat on the pile of orientals, watching her. She was moving quietly like she does, watering plants, moving from one plant to another on her soft little black shoes. Her clothes are late-hippie in style: T shirts which show her ageing outlines, and flowery droopy skirts.

'Oh hullo, Petra,' she said, looking up. 'How are you now?' She must have come upstairs while I was asleep. Since she had seen me, I began to tidy up the carpets for her, lifting them and rearranging them. The term oriental carpet is used loosely to include all forms of hand-woven floor covering, but this leads to confusion because the trade calls anything over forty square feet a carpet and anything smaller a rug. In a practical sense, what you roll up is a carpet, what you pick up is a rug. Stella was half-way up the stairs and watching me as if I was about to pinch a rug at least. She always looks like she has just come in from the rain, having this curly perm which is usually greasy. We'd hardly spoken since the day of the candlestick.

'I'll finish off if you like,' I said, 'and lock up and everything.'

I might have known it wouldn't work. 'No, no, don't worry.' She has this kind of bruised look to her face like she's afraid of offending people. Sometimes though she likes to go off early, having kids at home and a husband who isn't that keen on her working.

'I mean it's OK,' I said. 'There probably won't be any more customers and my mother and Henry will soon be back.'

'Oh, not till six, I think they said.'

One of the best things about Henry's absence, I must say, is that I can work in the shop and Stella can't say anything. She's working for my mother now, but then she was working for Henry. After five, when she'd done the watering, a bit of dusting, she took the velvet-lined jewellery trays out from under the glass counter and carried them into the office.

'You're sure you are all right?' she called upstairs.

I came down and sat on the high stool where my mother usually sits when her legs are tired.

'You really don't look well,' said Stella. She was in the office, turning the knob of the safe. The jewellery is nothing of terrific value – the jewellery that we sell, that is: silver lockets, craftsman-made heavy rings, etc.

'I'm OK,' I said.

Unless you put valuable small items of stock into a safe at night, you have to have special glass at the window or wire over the glass or screens across the window for insurance purposes.

'Henry doesn't look well either,' Stella was saying, bending to slide the jewellery trays into the safe. Stella is always deeply concerned about people's health. Her ambition is to have her own healthfood shop one day. 'And how do you think your mother is these days?' she said.

'Oh, fine,' I said. 'Well, fine-ish anyway.'

'Perhaps the day out will have done her good,' she said. It looked like it was going to be one of those long-drawn-out conversations where Stella tries to ingratiate herself with people, showing them that she is the world's most empathetic person. Well, she had a long way to go with me.

'But how are *you*?' she said again. She'd sat down behind the cash desk. Ten minutes left of opening time and I thought I'd better not seem to be pushing her, so I wandered over to the rail of clothes: Indian skirts and tops and caftans, etc., of which we keep a few.

'It is the weather probably,' I said. She was sitting looking at me. When looking at people, she sits with her chin in her hands and gazes at you steadily as if you are about to say something tremendously revealing of your state of mind. 'I'm ever so glad that things have settled down again . . .'

Now I don't take kindly from people outside concerning themselves with things so I didn't answer her, but played with the glass marbles of the solitaire game, lifting marbles over other marbles, dropping the cancelled marbles into the runnel round the edge of the wooden tray. I looked at my watch. Stella sighed. She sighs a lot. This sigh may have been because I

127

wasn't speaking to her or it may have been on account of what she claims to be a deeply uphappy relationship with her husband with whom she only stays on account of her children. 'It's never been easy being oneself,' she said. 'Especially in your situation.'

My situation, I was thinking, is that I'm not going to get her out of here. It was five-twenty-five and it would have been so easy if she'd left then and let me have a half-hour or so.

'People say that they envy people of your age,' she said, 'but I don't think it's at all nice being your age, do you? Not these days at any rate.'

These days Stella keeps pretending heartfelt anxiety over Henry's absence. I can see that they needed to employ a conscientious person who is devoted to their cause. But she may never know the true reason for my mother's choosing her.

She switched the main office light off and locked the office door. The red bulb of the burglar alarm came on. She switched the main shop light off and waited at the bottom of the stairs as if demanding me to go with her.

The true reason for my mother choosing Stella: that she is probably the one woman in the world who Henry doesn't fancy – apart from me that is. When they were discussing who to employ, Henry said 'Let's have a sixteen-year-old Philippino, please,' and my mother smiled obligingly and hired Stella.

Among my mother's supply of pills are these red ones which she takes to lift herself. God knows what they have got in them, though officially they're some kind of cold cure. I took one that night. I had to keep awake, didn't I, and noticed as I washed the pill down with a drink of orange juice that there was a warning, telling pregnant women not to take them without consulting their physician.

OK, I thought, OK, little foetus, little greedy gubbins, here is your pill. I'm sorry if it damages you, but you are on the way out anyway. No, I don't mean to joke about it.

Dark clothing: black sweater and jeans were the next requirements. In these I lay on my bed, waiting for the telephone to ring, then, when it didn't, I gave it nearly an extra half-hour for safety. There was not even talking from next door that night, and anyway the sound of rain was drowning everything.

It passed over the skylight like a thin waterfall. Then it spluttered out of the gutters, spilling over and splashing on to the pavement below. Like the time Sergeant Troy put flowers on Fanny Robin's grave and the rain gathered strength so that the church gutters couldn't hold it all. All the rain could do then was to burst out through the gargoyle's mouth in one huge torrent, with such force that it shot on to the grave and washed away the snowdrops and the other flowers that Troy had planted there. Nature trying to say something, Mr Forbes would say. Nature trying to say something like it was too late for apologies. No reversal. What's done is done. One life, one death.

Darkness was in all the corners of my room. Tammy from Colorado told me that when you did a job you had to breathe deeply: 'Always deeply, kid. Start breathing that way long before you start the job.' So I started breathing deeply at 2 a.m.

'You got your breathing right, OK?' I heard Tammy's voice. 'You gotta get your head right next. All righty then?'

I had the safe combination written on the inside of my wrist. Tammy said: 'Don't trust your memory. Check everything. Then double-check.'

So I'd checked that I had the penlite torch, socks on my hands for opening doors and muffling them. I knew that on the flight of stairs my heart would hammer and the pulses in my head would beat. I'd breathe deeply. The keys: there are two sets for all the doors, Henry's in the corridor and my mother's in the kitchen. I'd take the kitchen set.

I was there: in the kitchen: reaching inside the cupboard, first for the keys, then for the fusebox, shining my torch on the switch which governs the burglar alarm. Then in the corridor, knowing the squeak and creak of every floorboard – both there and on the balcony.

The light in the shop was dim like it was the night when all this started and I was locked out. The spiral balustrade: I had to let this take my weight rather than the treads because they have been known to clank. Now I was dead still on the shop floor, breathing deeply, slowly, getting my lungs right. 'Count to a hundred,' Tammy said. 'Between each stage, count to a hundred. Stand still and count.'

I was slipping along with my back to the wall but hardly touching it. Still raining and a car went past. Then footsteps came along the pavement and a figure passed with an umbrella up. Drops from this were bouncing on the pavement. I stood behind the grape-ivy which is seven foot tall in the centre of the shop. The footsteps went. I counted up to a hundred again with the office key ready pointing at the office door.

The office is a small square room leading off the shop. It has no windows and is only a cubbyhole with a ventilation grating in the wall. The insurance man said there was no need to have a burglar alarm on the safe, only on the office door. I muffled the door handle, turned the key, slipped in, remuffled the door, fitted the key inside again and took the torch.

No. I had to wait. Wait like I planned and listened, counting to one hundred as per plan.

The office is small and cluttered, so everything which I might have knocked over I moved – the chair back from the desk. Heart knocking but I was telling myself to remember that jewellery came down through the female line and would be mine one day. I remember my grandmother telling me about the jewellery coming down through the female line. I was clearing the desk to make room for things out of the safe. I moved a diary, a calendar, some pens, a tin of paper clips and the telephone which I put on the floor in the kneehole of the desk. There was a photograph as well: an old photo which had been there so long that no one ever looked at it. My grandmother, my mother and myself in the garden at King's Radlett. My grandmother in a deck chair, then my mother on the grass in front of her, then me held in between my mother's knees, me

130

aged not more than one year old or so. I'd got my hands up as if I didn't want to have the photo taken. The sun was in my eyes maybe. I checked the numbers on my wrist again. My hands were on the revolving knob. I turned. It clicked. I pulled the door. The door swung easily. Socks on my hand to lift the cash box first, raising it towards the desk in both hands, lowering it on to the desk with both hands, letting it rest there. Was it that pill that made my heart knock in that exaggerated way?

The jewellery boxes, several of them. This was the one. I pointed the torch to check and opened it. Check. Right. The earrings? Shine the torch again. Correct. I closed the box and wedged it in the tightest pocket of my jeans.

I was dribbling and gagging with the torch in my mouth, so I took it out and laid it carefully on the desk so it wouldn't roll, then put the boxes back, the cash box lifted slowly in two hands again. I took a break to wipe the sweat off my forehead with one socked hand. Then knelt and closed the door and twirled the knob. Sweating again, feeling sweat run down my nose. Tammy didn't warn me about all that sweat, so I knelt and counted to a hundred, clutching the edge of the desk to steady myself before moving things back into place. Tammy didn't warn me about the weakness in the legs either. I was leaning heavily, head down, counting to my fifteenth hundred, pressing down hard, when there was a crunch of breaking glass splintering under the socks on my hands.

Grandma Leadbetter, my mother and me, snapped by my father possibly, framed by my mother probably, broken by me certainly. There she was, holding me between her knees that sunny day as if I'd just been born, just sprouted out of her, a part of her. That person who was there between her knees in the sun was someone else, not me. Mother, I may once have possibly been part of you, but what I am now is not to do with you.

I took the calendar and slid the whole photo on to it, moving slowly round the desk on hands and knees to slide it in between the desk and the wall. Slowly, slowly, stop and count. Slowly,

131

slowly, breathe and count. Take it easy, Tammy said. You think your breathing will be heard by others, but it won't. I crawled, checking for splinters and for grains of glass and there was hardly a sound except a car passing somewhere and the town hall clock striking three o'clock. The rain couldn't be heard any more. Nothing could be heard any more.

Once I said: 'Why do you keep that silly photograph?' and she said: 'I don't know,' but went on keeping it. I said: 'You look better now than you did then,' and she said: 'I felt awful after having you as well as looking awful.' 'Was it bad having me?' 'Not so bad,' she said. But I suppose people can't tell their daughters how bad it is in case daughters get scared and frightened off having babies ever.

Did you faint sometimes, mother? Did you sometimes get a rushing in the ears, in the whole head so that it seemed like floods were coming up from under the floorboards like tide pouring into your ears, like swishing into your brains and filling them so that your head weighs a ton and you need to curl up and float? Did you get that ringing in the ears, that kind of ringing which seemed to shut off all other sounds, the kind of ringing which seemed like all the telephones were ringing everywhere, ringing in the office in the middle of the night just after the town hall clock struck three?

Where was the telephone? I had to find the telephone. Under the desk of course. I reached and was lifting it. Lifting it and hearing the woman's voice calling out in the middle of the night, saying: 'Is that you? Is that you?' so I didn't speak to say who had lifted up the phone. My stomach was full of a hundred different pieces of pills and machinery and the taste of orange juice was not helping things the way it was returning. The huge bird was dragging me again, so I couldn't even replace the telephone. This bird had got hold of my feet and was pulling at me, hauling me, the whole of me away from under the desk and all the lights were on.

So this could be where it ended. This was the final falling where there would be no shelf or ledge on which to land. But what a soft landing down there as if you were already in your sleeping bag, which seemed to be full of feathers, deep enough for falling into from Everest.

Henry held my head and my hair away from my face while I was throwing up in the downstairs loo where he must have carried me and afterwards I was on his knee so it seemed, him telling me what a silly girl I was and stroking my head. He was in his towelling dressing gown and silk pyjamas, but only the bottom half of them. My head was on his shoulder.

'Don't cry,' he said.

And I said: 'For once I am not crying.'

He was telling me that I was preposterous and arrogant, but it was in a kind way that he was telling me this. It was like the times years ago when he used to tell me what I was really like, even pointing out the good things about me like determination and consistency which he envied me.

He patted my back rhythmically like he patted Daisy's back when she was a baby, like I've seen him pat my mother's back when she's upset. He asked me who the baby's father was, who the father of the fish was, but I wasn't going to tell him. So he stopped patting my back rhythmically, but didn't turn me off his knee.

He was warm, fresh out of bed. That dressing gown was the expensive striped one that my mother gave him for his last birthday when he became the same age as her for a few months. He smelled like my mother as well. It would be awful being sick with a stepfather holding on to you if he smelt completely alien, which Henry never has. He seemed to smell the same as her right from the start.

That woman on the phone had a voice rather like my mother's voice.

'You're such a silly girl,' Henry said.

'I know.' I was sitting, hanging my head and telling him I knew I was a silly girl.

133

He stroked back my hair again and said: 'Aren't you just?'

'I know I am a silly girl.' I swallowed.

'What a dum dum you are!'

'Yes.'

'Daft, Oliver!'

Oliver. He was calling me Oliver. He didn't like Olivia, my second name. Nor did he like my first name and said that Oliver was what I seemed to be to him. Whenever we made up differences he used to call me Oliver. He said I was always asking for more – more differences, I suppose.

But when Henry isn't angry you begin to wonder why he isn't getting angry. When Henry's forgiving, you think it's all too much and you can't believe its happening.

He must have put the telephone back on its cradle when he dragged me out from under the desk.

'You'll never know how daft you are,' he was saying.

He'd got the box. I must have handed him the box. He took the earrings out of it and they swung against the light showing rainbows in their prisms. Then he returned them to the box, lowering them into their blue velvet bed and put the box in the pocket of his dressing gown.

'I would have got them back,' I said. 'I would have pawned them and then got them back somehow.'

'Why on earth didn't you tell your mother?' he asked for the twentieth time.

He must have heard the telephone and come downstairs to return the call, which is what my mother used to do all those years ago.

'I didn't think she was up to knowing about it,' I said. 'You know how she is these days.'

I was still on his knee, but was waiting for him not to want me there any more. It was like hugging my mother but feeling the canyons in between us. It was like he wanted me there but didn't want me there. It was like he was thinking that I was his at last but was waiting for me to show him that I wasn't his. While I was waiting for him to decide that I wasn't his. In fact there was so much waiting going on that it seemed I shouldn't stay on his knee for another second, though I wanted to be there, I think, at the time.

'No, I don't know how your mother is these days. Come on. Let's go and tell her now. You need her and she needs to know. We'll wake her up and tell her now.'

How could he not know how my mother was these days or had been recently. Or how could he lie in his teeth so blatantly?

'Your mother loves you, Oliver.'

That isn't anything to do with you, I wanted to say. None of this is anything to do with you, I wanted to say. It's nobody else's concern except mine and marginally my mother's, I wanted to say. It's absolutely nobody else's concern. None of this is. None of any of this whole mess. It isn't Patrick's concern or any of the Leadbetters' concern. It isn't any of anyone's relations' concern. It would not even be my father's concern: least of all his. My lips are sealed to everyone and no one had better come on strong about it or try and help because help isn't to be given in this matter and it may go on for ever, but if anyone tries moseying in on the action I will be there armed to the teeth with a machine gun on a mountain pass to slay intruders so they fall as they come out of the canyon, fall on top of each other. Piles of dead there will be.

And if I come to court like I sometimes imagine being in court, I will stand in the dock and ask the court to be cleared of any persons interested in this case and demand my lawyers check the jury through and through before they call the witness for the prosecution: Henry Harrison. Call Henry Harrison. And did you on the night in question come across the prisoner, Petra Frobisher, committing the said felony?

'Come on, Oliver.'

Not Oliver! Not Oliver this time. Henry Harrison wanting Oliver to go upstairs with him to mother so that everyone could be cosy together in the middle of the night, making things right for ever which they never could be anyway.

'Come on.' He tried to turf me off his lap. I stood up and he stood beside me. He had the trousers of his silk pyjamas on, but his chest was bare and open. I hate him having so few clothes on close to me because it makes me feel I'm like my mother and have access to that body which I shouldn't have. It also made me think of other people like the woman on the telephone who may have had access too, so I had to go and sit down at my mother's bench with my hands between my knees to stop my knees from banging together. The raffia blinds were not rolled down and the rain was bashing at the remains of the virginia creeper and I was not going to move from there.

He only wanted to get me out of the way so that he could use the telephone. That woman sounded desperate. My teeth were chattering. I put my head down into a pile of cotton cuttings on the bench, head on arms, shoulders jerking. It had been years before this moment that I'd been upstairs in the dark planning things.

His voice was different and he didn't call me Oliver any more. He sighed. He sighed like all the world had failed him again, like the prime mover had moved against him and flung shit into his face. Like he had decided life was not even as much as a fish any more. 'You have arranged to go somewhere?'

'Yes.'

'And it's all right? Safe?'

'Yes, perfectly. Jane's coming with me.'

'Your mother should be with you.'

'I've asked Jane.'

His voice sounded like he was trying one more time. 'Come on. Let's go and tell your mother. Come on, love.'

He forgot himself and called me love.

'Come on.' He was touching me on the shoulder. 'Come on.' He was commanding me and not inviting me.

I heard him move away from me and sit down again. I heard the swivel of his chair and another sigh. Henry's sighs are like the sighs Daisy heaves when she is about to throw a screaming fit. There is a countdown to the screaming fits like there's a countdown to the end of Henry's sighing and the beginning of his anger.

'Come on.' He was trying to be nice again. 'OK,' he said. He took his hand away. 'OK,' he said, but nothing was OK in his view. That was evident from the dead sound in his voice. The countdown was ending. Two seconds and it would be too late to go.

He said: 'I wanted it to be all right for everyone.'

'I know you did,' I said. I hadn't cried up till that moment, but I cried because he'd never believe that I would have rather been his child than anyone's. I've overheard Henry saying that my father must have been an ineffectual twit. I've heard my mother agreeing about that. They blame my father for the way I am, but who chose him? Who made me part of him? The answer's obvious.

'You've never given me an inch,' he said.

'I've given you a mile, but you didn't notice it.'

'I haven't asked for much from you.' I could hear him moving around on bare feet. Then I could hear him in the office opening drawers and shutting them and was wondering if he'd notice that the photograph was missing.

Say this for Henry Harrison: I knew he'd never tell my mother if I hadn't told her myself. Say this for me: he knew I'd never tell my mother about the woman on the phone. Say there was something like a bargain. One tiny thing which could defeat the cock-up theory of the universe.

Henry was back beside me holding a glass of brandy from the bottle which they keep downstairs for special customers: 'Drink this.' Then he was back behind me sitting down with his head in his hands. 'Why do I bother?' he was saying. 'Why didn't I keep out of everyone's life?'

'Don't say that. You are in everyone's life. You are in Daisy's life apart from anything.' I was sobbing and the brandy was making me feel sick again. How could my mother ever take those pills and drink and stay upright, I wondered. 'You make things wrong, but often you make things right again.'

137

'Like this?' He pushed something towards me, a piece of paper. It was a cheque. I lifted my head and read it. It was made out for £200.

'That's much too much. That's overkill.'

'OK. Be overkilled.'

And I'd been about to tell him that he was the only person who had ever told me anything worth knowing. Except for Mr Forbes possibly. I was thinking: what did I know before I knew Henry? What did anyone know about anything before they knew Henry? And how can I know what it is I've learnt from him when I don't remember what I knew before to compare it with? He pointed to the cheque: 'That's everything you'll get from me,' he said. 'That's it.'

'It isn't money that I want from you.'

'That seems to be all I've been able to give you over the years.'

One thing I remember about sitting on Henry's knee. He must have been sketching earlier like he often does. There was a pen caricature of my mother on the desk, but it was as she used to look when he first knew her, before she wore her hair up. Later he screwed it up and threw it in the wastepaper basket.

TEN

Our GP was a pushover. He said: 'You want me to sign this?'

'Yes, please.'

He pulled it towards him, this letter telling them they could go ahead. 'You have discussed it with your mother?'

'No.' I sat with my hands between my knees.

'Um ah,' he said.

'She isn't very well,' I said.

'Oh really?'

'I mean mentally. I mean not something that she'd come to you about.'

'We are supposed to deal with the mind as well as the body,' he said.

'Well, yes, I'm sure you are. I mean they are linked, aren't they?'

'Much to be said on that,' he said as if he wouldn't deign to discuss such things with me. Then he stared into the distance until he heard a bell go in his partner's surgery, which I suppose made him realise he wasn't dealing with patients as fast as his partner.

'Have you discussed it with your father?' said the doctor.

'No. He's in America.'

'Ah, yes.' But no way was he going to say anything about Henry who had left the practice after having a disagreement about the treatment of a boil, which, according to Henry, was made worse.

'It's a very serious step to take,' he said.

'Oh absolutely. I know that. I've thought about it a lot. I've been losing sleep about it actually.'

He drew a pad towards him as if about to prescribe a sleeping pill, but then pushed it away and picked up the letter again and read it over several times. 'It's a weird, sad world,' he said.

Far be it for me to argue, I was thinking, though I didn't have to pretend to be nervous and was shaking quite a bit. I had been careful to make an appointment with this doctor instead of with his partner, however, who as well as dealing with patients in record time, is a member of some anti-abortion group. This information came from Jane as usual.

'I'm not in favour of all this, you know.' He consulted my notes which the nurse had brought in. 'You're on the pill?'

'Yes.' I looked at the floor hoping he would not ask why I had not taken it at the appropriate time. But my mother always says doctors should not be moral judges and I was not going to be morally judged by him. My mother always says doctors are there for getting what you want out of them, like the right pills. Henry says she treats doctors like they were servants. He has rows with doctors because, I suppose, he feels inferior to them. The next time he has a boil – and he does get them once a year or so and can't take antibiotics – he'll have to go to an emergency outpatients' place.

'I'm not at all in favour of this, you know,' the doctor said again.

'I have had counselling,' I said.

He looked a bit more put out at that than he had before. Jane says doctors do get worked up about these things because it is a negation of their life-preserving skill or whatever. He made

140

some notes: I guess about the date of my appointment at the clinic since he has to be on duty during the evening of that day: this is a rule that the clinic makes.

I've thought about Henry not taking antibiotics, not being able to, and thought how awful if he was found dying of pneumonia in a ditch somewhere and having penicillin pumped into him. Some doctor gave him a card once, a card explaining he could only be given whatever special antibiotic it is that isn't penicillin, but as often as not he forgets to carry the card or leaves it in the wrong suit pocket. He is known to be very careless of his own well-being.

There was a silence when I got back home. I could hear it and feel it. Sometimes the silences go on for so long that you're used to them and forget what everyone's voices sound like. Except for Daisy's since she doesn't seem to twig the silences or is so used to them or has grown up with them, that she seems not to think they are worth acknowledging. God knows what will happen when she's old enough to take part in them, though by that time I'll be gone for Christ's sake, won't I?

But this time it wasn't so much a silence as a feeling that in his mind I wasn't there, like I was transparent, like a piece of his brain had atrophied, the piece that received optic nerve messages telling him his eyes saw me.

Once there was a silence which went on for weeks and weeks, before Daisy stayed up for supper, which was then a terrific strain. The only words spoken at such meals were – for instance: 'Do you want more potato?' and as often as not he wouldn't answer, so you gave up saying it and he never had more potato. But one day after weeks and weeks it happened that I caught my mother's eye before saying it and looked at her as if to say: it's not worth saying it, but I will say it all the same. So I said it and he said: 'Yes, please.' Just like that he said: 'Yes, please.' I caught my mother's eye again and she was choking into her stew just as I was choking into the potato dish.

It's odd how I can catch her eye and we can both laugh

141

privately but never laugh much when we are alone together, when it is as if he's standing there behind us and we're thinking of what he would say under similar conditions.

That evening before my London trip it was a bit like this. I think she wanted to get out, away from things and silences. She'd found this piece of paper which I'd used to write a shopping list for her. It was a photostat from college.

'We must go to that,' she said.

'No point,' I said. It was a careers conference that very evening organised by the PTA. 'It's only for people who are definitely not going to university,' I said.

'All the same,' she said. She seemed intent on taking notice of me, presumably to make up for Henry's neglect of my existence.

'OK,' I said. It occurred to me that it might take my mind off the next day's ordeal.

She actually talked in the car as she drove me there, asking questions about the different staff who would be there on duty for the meeting, but she fell asleep in the assembly hall during the main address which was by a man from the Central Electricity Generating Board about careers in electronics and so on, although she had been making notes to start with.

'I told you it would be useless,' I said as I nudged her awake.

'But aren't we going to have individual discussions?' she whispered.

About a week later when the whole thing I am describing was over, Mr Forbes said: 'Was that your mother you were with that night?' and I said 'Yes,' and he said, 'She is very beautiful. She has amazing lips.' He is always on about people's lips, about people in Hardy having these amazing lips, women having these amazing lips.

But that night she didn't talk to him. She talked to several other people, doing her high-handed doctor-dealing façade of knowing everything there is to know, a kind of gracious act which Henry says is the true Leadbetter coming out in her.

Parents were supposed to circulate and talk to staff who had

142

their names on their lapels and mostly looked bored out of their minds. My mother fastened on to the art teacher describing how, with very little art training, she had learned to make these wallhangings, telling him that most people had natural aptitudes which weren't properly brought out by most kinds of education. The poor bloke's eyes were crossing with boredom. Then she collared the domestic science woman and expanded on how they ought to make domestic science compulsory for boys and that sexual equality (which she preaches but never practises) had no future without measures of that kind. This woman was equally pissed off by the conversation. She was having it off with the art bloke anyway and presumably itching to get away and into his arms in his Volvo.

To hear my mother talk of sexual equality, you'd think she was a raging feminist, which she is far from being – when it comes to Henry anyway, although she bosses Patrick quite a bit. Maybe she never expects great wonders from the men in her life, viz. Henry who walks over her and Patrick whom she treats like a lost cause.

She went on being very up and chatty in the car and seemed to think she had done very well, although she had not talked to anyone about me or my career as far as I could make out. But she seemed energised by having thrown her weight about and suggested that we went for a drink on the way home. I took her to the cocktail bar but after one drink she was ready to leave again.

In the bar she was talking about what I was best at doing which in her view was arguing or debating and objecting about the meaning of life and she kept saying how university was the only place for me. All of which I knew already: she can't seem to tell me anything new about myself. It was very odd sitting there thinking she had no idea what I was going to do the next day, rather what was going to be done to me the next day.

Patrick had only just started coming round again after the September disagreement or row or bust-up or whatever you might like to call it. He'd got over better dead than Leadbetter night and was in the lounge with Henry when we got back. He was visiting tentatively you might say, like testing the Henry water with one toe and being helpful and obsequious.

Daisy was still up. She was going to a fancy dress party and Henry had made her a spaceman's outfit out of foil and sellotape and cardboard boxes chopped to shape. Mess was spread out everywhere. Couldn't they have done it in the workroom, I was thinking, and my mother, I guess, was thinking likewise. But they had been watching television at the same time.

Patrick, useless at this kind of thing, was painting Daisy's wellingtons with silver paint, standing on a piece of newspaper.

It was long past Daisy's bedtime but she was standing, being fitted, rolling her eyes in agitation and excitement. The outfit was stupendous actually. She'd said she wanted to be a female robot or a space queen. The helmet Henry made her had a gap in it so that her hair came out of the top and swung.

Henry, also feverish, hardly noticed us or asked how we'd got on at the careers meeting, not that we could have told him much since it seemed, in retrospect, to have been a non-event, like most things were without him around either making the occasion great or making it disastrous.

'Look! Look!' he was saying, making Daisy turn round.

'Yes, marvellous,' my mother said.

'Say that again,' he said.

'It's marvellous, I said,' she said.

She had to say how marvellous it was.

'What I won't do for you!' he said.

'It's absolutely marvellous,' she said again.

He seemed so carried away by his own enthusiasm he seemed to have forgotten I was there and he was breaking his silence-in-my-presence-rule.

'What I won't do for you!' he said again.

She didn't point out that it was for Daisy more than for her. She kept on looking over where Patrick, kneeling on his newspaper by now, was only just avoiding splashing silver paint around the precious floorboards and rugs.

'All love!' he said. 'It's all for love! Love glued it together.'

Daisy fidgeted. 'It's itchy itchy itchy,' she said.

'The party's not till Saturday,' my mother said.

'Ah well.' He stood back from Daisy with his head on one side to assess the whole effect.

'It's really splendid, isn't it?' said Patrick, holding up his paint brush and looking over the back of the settee.

'I suppose,' my mother said as tactfully as she has ever spoken, 'that it could be finished off . . . say tomorrow sometime . . . in the workroom say . . .'

'Well, actually,' said Henry.

'I mean, it is quite late,' my mother said. She bent to pick up slivers of foil which were scattered everywhere.

'We'll tidy up,' said Henry.

'Oh it doesn't matter honestly . . . tomorrow . . .'

'I've got that man to see tomorrow,' Henry said.

My mother was still bending down. She stayed bending down with her hand stretching out for a piece of sellotape which was stuck to the side of an armchair. 'Oh yes,' she said as if she had no idea he had to see a man tomorrow. 'I can't remember where you said you had to go to see this man . . .'

'I told you, didn't I?'

I remember Patrick was cleaning paint off his trousers with some paint-remover and beginning to talk about a movie they'd been watching. As far as I can remember one like *Brief Encounter*. 'Great old movie we've been watching, haven't we, Henry?'

'How nice!' My mother was having difficulty with a simple thing like removing yet another piece of sellotape stuck to her skirt and spending a lot of time over it. 'You didn't tell me actually,' she said.

'Whoopsie,' said Patrick as he spilt some turpentine.

I wasn't really listening. This time tomorrow – I was thinking. But Henry said the man he had to see was to do with orientals – say an agent or importer. About Afghan stuff I think perhaps. They still get stuff from Afghanistan even since the Russians overran it a couple of years back. It must have been Afghanistan because Patrick said: 'Afghanistan? I didn't think . . .'

'Oh yes,' said Henry, 'it still gets through.'

I wouldn't have remembered this, except that in her diary where she's put the red triangles there's a note which says 'query Afghanistan?'. But she would have been querying the supplier of Afghan stuff, rather than the supply. And later on that night when I went downstairs and passed the door they were still talking about Afghanistan and more recent international politics, such as El Salvador, etc., though my mother was not contributing and looking scared. In fact Patrick has queried me about Afghanistan. Let him think it was all to do with Afghanistan, I say.

That London place: I'd rather not describe it really. Only say that the worst part was knowing I was going there, but making myself in my head look forward to it being over rather than dreading the event itself. That was the way my mother used to make me mind less about going to the dentist way back when she used to take me to appointments.

It seemed daft going to London and not wanting to go. The last time I'd been there was with Ginny when she bought me the clothes and it had been blazingly hot and she nearly passed out in Miss Selfridge's. We had to keep stopping for iced gins, with her telling me it was even hotter in Adelaide than this most times of the year.

The London place: I knew it wouldn't be like people were blaming you for being there: no moral judgements since you had been counselled already. It would be more like a dentist's where you'd never been before. The only interesting thing at first were the other people in the waiting room. One woman looked incredibly rich and posh like she ought to have gone to

146

some much more exclusive clinic. And one girl who seemed much younger than me.

For home, I had made up some story about a college trip to do with sociology. I'd left a note saying: 'Forgot to tell you last night . . .' etc.

The robe they gave you, in which you had to lie around afterwards, wasn't bad . . . sort of white with a nice neckline.

Jane was shopping all this time. She'd got a day off from work in exchange for a day off her annual holiday. She went to the Miss Selfridge's just off Regent Street, but said that apart from new baggy trousers in a kind of tartan there wasn't much there this time. She had to come with me. Someone did. That was a rule.

Afterwards it was a bit like being at a school camp, girls together in a room in beds. Well . . . three of us together: the rich woman and the girl who turned out to be sixteen but who seemed more like fourteen and came from somewhere like Birmingham, and the rich woman carrying on about having been promised a room of her own. The girl had been three times to other clinics but hadn't told the people at this one, so was whispering.

Jane said she spent more time in Heal's because the clinic was near Tottenham Court Road. In Heal's she said some of the stuff was even nicer than the stuff we had at Harrison's. 'Of course it would be,' I said. 'Harrison's is only a little tin-pot set-up in comparison.'

The girl kept whispering that her friends all said she'd never have a proper full-term baby if she went on like this. She was at school doing O Levels but about to leave. She said her friends said her insides would be shot to pieces if she went on this way.

But the actual thing was nothing. Well, it wasn't nothing. It was quite something when you think how much it cost and how many hours of training went into the doctor and the two nurses that were around, one of them Philippino like the girl who Henry wanted to look after the shop instead of Stella.

The first injection made me chatty and quite cheerful:

147

'Where are you from?' I said.

'I am a Philippino,' said the nurse.

Under the anaesthetic it seemed that I was in a very strongly lit place but I couldn't remember where it seeemed to be when I woke up.

I remember being told ages ago that someone once had heard them shut the pedal bin just as they were coming round. I don't think I heard the pedal bin. I don't think there was one. But I came round thinking: that was life that was and trying to remember where the bright place had been.

Jane said, 'What was the procedure then?' This was in the taxi on the way back to Waterloo. It felt odd being in my clothes again. I told Jane about the girl who thought she might not have any kids in the future and Jane began to talk about this lovely curtain material she'd seen in Heal's, but she kept on looking at me carefully. She was observing the clinic's rule most conscientiously.

I remember the taxi crossing the bridge near Waterloo and seeing the lights along the river and the Houses of Parliament lit up where they made the law which said you could have abortions and where people were always trying to change the law back so that you couldn't. And thinking that it might have been my mother doing all this if I hadn't left her that pill, but how she would have had Henry with her, driving her probably and stopping every now and then to see if she was all right, holding her hand while driving and buying her post-abortion presents.

Jane had talked to the receptionist: 'What a lovely job it would be to do something like that, sort of fringe medical. I wonder what the qualifications are.'

'I don't suppose anything special,' I said.

'Just kind of motherliness perhaps,' she said.

'What irony,' I said.

She seemed upset about that.

The train wasn't due for half an hour, so we went into the café facing on to the concourse. My legs felt considerably wobbly, funnily enough, though I'd felt incredibly exhilarated crossing that bridge, though it wasn't Westminster bridge where Wordsworth felt exhilarated I don't think. Nor was it the time of day he was on it.

'You had no breakfast,' said Jane. 'And your metabolism will take time to adjust itself.'

Most of the café windows had frosted glass, but someone had smashed one – a vandal probably – and there was clear glass in the window we sat by. There were curved seats and we had an alcove to ourselves at first.

Jane was going on about what a marvellous woman Marie Stopes must have been. 'So determined,' she said.

Perhaps the strongly lit place was lit by sunshine and was a staggeringly hot bright beach. Jane was talking to me asking if I was all right. I'd offered her some of the surplus money from Henry's cheque for losing a day of her holiday, but she wouldn't take it. It must be terrible having only three weeks a year. But I did pay her fare.

'I feel like a drink,' I said. 'Perhaps my metabolism has adjusted itself in record time.'

Jane said: 'Oh, Petra, no. Not after a general anaesthetic.'

I looked around at all the people who had been having ordinary working days in London or just shopping. Perhaps where I'd been in those ten minutes was a dream of the mountains in Colorado, but the word 'Afghanistan' cropped up in my head because of the way they'd been talking about it at home the night before. When I came round it seemed that the nurse had only just finished saying 'I am a Philippino.'

From the café I could see people on the concourse walking, some of them with furled umbrellas, walking ahead not knowing what was going on in other people's heads. The café had brass rails and short green curtains round the alcoves. The seats were buttoned leather in a style like some of the stuff we used to sell in Harrison's, though everything now is lighter and more flowery. The more gloomy my mother gets, the lighter the materials she deals in.

Jane was saying: 'And the lighting in Heal's! Honestly, Petra, it made me drool with wanting to have lamps like that . . .' I seemed to see Jane running after lamps which eluded her and bobbed away from her. Then I thought I saw someone like Henry walking past the windows of the café with a woman beside him. How was I to know that my mother hadn't taken it into her head to come with him today?

Jane was saying: 'Well, I don't suppose I'll have my own house, not for years and years, but when I do I am determined I shall go back to Heal's to choose. I don't mean that you don't have lovely things in Harrison's . . .'

It's over, I was saying to myself. The fish has gone. I do feel marvellous, I was saying to myself. I shall have my hair cut short and come back to get baggy trousers at Miss Selfridge's for the spring.

The man who looked like Henry seemed to be looking up at the mainline departures board opposite. He was wearing a big navy blue overcoat like the one that Henry wears. The one he wore in the shop the day the candlestick went missing.

Then this man went back to stand near a woman in a fur coat, but not a fur coat like my mother's. Thank heavens, I thought. The fur coat was black and curly and the woman's hair was on her shoulders and almost the same colour as the coat, but not curly.

Jane was saying: 'Geoff's mother's house has really quite nice furnishings, but too much dralon and identical textures to my mind. Are you sure you are OK?'

The tea tasted really smashing and was the best tea I'd had for months. I'd made the deadline. Under fourteen weeks. The September party would have been exactly fourteen weeks ago that Saturday.

The man and the woman both turned, but a trolley swished in front of them. The next time I saw them they were kissing and his head was bent over hers. I still have no idea who she was, but my mother has marked a red triangle against that day, where it also says: 'H to London. P to sociology trip – Salisbury.'

150

The fish has gone, I was saying to myself while Jane was telling me that Geoff's mother had shown her all the family photographs last Sunday lunch when she was visiting, and how Geoff had this blonde curly hair as a baby and was fat and gorgeous, but had nearly died as a result of an allergic reaction to a whooping cough injection at three months.

I suppose I knew it was Henry by the departures board all along, but wasn't allowing myself to worry about it.

'My goodness me! We ought to go,' said Jane.

The café was beginning to fill up and women with shopping bags were sitting either side of us.

'We really ought to go,' said Jane.

'No,' I said.

'Why ever not?' she said.

'Don't feel like it,' I said.

'Oh Petra, what is happening?'

'No, nothing's happening. I just need to sit here.'

We were hemmed in by these women. Also, if I didn't look out of the window, I had to look at Jane and didn't want her to be looking straight into my face. There were other directions in which I could have faced, but dead in front of me was this bloke looking us both up and down, a leery, lecherous bloke with a straight moustache like a Hitler look-alike and I didn't want to gaze at him either. So it had to be the window where I could see Henry with his arms around the woman's waist, slowly pacing towards the iron gates of the platform barriers, and her stopping and putting up her arms to cling around his neck. Then he drew her towards him in a comforting way as if he was going to pat her back like he patted me when I was sick, like he patted Daisy when she was a baby and often still patted her, or patted my mother when she was really upset about something or had said something really stupid but laughable.

'There isn't another train for an hour,' said Jane.

For a few minutes the two of them sat down on a station seat and his head was turned towards her and his hand was on her cheek briefly.

'Not for a whole hour,' said Jane, 'and you know the rule is that you have to be home within two hours of leaving the clinic.'

'I'm breaking the rule in that case. We'll catch that one.'

She didn't go on about the train any more, but I remembered she was meeting Geoff at eight and going to a do at the Rugby Club. 'You go,' I said.

'And leave you here? Please, Petra, listen . . .'

I didn't really want her seeing Henry with the other woman either. The man with the Hitler moustache had shuffled off but was still looking over at us as he queued at the self-service counter with a tray. So were other people looking at us, namely the women in our alcove with their shopping in carrier bags jammed up against our legs and theirs. The place was so packed that some people were standing balancing cups of tea and plates with doughnuts and eclairs on them.

'You will be better in the fresh air, won't you? Even if we don't go on the train, let's move. I'm feeling fairly claustrophobic in here myself.'

All the women round us were staring. At least they seemed to be. One of them must have asked Jane if I was all right. 'Yes, I think so, but she needs some air. She's had . . . had . . . had a shock, you see.'

'I haven't had a shock,' I said.

Henry was standing up again near the seat directly facing the café window. It was some way away, but he might have seen me and I wanted him to see me watching him over the woman's shoulder. Then I didn't want him seeing me, so I held the empty teacup in front of my face. Maybe he'd think he might have seen me and he'd be doubtful whether he had seen me or not and worry about it and it would haunt him down all his days that I might have seen him being furtive with another woman.

That bright place where light came through your closed eyelids: it was hot: it might have been Afghanistan or Mount Evans or the Philippines. Shouldn't my mother have let him have a Philippino girl to stop him doing all this?

Or was it like out there by the barriers, because the noise I'd

152

heard under the anaesthetic was like the station noise with music and announcements? Or was it the operating theatre itself and I was conscious? No, that was this morning. About ten o'clock was the time they did it and we had to get there at eight a.m. which had meant getting the very early train. Henry wasn't on that train so must have caught a later one.

She was taller than my mother and he didn't have to bend that much when he hugged her again. His face was looking out beyond her and I went on looking at him with my empty cup held up in two hands in front of my face.

If he's with her there may be no silences.

'I'm sorry, I can't make her move.' Jane was tugging at my arm, leaning across all the mess of cups and plates and old paper wrappings on the table. 'Give me your cup, Petra. I'll get you some more tea.'

If he's with her, he will not have to blind himself to my existence any more.

The cup was taken from me, thus my face revealed to Henry in between people passing, but I'll never know if he saw me or recognised me, although it seemed to me that he did. The expression on his face seemed to me to fill my mind with what was in his mind. Which was. Oh shit. Oh God. I'm done. She'll shop me, won't she?

Or maybe it said: poor kid looking sick. I know where she has been, but can't do anything for her with this woman on my hands. This woman needs me anyway and Petra doesn't need me anyway. She only needs my money anyway.

Two-faced Henry who is not two-faced intentionally because he isn't anything intentionally. He is. That's all. He's like the frogs in *Life on Earth* and unintentional. A random frog, the slug he thinks he is, the God he thinks he is, the God some people think he is. He's life, that's all. That's life that was in the bright place under the station lights when I was feeling not exactly sick but feeling something in my stomach on account of what had gone from it. No air, sweat pouring down my face, Jane saying: 'Yes, she's had a shock' and dragging me outside,

153

me tripping over people's shopping, passing the Hitler look-alike with a doughnut half-way to his mouth, me shaking off Jane's hand. 'It wasn't a shock. It was planned. It was intentional. It was inevitable. I mean it wasn't planned. It was unwanted, but I planned.'

Jane didn't see him and we waited sitting at the far end of the concourse till the train had gone. The woman in the black fur coat stood beside the barrier, then walked towards us, passed us, then walked back again, wandering around like a fart in a bottle, as Henry would say. Eventually she went towards the entrance to the Underground. Close to, when I saw her, she was not really like my mother at all, but like some of the sketches he used to draw. Her face was broader than my mother's; her eyes were steadier, her lips were thinner. Close to she was trying not to cry maybe, but quite unaware of me and thinking maybe: oh my love – I've lost my love. Or shit – he's got away from me, gone home.

Court evidence: And did you, Henry Harrison, on the day in question, visit London to meet a lady of unknown origin and leave her there? It shall be noted down.

That evening at home my mother was smiling and believing him apparently. He was sitting with her and the telly was on. I passed. I was passing the door. They were holding hands. He was telling her about the lunch he'd had. Well, he could have had lunch. There *was* a man he was talking about. There always would be a man he'd seen as well to make the story right for her. Like any fool who had ever been to see a man could make the story right for her.

'All right?' she called out to me. Then, when I didn't answer, she came out into the corridor as I was going on upstairs.

'Yes, fine,' I said, not turning to look down at her.

She went back to him. I heard him say: 'Where has she been?'

'Oh, on some sociology trip.'

'Where?' he said.

154

'Oh, Salisbury, wasn't it?' I heard her say vaguely, but had she been in a normal frame of mind and really believing him about everything, she would have asked me about the trip. For which I was prepared. Any fool can invent a sociology trip once they have been on one.

ELEVEN

About the time that Henry left, however many weeks or days ago that is, there was all this going on in English about tragedy and comedy. We'd just started doing *Lear*. This was on Valentine's Day, I think. Yes, we were doing *Lear*. People die at the end of tragedies, said Mr Forbes, and marry at the end of comedies – or at least pair off.

'Why does it have to be either?' I said.

'Why does what have to be either?' said Forbes.

'Why does life have to be either tragedy or comedy?'

'Perhaps I'm talking only about literature,' he said. 'It might be worth reminding you that this is a literature class.'

'But you're always saying literature has to be like life,' I said.

'I'm thinking of retiring,' he said.

'Oh dear, oh dear,' said everyone in the class in chorus, since he's always saying that. Either that or that he wishes he'd gone to Kuwait where he once got offered a job.

'No,' he said. 'I've changed my mind. I shall continue to draw the salary, but Petra can take the class for me.'

'Groan groan,' said everyone, since that was an old and sarky joke.

'I was only trying to say,' I said, 'that life could be neither. It

156

could be like cock-up and conspiracy. I mean cock-up *or* conspiracy,' and I went on about the prime mover and all that like all the arguments we'd had at home and Patrick's theory about the Austro-Prussian War. But I was getting sharper than usual looks and signals from everyone and my voice just trailed away until Mr Forbes cleared his throat and went on about what tragedy meant all over again.

Sod them all, I was thinking, but didn't actually mind that much on account of the letter I'd received that morning from my father telling me about this money that was coming to me, namely £2500 on my birthday.

Now I come to think about it, that was also the day on which we heard that Mr Forbes' wife had gone into hospital to rest until she had the twins. She'd had a scan to prove it was twins, but because of high blood pressure and possible complications she was in Southampton General.

Meanwhile Mr Forbes was back on tragedy and the breaking of tabus like incest, murder, fratricide, etc. and I was working out what to do with the money when it came. Its source, my father said, was an insurance policy which had matured. I was making a list of all the things that I might do with it. I was sitting at the back of the classroom I remember and gazing at Tracey's hair in its corrugated waves, sticking inches out all over her head. She's got straw-coloured hair and it looked as if a hundred yards of gold fuse wire was messed up into a yellow birds' nest and the sun shone into it.

Someone asked Mr Forbes if *Far From the Madding Crowd* couldn't be called a tragedy because of Farmer Boldwood shooting Sergeant Troy and going off his head in the end. Yes, he said, it probably could, especially as it included the tabu of adultery as well – that of Sergeant Troy and Fanny Robin.

Tracey's hair was done with an electric crimper, but no way was I going to copy her. Anyway, you can make your hair stick up with gel much easier. Apart from looking at Tracey's hair I was considering whether I would buy a motor bike since I wouldn't need to pass a test for that; not to start with at any rate.

Then I noticed Mr Forbes had stopped talking about tragedy, tabus and that and was holding up this card. It was a valentine card. He said someone had sent it. 'If anyone knows anything about this, may I say thank you?'

There was a general buzz and murmur. People were exchanging glances. Tracey turned and looked at me as though she thought I knew the sender of the card or had sent it myself. Mr Forbes was looking at me too.

'Maybe,' I said. 'Maybe someone sent it as a joke reference to *Far From the Madding Crowd* because of Bathsheba sending Farmer Boldwood one and Farmer Boldwood falling desperately in love and going mad with jealousy and causing all the deaths at the end?'

He was staring at me. 'Oh yes, I see,' he said. 'Stap me! How thoroughly obtuse of me!' He rolled his eyes in a double-take and put the card away again. 'What good will such a message carries with it in that case!' he added.

'Oh well, that explains it, doesn't it?' said Tracey, twisting round to gawp at me.

'I should be grateful, I suppose . . .' said Forbes.

'Yes, shouldn't you!' said someone.

'Or be scared out of your mind,' said Tracey, still looking at me.

'I should at least be grateful,' reiterated Forbes firmly, 'that whoever sent it does at least remember the plot, some of the plot of the story. I wonder what happens next.' He was packing up his briefcase at this point.

While his wife was in hospital, Forbes' older kid was spending the days round at Jane's mother's house, but there was to be this list or rota for babysitting for him in the evenings while he visited Southampton General. As I left they were discussing it. *'You'll* be wanting to babysit as much as possible, won't you?' said Tracey to me.

'No, certainly not,' I said. 'You can count me out except as a reserve.' But they were still giggling as I left.

The only valentine I'd sent was to Giles at school, a rude one

158

to embarrass him in front of his holy friends. We'd had a row in the Christmas holidays – not about him not sleeping with me any more, but about homosexuality, about which he'd become intolerant, saying that it was an extra dose of decadence that this country could do without. Otherwise Christmas had been OK, with me and Henry kissing under the mistletoe and giving each other presents as we always did and meaning it at the time. At least I did, mean it at the time I mean. It was like we had kept our bargains and were keeping distances and were keeping a face on everything for my mother's sake and Daisy's sake. And the telephone calls had stopped and everything. Although, in retrospect it was maybe we were only papering over the cracks or maybe it was like the underground nuclear waste in Colorado, lurking ready to spill out again at any moment.

That Valentine's Day when I was unpadlocking my bike in the yard in this very bright sunlight, I saw Mr Forbes getting into his car on the far side of the courtyard where the staff car park was. Then his car came nosing out between a row of yellow privet bushes. As I turned my head I remember noticing that I was trying to make my neck look longer, which is always a sign that I want someone to look at me especially. It was actually the day after I'd had my hair cut short and my ears pierced to celebrate the return of spring and had these gold sleeper rings put in my ears. He was looking at me kind of ruefully over his steering wheel. Perhaps as well as my interpretation of the valentine card, he'd heard me say I'd rather die than babysit for him.

There was a girl at our school once, several years ago, who went off with the physics teacher and lived with him in Petersfield, but left him six months later. I saw him once, looking pathetic after she had left him. He had to leave physics teaching too, or was doing it at another school somewhere.

I suppose a pupil/teacher steamy do might be breaking a tabu, but I reckoned Mr Forbes could always get another job, in, e.g. Kuwait, teaching jobs being short in this country at this time.

But mostly as I biked away I was thinking about the idea of a motor bike and holidays and shooting along wide French roads with poplars along the side and rolling land all around as far as I could see.

That afternoon I rode. It rained on and off and there was a rainbow followed by a greenish light, Troy acting restless and unpredictable, ears flicking even when on a good hard gallop up to the beacon. I'd forgotten my crash helmet, so went bare-headed, knowing somehow there was no danger, though the ground was hard and the temperature only a few degrees above freezing. I remember thinking I could have gone on galloping till dark arrived and there was nothing more anyone could want than that. The hint in my father's letter that he hoped I was considering the idea of college in America seemed feeble and pathetic.

When Patrick questions me about the evening of that day, I tell him how I went home and then took Daisy for a walk or rather a run or scamper in the park. I tell him that Henry was selling a man a carpet and the shop stayed open late because of this. From between the avenue of conifer trees in the park I could see Henry rolling up the rug, knotting it with string and chatting cheerfully to the man.

Daisy was doing handstands on the grass, staying balanced upside down for a count of five or ten or so. I could stay balanced just as long although I hadn't done handstands for years.

She said her chest felt funny as if she was excited about something. Then she did another handstand and the black dog bounced out of nowhere in the dark and sent her flying. She lay on her back, too winded to scream out, too surprised to cry, too flattened and shocked to be scared.

'You say he didn't take the car?' says Patrick.

'You've seen it. It's still there.'

Then I was in the kitchen alone with my mother. She was cooking and the time was six-ish and the blinds had just been drawn. Lighting-up time for that day I see was five past six and perhaps I glowed a little from my exertions in the park where it had been cold but very still, the kind of night you can imagine surviving in the open, whereas all the other nights for weeks had been raw and windy and impossible.

Wearing her red plastic apron, my mother was watching the saucepan. Steam was pouring everywhere. She was boiling spaghetti. Henry was still down in the shop and Daisy was watching television.

'I've had this letter from Daddy.'

'Yes. I saw it in the post today.'

She turned the gas down to let the spaghetti simmer and she looked at her watch, lit a cigarette and blew the smoke towards the blinds. It curled around the bottom of the blinds where a little air came in.

'It means big money – well, for me big money. It was an insurance policy.'

'I remember that policy,' she said. 'That's lovely, isn't it?' or words to that effect. She never sounds too excited. Being a person who expects the worst, she doesn't dare get thrilled by expectations, I suppose. 'What will you do with it?'

'I haven't thought.'

The sauce she'd made to go with the spaghetti: it was keeping warm in the oven; you could smell it. She's nifty when she's got her cooking head on properly and uses fresh herbs to give things tangy flavours.

I sat on the table and there was a normal feel. My mother had an especially thoughtful look, but always looks like that when smoking. It's the mannerisms and the sharpish drag she gives a cigarette, as if she wants to look decisive.

'Not enough for a car, really,' I said.

'No, not enough for a decent car,' she said. Sometimes it is annoying, not to say exasperating that she refuses to get too excited about anything. I suppose she wouldn't have lasted two minutes with Henry if they both got excited.

'You'll be relieved,' I said about the car, because I guessed

161

that no one wanted me to have one, with two cars already in the yard and not much room for manoeuvring for parking.

'I might go on a terrifically long journey,' I said, imitating Daisy's way of talking and making my mother laugh, which was unusual when we were alone without Henry or without Daisy. Because they are the members of the family who make most of the jokes.

At some stage during the conversation I got up and fetched the long-spouted can and watered the plants and noticed that the monstera had made more new leaves than usual for that time of year, which meant it had benefited from the calm atmosphere that had reigned since Christmas.

People who talk to my mother don't expect jokes. They expect quiet sympathy and friendliness, which she is very good at giving, so my friends say anyway. Though they don't realise she isn't listening most of the time and will probably have forgotten their names next time they come. But that evening she was listening for sure and not as cracked as she is now. For once I wasn't feeling ratty with her fading dottiness.

It wasn't close or particularly sincere. For instance I didn't tell her that I really planned to buy a motor bike or that it had occurred to me I could pay Henry back the £200 he'd given me in November. We talked about suggestions that I might spend some time in Italy because I thought I'd like to learn Italian and more about pictures as well as going to university if I got into one.

I had my feet on a crossbar of the kitchen stool. She offered me a cigarette and then switched on the ventilation fan. The radio was on quietly, on Radio Three, but not too classical as we talked about improving ways of spending two thousand five hundred pounds.

Henry used to say that she and I never talked as people who are close should talk. He may have been right, though who knows what people who are close do talk about. At any rate my mother and I do talk about a good many things easily, even if it is only why we have run out of Weetabix or who has spoiled the cheese by putting it in the fridge.

I was tapping my toes on the crossbar of the stool to the music and she told me about Italy, about the time she'd been on honeymoon with my father there, which seemed ever so odd because although I knew they'd been there, she'd never talked about the actual place. While we knew tons about Henry's honeymoon with Vivienne the flower arranger who had passed out in the heat of Athens and gone off sex in Rhodes.

There was this extraneous thin sound. It was, of all things, my mother whistling to the tune of the music. The music was Mozart or something. With a trumpet in it. I was looking at the copper saucepan on the dresser. The spotlight made it almost purple. There were blue mugs on either side of it with all our names on them.

'Yes, I'd like to go to Italy.'

'You can go anywhere you like. As long as you keep in touch.'

'Isn't the spaghetti cooked?'

You could always hear him coming from the click of the latch of the door from the shop into the corridor. You would know it was him by the footsteps anywhere.

Years ago I used to hang around the kitchen even when I knew they wanted to be on their own. I used to wait and see how long before someone asked me to get out. My mother wouldn't ask me to get out however much she wanted me to go, however much it was obvious she wanted me to. No, my mother would wander round and keep on cleaning things, wiping surfaces over and over again without speaking, although you could feel the irritation rising in her. I'd be willing her to say 'Get out!' and she'd be willing herself not to. Or maybe she'd be thinking up some errand she could send me on which wouldn't sound too useless or pointless. And if Henry was in there, he'd begin to breathe heavily and fidget and shake the newspaper loudly as I stood leaning, watching to see how it was affecting him and if he'd leave before I did.

He never threw me out. He's hardly ever laid a finger on me.

163

I should make that clear to Patrick. Maybe when Patrick told me the other day that the police will only search properly for loony people, he was asking me in a roundabout way if I thought Henry was dangerously loony. Like I've said, he breaks so-called tabus of manners, but he doesn't lash out physically, though you often see him wanting to.

As for more serious tabus, there was adultery: there isn't now – at least not with my mother any more. I can't quite see the significance of tabus in any case. I was talking about them with Liz the other day and she said she reckoned they were only rules to protect society – like not eating dogs which could give you worms and so on, and mainly for the benefit of men, particularly the one about adultery, because in a patriarchal society no man could be sure any child was his to inherit his worldly goods if his wife was screwing around. I can see that murder needs to be put under the heading of a tabu, however, or no one would feel safe at all. But if people couldn't commit adultery, they surely would go mad.

So Henry came into the kitchen and since my mother went on whistling, it could be that we could go on talking normally about my future, but I put the letter folded into the newspaper on the dresser opposite until I'd seen how Henry looked when he came in.

He didn't speak, but that was not unusual. My mother turned from the cooker to look at him and went over to bend and kiss the top of his head as he sat at the table. I was leaning on the dresser opposite. My mother still went on whistling, but it seemed like she went on whistling so as not to make it as if the atmosphere had changed when he came in. He hadn't responded to the kiss on top of his head. Sometimes he used to put an arm up and touch her when she kissed him like that.

'Chuck me over the paper, will you, Petra, please,' he said. A bit cool that. Not over-friendly, the voice.

'Oh, yes. Where is it?' I kept my voice level.

'Behind you on the dresser,' he said.

'Oh, yes.'

164

I slipped the letter out of the newspaper and shoved it in the back pocket of my jeans. He saw me do that, but went on holding out his hand for the newspaper, still with a kind of weary and resigned look on his face, as if suspecting subterfuge, as if to say that this was what his life was like, being kept out of things.

My mother lit another cigarette and was dropping ash down the plughole of the sink. The spaghetti smelled like it was over-cooked and I was thinking that I'd show him that I wasn't keeping him out of anything. So I took the letter out of my pocket and smoothed it, saying something like: 'Well, I'm in the money at last.'

I even thought of asking him for advice on what I should spend the money on, but thought he might think I was flannelling, so I explained how the money came and made a joke about it, something like: 'I'll see you and my old mother don't starve.' I put a bit of an accent on, like the King's Radlett accent which I can slip into quite easily.

He didn't react or say anything. He was probably tired. I don't know why on earth my mother stood and let the spaghetti burn.

Henry said: 'So you'll be shaking the dust of Harrison's off your feet?'

'It isn't that much money,' I said.

Sometimes it's a good idea to get out before the warning signals come. At that point, if you leave, you go on believing there might have been no flashpoint, if you leave while things are normal still. I left, although I knew I'd have to come back if I was going to eat with them. But as I left and was on the bottom stair, I heard him say: 'We'll use her room for extra working space.'

So I looked back in to show him I'd heard. 'Yes, do use it for extra working space,' I said.

My mother said: 'Let's have a drink.'

Then she offered him a cigarette.

He said no thanks to both of these.

165

She was picking bits of good unburnt spaghetti from the burnt spaghetti, which was most of it. The saucepan would be ruined.

It was a case of putting the stereo on loud again. Bob Marley this time, which drowned the ringing in my ears which I hadn't had since the November rows. Then I began to tear posters off the wall. The room I reckoned was full of things which could be thrown away, so I started shoving these and the posters into a plastic bin-liner which I'd grabbed from the kitchen long before.

I'd often started packing for leaving home before, but this time I was making piles of photographs and cuddly toys and clothes and games: some piles to throw away and some piles to be given to Daisy. Then thought: oh well, Henry won't want Daisy to have things contaminated by having been mine, so everything I could lay my hands on, except the stereo, records and some books and clothes, went into the black bin-liner. I couldn't decide whether to keep the silk shirt he gave me for Christmas when we kissed under the mistletoe and seemed to mean it at the time.

Sometimes when I've been packing to leave home, my mother's come and pleaded with me, whispering that I should hang on and it will all blow over, but I wasn't giving her the chance this time. I'd hear no gentle knocking on my door. There'd be no chance for her to mediate.

This time I meant it. I was going round to Bentley's with a suitcase and a bin-liner and I'd leave an extra pile of heavy things with a note to say 'to be collected'. Which I hadn't done before. I stuffed important papers like my passport into my shoulder bag. Then thought about my cheque book. I found it, sat down and wrote in it: 'Pay Henry Harrison two hundred pounds' and wondered if I should make it more for interest. Hadn't it been a loan? But I left it at £200 and put it into a stiff white envelope from a set of writing paper I'd been given at Christmas and went downstairs. I owed it to him, didn't I?

166

Everything in the lounge was amazingly tidy and neat like it often is when Stella has popped up to clean. The white curtains at the far end had been washed.

The carpet in front of the gas fire is pale – reds and blues, but softish hues. It's antique, Caucasian, a soumac rug – near pinkish as it shimmers in the glow of the gas fire.

I hadn't thought of Daisy being there. He was on the long settee with her; she was lying across him with her head in his lap. His hand was lifting up her hair and letting it fall, Daisy being quite indifferent with her head turned towards the television. It was a quiet calm place – with everything in place. The volume of the television was subdued. The brass carriage clock, a Leadbetter clock, on the mantelpiece was not wound up. It never is wound up, Henry, as I've said, not liking to be reminded of the passage of time.

I held the cheque in its envelope and sat down on the floor, leaning against an armchair, hands round my knees.

At first his hand moved more slowly as it lifted the thin strands of Daisy's hair and let them fall again. Then it stopped altogether. He was still watching the television. Distant sounds of panscrubbers in use in the kitchen could be heard. They must have had a meal with the sauce which would have been OK – and what was left of the spaghetti; I was thinking how I might have been hungry, but wasn't hungry.

The television showed people running like in the Olympics, but it wasn't the Olympics. This made me think of Sebastian Coe and Ronnie and the aftermath of that and how this was the after-aftermath and how there would always be aftermaths and after-aftermaths and how the thing with me and Henry might never end. Because if life's a tragedy, the only way for things to end is with death, and if life's a comedy, no one was going to pair off in our situation, only break maybe a pairing off, since I guess that with the rows they've had about me, their pairing off has been strained no end.

Henry and Daisy must have been watching ITV because there was a commercial break during which I said: 'This is for

167

you' and held out the envelope towards him. He didn't reply or seem to hear me, though Daisy turned her head to peer up into his face before putting her thumb back into her mouth. I said again: 'This is for you. What I owe you,' and stood up facing him, holding it towards him. I could always meet his eyes and know more about him than anyone and he knew more about me than anyone. He knew I meant it, giving it to him. It was the thing I meant to do, and, thinking about tragedy, for instance at the end of *Lear*, Edgar, after clearing up the dead, says that everyone has got to speak what they feel and not what they ought to say – or words to that effect.

So I went on holding the envelope out. Henry stopped stroking Daisy's hair. He lifted her head. He put his arms under Daisy and lifted her up, kissing her cheek and laying her back on the sofa. Daisy's face did not change. She was used to that. I held the cheque out, willing him to turn round and stop staring at the TV screen. But he didn't. He went on staring at it, even though he was on his feet, standing up and moving towards the door, leaving me with the envelope and Daisy still watching television.

There was music on and the titles rolling of a chat show, faces of people making jokes and people creased up laughing in the audience. In the corridor I heard Henry's footsteps going towards the shop. I heard him stop and pick up his keys. And I went after him. He hadn't locked the door behind him and I reached the shop floor as he reached the door into the work-room. I ran, in case he locked that door. The hangings over-head were moving with him rushing through and me rushing through. It had to be done. I pushed my way in as he was about to shut the door, but he pushed past out again and dodged towards the outer door on to the pavement. He must have had the keys on him for that, but still would have to fiddle with the bolts, so I belted up the stairs to go round the yard and head him off, passing my mother looking wild-eyed in the kitchen, taking off her apron. Then I went on out and down the steps and round the alley-way and saw him on the far side of the road. He must have had to wait until some traffic passed. So did I – have to wait I mean, but could see his white arran sweater and his pale hair going on up the slope.

Some people finish what they have to do. Some people are consistent, totally consistent. Some Leadbetters do not give up or fade or stand wide-eyed and weakened in the kitchen with no fight left in them.

It was as if every lorry or juggernaut or car that passed along the main road while I stood there, was telling me not to go on, but that would have been what I ought to have done and not what I felt.

Henry, having had a good head start, was almost at the top before I'd crossed the road, and when I'd crossed it, I couldn't see him at all, so had to get up all the speed I could. At the top I guessed he might have gone on down towards the station, but I took a risk that he'd been cunning, letting me think that's where he was going, while he was really hiding in the wood.

Dead leaves covered the ground and crackled and a huge bird flapped around. I went on and the bird kept flapping high in the trees. Surely Henry wouldn't be there. He hates country places, even though this isn't real country. But no one likes big birds dodging in the tree tops or getting their feet in dogshit of which there were piles in that wood.

Maybe I was crying. Maybe my mother's face had set me off. I know I was panting and getting torn at by branches and twigs and thinking what a rotten place that wood was in the dark. So I climbed a tree which was a tree I'd often climbed and stood in a fork of it and listened, the soles of my trainers gripping the bark. Chances were, if he were in the wood, he was crouching down dead still. But I was standing up dead still too and listening for every minute noise. I knew the big bird was a barn owl and that in summer there were bats in the wood. I knew the sounds of the wood like Gabriel Oak recognised the sounds and signs of his kind of countryside, like he knew the stars and

169

constellations and could tell the time of night by their position in the sky.

A kind of powdery sky with pinprick stars. Being high up on that hill on that tree in that wood made me nearer to all that sky. Some night skies make you full of wonder, but that night sky was sharp and gritty, spread out over me, roofing everywhere, no way out of it or through it. It was covering the whole of southern England, reaching to the Channel and to Cornwall and to Kent, sweeping over Portland Bill, enclosing everyone who was in all those places. It was stony, gritty and impenetrable, so that the only people who could lift their heads up out of trees and look down and survive were those like me who were going for broke. While everyone else was lying prone, slain on their backs and waiting for the space invaders.

So I was listening. The branch I held on to felt cold, but I did not. Feel cold I mean. Occasionally the traffic became heavy down on the road, but that was a different quality of sound. Times I'd witness sexual episodes between people in that wood. Not that I went out of my way to witness them, but I could tell the sound of copulation from that tree and at what stage it was, although I gave up overhearing such things years ago and would always announce my presence and leave if it looked as if it was going all the way with couples, particularly if it was anyone I knew.

So I was ready poised to flush Henry out, antennae tensed for every crack of twig or scrunch of leaf or rustle which might not be a squirrel or a bird or mouse or falling leaf. But the only sound was one I didn't particularly want to hear, or didn't want to hear at all. Or wasn't that a sound or was it there or wasn't it, this breathing sound? Not my breath but the breath of someone having difficulty in breathing, like someone who's not sobbing, but is maybe trying not to sob. No, more like someone near me was very, very scared.

For Christ's sake, couldn't he have stood up and said: 'Come down. I know you're up there. Get out of my life!' Though he only had hours to wait before I would get out of it. I would get out of it. I knew I would get out of it. I did intend to get out of it.

The breathing was a bit like the way Daisy breathes before she gets hysterical – in–out–in–out – a panic sound. There was no traffic for a time, but I wished some would come and drown the breathing. Didn't he want to be a soldier? Hadn't he often said he wished he'd landed on a beach with bayonet poised? Didn't he once tell me that his father told him that to make yourself kill the enemy in front of you, you had to roar and shout and yell as you ran and stabbed?

I wished clouds would come and cover the stars and crescent moon. I wished people would come walking in the park or call to each other from streets down there or even that the black dog would come bouncing along and paw the bottom of the tree and whine and yelp at me. That would be ordinary. I wanted something ordinary.

But nothing interrupted it. The silence thickened and the breathing seemed to come up through it, come from all around and under me as if it was some kind of rhythmic dynamo cranking the world around.

He must have been hiding in a clump of rhododendrons, like a fox hides, like at the end of a hunt when the hounds are pouring in baying and closing in and making this amazing sound echoing all over the landscape, which curdles your blood and you are having this terrific time. Then suddenly you think about the poor bloody fox and have to tell yourself that it's not as bad as being trapped in a gin or maimed by gunshot.

I shut my eyes and opened them and everything was still the same. The tree, the sky, the feel of the bark and my feet clinging on to it were real. Remember thinking this is it or this is not it and the only thing that might not happen was a death because I wasn't armed. I hadn't hounds with me or a machine gun. Him being in there, making that noise made me want to make the same kind of noise, to echo him, to show him that I knew he was there. But it also made me want to whoop towards the bush and fall on him. Half of me wanted to stand up there in the fork of the tree shouting 'View halloo I know you're there!' and to cheer myself for having tracked him down. But I was running down the slope instead, thumping my feet on the hard ground as I ran, choking in the cold air and leaving him because there wasn't anything to do anything about.

I left the cheque in the workroom and it isn't there now. He must have taken it when he went back for his suitcase. He couldn't cash the cheque yet anyway because it was postdated to my birthday which isn't for a month or so. Or for all I know he tore it up.

Patrick talked about money today. He doesn't know about my cheque of course. He said: 'Your mother will know if, say, Henry has cashed a cheque off a joint account.'

'He hadn't up till last week,' I said. 'I read the bank statements.'

Patrick blinked. 'He could always have another private account about which no one knows, I suppose.'

'He must have, mustn't he?' I said. 'He wouldn't accept money from anyone else.'

'You say you were away the night he left?'

I nodded. All I tell Patrick is that it so happened that I was with friends that night and the next day Henry had gone.

Petra Frobisher. The prosecution wish to question the evidence of the prisoner. Has she considered that, were Henry Harrison to pay such a cheque into a joint account, Alison Harrison would have questioned both the source and the reason for such payment or repayment?

Witness nods thoughtfully.

Witness is withholding information, m'lud. For instance, how does she know he went back for his suitcase?

Well, he must have, mustn't he? It isn't there now, is it?

172

TWELVE

There aren't that many good shops in town, but I've taken to going in at lunchtime with Liz to try on jeans and flying suits and canvas boots in this new boutique. They had new summer colours in yesterday – pale towelling sweat shirts in fresh colours with stripes.

'You going in home after this?' said Liz.

'Not specially,' I said.

I bought a sweat shirt with pink stripes and Liz got one the same but with green stripes. We kept them on and shoved our old sweaters in a plastic bag and got on our bikes.

Forgot to say that the woman in the boutique looked miffed when Liz came out of her changing cubicle with nothing on her top half – to lean over and say something to me in the next cubicle, although, with breasts that size, she might have been a boy.

'You going to ride that horse you were telling me about?' Liz called out as we were heading down the Portsmouth Road.

'Might be,' I said.

I decided it might be more tactful to take her to King's Radlett than to my home at this particular time, but I'd said I'd go and see Patrick at lunchtime. Liz sat on the floor reading old

173

geographical magazines and eating a sausage roll she'd found in her bike basket, while Patrick looked dead uneasy, but he certainly wasn't going to ask me any awkward questions while she was there.

'You seen my Mum today?' I said.

'Your mother? No.' His eyes were flickering towards Liz as though he feared it might be indiscreet even to speak Henry's name in her presence. He was at his desk making notes. I leaned over him. 'Henry is never six foot two,' I said.

'It says that he is on his passport,' Patrick said.

'Then he's shrunk, must have shrunk,' I said. Liz giggled.

I picked up the passport. I'd found it for Patrick and my mother knows I found the passport and took it to Patrick and why I took it, but she is preserving her silence on all matters concerned. Patrick said yesterday that he's going to the police on Friday.

As we cycled out of town there were celandines beginning to come out on the short grass verges, also patches of dandelions. On the gradual hill out of town there were early lambs dotted around in the fields either side, and a hiker standing above the chalk escarpment just before you reach the village, where you have to push your bike. Because it has become a habit to give searching looks at every man I see these days, I stared at him. But this man walked along the top of the escarpment and then came downhill with an easy lope which was nothing like Henry's walk.

I needed to avoid seeing Gerald in case he began quizzing me about Henry and the cottages again. Let him wait until the news breaks on Friday, I decided, as I led the way along the lane and down through the drive of Rad Cottage, across the orchard and the footbridge to the paddock. There we sat and looked across at the cottage, which was empty still, waiting to be done up, though the doves that Mavis keeps there in the outbuildings were fluttering and cooing. Liz took to the doves. She was more interested in them than in hearing that I'd lived there once.

Nor was she that impressed with Troy. 'What, that stringy old thing?'

'He can't half go,' I said.

'Soon will, I shouldn't wonder,' she said.

'He isn't that old.' I ran towards Troy and he shied away, did his skittish gambolling as if to show her that he still had life in him.

In the end I didn't ride, so we sat on the edge of the stream on a log until the damp came through our dungarees. She seemed bored. Country isn't a new experience for her in any case. She was telling me about living over beyond Basingstoke before her mother had met this bloke they live with now.

I was about to ask her if her mother, in spite of the fact that this bloke is, like Liz says, always half pissed, would go barmy if he suddenly walked out on them, but remembered what she'd told me about her mother being nutty already.

'I should be so lucky he'd bunk off,' she said, dragging at stalks of grass and chewing the ends of them.

What I like about being with Liz, although I am unsure of her in some respects, is that she is neither hopeful nor unhopeful about anything, but just gets on with things she feels like doing.

'If my Mum's bloke fucked off I wouldn't care if he'd been hacked to death by a schizophrenic or run over by a juggernaut,' she said. 'Remember that bloke who got tied to a bed and raped by a Mormon woman?' she said by the stream.

'Maybe my mother's right and he will just turn up,' I said. 'He took so little with him, though. That's what's odd.'

'Sometimes,' said Liz, 'nothing in your hand is a cool cool thing to have.' She was quoting from the movie *Cool Hand Luke* which is a kind of primary source for her. She once said that she tried eating dozens of hard-boiled eggs like Paul Newman did in the film. She achieved ten, but said she was sure she could manage more.

'Paul Newman didn't really eat them,' I said. 'They'll have shown him putting them in his mouth, then stopped the

175

cameras and let him spit them out between takes. So it might be that no one ever ate that many eggs.'

Later we talked about the cock-up theory for a bit because she'd used it in an essay for which Mr Forbes had only given her C minus.

'He can piss off too as far as I'm concerned,' she said.

Her attitude makes me feel soft compared to her, almost an idealist compared to her. I said: 'If everything is a cock-up like we have been saying we believe it is, that doesn't seem enough somehow. I mean no one statement ever says it all.' I was thinking of the September argument with Ronnie just then, but went on: 'I mean it's sometimes nicer, isn't it, like today, and some people get pleasure out of being hooked on people as well as going barmy on account of it, and some people hope and that, and the sun comes out and people remember feeling pleased inside when someone has been matey.'

She was chewing ends of grass like grass was the flavour of the month: 'People are matey because they want things from people.'

But she doesn't seem to want a lot from me.

'If I was ever going to be religious,' I said in the paddock, 'I think it would be to worship that Greek god Pan or whatever his name was, the one with horns and hooves and who represents nature and sex and virility. I saw about him somewhere . . .'

'You told me you had gods you found yourself,' she said.

'I never did.' Then I remembered I'd got high with her at Bentley's a few nights back when he had got some good stuff to smoke from the mate with whom he works at window cleaning.

'You said you fancied Forbes as well.'

'I couldn't have.'

'Whoever sent that valentine to Forbes,' she said, 'must have been missing an important chunk of their mind.'

'Right on,' I said or words to that effect.

Back in town Liz said to me: 'You coming out again tonight?'

'I might,' I said, but it had got colder and I wanted to be inside. I'd been thinking on the way home of the class discussion we'd had this morning, based on the faults in Liz's essay. Mr Forbes had said that he believed in miracles. And I'd said what on earth? And he'd said that it could be said it would be a miracle if any of us, particularly Liz and me, vouchsafed any trust in human nature. 'Would it?' I said.

My mother wasn't in the shop. Stella was. My mother was in the workroom working furiously on this hanging which she hasn't finished. The woman who commissioned it keeps on ringing up. My mother went on sewing and I got on the exercise bicycle, having first removed the dust sheet from it. I was watching her and wondering about the ageing process she was undergoing at the speed of light, rather at the speed of decay I should say, especially around her eyes and chin, although she hasn't got that really old leathery look yet. I suppose it could be called a miracle if she started looking younger again suddenly.

Another odd thing I noticed for the first time: that wallhanging has a border of little red triangles, which she's only just begun to add. Her head must be just bursting with little red triangles. I wondered if the woman had asked for them.

'Do you believe in miracles?' I asked my mother and explained Mr Forbes' theory that a miracle is nothing to do with loaves and fishes and suchlike, but to do with people acting out of character suddenly.

Added to my mother's ageing face, there could be some concern expressed about her boniness and loss of weight, reminding me of an aunt of Jane's who died of cancer recently. This woman became all over angular and sharp. Even her lips seemed to lose weight.

'I suppose that could be called a miracle,' she said but without any conviction or real interest, so I pressed on and told her about another discussion we'd had on the prime mover and whether it was masculine or feminine. 'Mr Forbes called it the Great She in the Sky,' I said.

'Not really,' said my mother, obviously not listening to me.

Jane said her aunt's husband had become redundant and lost pride in himself and was causing her a lot of worry, Jane said, pain and anguish and the rest of it. Jane said the cause was obviously physical, but that, since the study of the connections between body and mind was still in its infancy, who could say? 'But we do know the cell structure goes berserk,' she said.

There was no real point continuing to discuss vital matters with my mother today. Nor ever again possibly, since, if Henry doesn't come back, she'll never get her thinking head on again. Jane said her mother used to say that the aunt had been swallowing pain and it had turned into a cancer. Jane said her mother was hopelessly unscientific in her outlook, but there could be truth in it.

While I was on the exercise bicycle, a sudden brilliant thought burst out of me: 'If the prime mover was female,' I said to my mother, 'then she'd take more care of women than of men, wouldn't she?'

'I'm sorry,' said my mother.

'Sorry about what?' I said. 'Why be sorry? Why be sorry about anything? It's bad for people being sorry about things.' I got off the bike and threw the dust sheet back on it and left the room.

Jane said some people take vitamins against cancer. Vitamin E is good for preventing it as well as Vitamin C. She, my mother, has already got a good supply of Vitamin C, so I collected some cash from her bag upstairs and bought her a jar of E at Pevensey's, which Jane let me have on her account at cost. I put the jar on the kitchen shelf and hoped she'd take some since she will take almost anything.

Jane also told me about the clairvoyant whom I visited today. The only ESP experience I've ever had was when I was about six and my mother didn't fetch me from school. So I crossed the road to catch a bus, a dangerous main road. Later she said she knew, as she was driving towards the school, that I'd caught the bus although there'd never been any arrangements for me to catch it.

Jane said: 'You never know. My grandma found a cat she'd lost by going to this woman. It is ever so unscientific, but you never know.'

This woman lives way out of town off the London Road and I was pedalling there between pollarded trees and houses with bow windows, gardens and lawns in front of them and clumps of crocuses, way out where the houses got smaller and grottier. I was freewheeling, leaning back from the handlebars for a time between privet hedges, looking for the turning.

It was my mother's ESP if anything that knew I'd crossed the road that time. Although it may have been mine which sent the message, might it not?

This place was on the edge of town, the edge of everywhere, open to sweeping winds, with wide roads and narrow pavements, minuscule gardens and doll's house lawns. Once Henry said that it was coming into places like this that would make you realise why people bought the useless stuff we keep at Harrison's: 'Why useless?' I would say. 'What's style?' he'd say. 'What is the point of everything?' he'd say. 'What is the point of anything?' I'd say. And yet he wouldn't hold the cock-up theory I am sure.

I found the number and I leaned my bike against a privet hedge. Its handlebars slipped in between the leaves and twigs. The hedge was low. My head must have been visible from the front windows. Even clairvoyants need to see the postman coming I suppose.

Henry doesn't plan things. Henry didn't mean to go away and stay away. But then if he doesn't plan things, he wouldn't be planning to return.

The bell rang, giving a musical chime. The tiny damp garden had one round bed of pruned roses and someone had put horseshit round the jagged woody stalks. I felt dead stupid standing there and even stupider expecting help from someone who lived there.

179

'But even if I found out where he is,' I said to Jane, 'what good would that do?'

'Supposing one of you got ill. Say Daisy did. He'd have to know.'

'Clairvoyants couldn't find addresses out or telephone numbers, could they?'

'You never know. You really never know. The unknown is extraordinary, isn't it?'

The door was answered, then shut behind me. Thick heavy patterned carpeting led into a lounge from a narrow hallway with a smell of something. Or maybe an airless feel to it. The woman was wearing an orange nylon overall. She led me from the dark hall to a lighter lounge full of purples, lime greens, ginger browns.

It made me want to cut and run, to take a header through the white lacy flimsy curtains, take a dive like I took at the swimming pool once to try and rid myself of what is long since gone and nearly forgotten. There was this bursting urge to rocket out and up, break glass and charge across the rosebed and through the hedge.

The room was closeted and sterile and I seemed to fill the place. I could smell the sweat I'd sweated out of nerves and cycling. The woman's front-room clock ticked with a dead thudding noise.

'These are the loved one's belongings dear?'

I'd handed the Sainsbury's bag and realised straight out that she'd guessed the loved one's sex. I'd grabbed them quickly: the shirt was a blue one he used to wear a lot and pretty old. The hairbrush was obviously a man's.

The woman put her spectacles on, which was odd if she was going to see things inside her head. Then she sat holding the shirt and hairbrush on her knee. Her hair was dyed reddish and her face was powdery. Her mouth moved even when she was not speaking and her false teeth clicked. The imitation leather settee creaked as I shifted on it.

'I have good news for you, my dear. Such good news. Your loved one is alive.'

180

I gave some sort of smile I think. Everything there was muffled or swathed. She had plastic doilies everywhere, as if, although her job was to know, she didn't want to let things be seen clearly or divulge the texture of her belongings. Well, who would with things like that, I was thinking.

'The loved one isn't dead,' she said again, looking at me as if to test me that I'd come about a loved one and not a hated one.

'I see,' I said, not smiling this time, so as not to give anything away.

I thought I'd better focus on some object which would give my thoughts free range. If this old woman had the tiniest degree of ESP she might pick up any thought of Henry, any mental image of him that I had, rather than the emanations of the objects she was holding in her lap. The only thing around the room that was both unshrouded and worth looking at was this faded photo in a silver frame of some bloke in a soldier's uniform with a sort of army cap and slicked back hair. Second World War probably.

'Our minds must move as one, together, dear.'

I closed my eyes, then opened them and found I was gazing at these pudgy knees and varicose-veined legs and matted pink fur slippers, so I shut them again. It was going to be a waste of time and of the five pounds that I'd taken from my mother's open bag.

'Yes, shut your eyes, but think about the loved one, dear.'

I thought of Henry. I thought of Christmas and us kissing under the mistletoe and meaning it at the time. I thought about the wood and chasing him. I thought of Henry in the workroom.

The false teeth clicked, making a sucking noise. The clock ticked thuddingly, the plastic leather squeaked. The woman asked me for my name.

'My name is Olivia,' I said.

I thought of Troy instead of Henry and I conjured up this trip with Troy across the countryside, deciding I was in the paddock jumping him and the day was fine.

181

'The source, you see. You and I must work together on the source and nurture it . . .'

Then Henry's there and watching me. I jump again. The brushwood low jump and the brushwood high jump and he's watching us and Troy is in his spring-like jerky mood, likely to shy at anything. I'm slowing him and walking him, then trotting him along the boundary hedge, the Manor gardens on our right, the beech trees and the rooks' nests at the top of them.

'I see a light-haired man.'

Of course she saw a light-haired man. A strand of Henry's hair from the hairbrush lay across the skirt of her orange overall.

I want him watching me. But I don't want him watching me.

'I see a woman. She has large grey eyes.' Of course she saw a woman with large grey eyes. My eyes are fairly large and definitely grey. It stands to reason that I might well have a mother with those eyes as well.

'I see a little child with long fair hair.'

Don't give an inch. Keep trotting Troy, tight-reined. Control him and don't let him have his head. There's many children round with long fair hair.

'You know the child.'

Was she asking me or telling me? My eyes screwed shut, I'm letting Troy increase his pace. A gentle canter round the paddock, which he doesn't like. He'd rather amble or gallop at top speed, can't see much point in being urged to move and then held back. Hang on. Is Henry there? Still by the footbridge watching me?

'The kiddie is wearing little jeans and wellingtons.'

What did she say? Who's that? God knows where that was coming from. Must get away, head away from the paddock, try and hear in my head hooves on turf and rooks fading and tractors in fields, making myself see Troy's mane bobbing down in front of me and feeling the leather of his reins in my hands.

'A long low house with hedges round it and a stream beside

182

it. These emanations are the strongest that I've had from any client, Olivia.'

Now galloping. Get right away. The gate is open and we leave the field. Keep going, Troy.

'Keep thinking, dear. The vision is a bright one, dear.'

We're moving out and round the raspberry field. We're heading for the ridge, which stretches out and up in front of us, and since it's spring, I'm looking for the yellow gorse and bluebells in the dips.

'A car outside the house. An old car. Try and read the registration number, Olivia. I always say there's nothing so helpful as a vehicle registration number.'

Henry can't be with us now. He liked to watch the horse but didn't like the horse itself. He wanted me to fall but the time I fell he picked me up and took me to the hospital. I've said about the hospital. He knows I'm grateful for the hospital and for the riding boots and sweater that he bought me afterwards.

'A woman at the window of the house . . .'

The one with large grey eyes perhaps? Can't stop. Daren't stop. The ridge goes on for miles and you gallop, urging him with your knees. He puts his ears back and I am standing in the stirrups, jockey-like. We're moving well.

'But, Olivia, there's pain and anguish from this woman at the window as she watches the fair-haired kiddie run past from the bridge with its hand over its face. It's raining and the woman's looking out at the rain . . .'

It isn't raining. It is fine up here beyond the beacon, gorse flashing by, the dip where I sheltered in the thunderstorm. The hollow full of short bright bracken.

'You see her, Olivia. I feel you see her at the window, don't you? Can you see the number on the car outside?'

Beyond the beacon, where the ridge ends, there's a fence, a spur of hill and then the slope to the north, from which you see the narrow river Rad go winding on until it disappears into a wood.

'You see her, dear? Olivia? You see the kiddie going up the

183

drive between the hedges and the woman watching her from the window . . . oh, she wants the kiddie. Oh, how she feels for the kiddie.'

I can't go back because Henry's there. I'm seeing down the slope and beyond it a bank of cloud is approaching, blotting out the sun, and if I go in I shall ride into that dark cloud.

'The man is there, but he is shadowy. The kiddie is the one that means so much to her. The man is fading, dear. The woman feels he should not be there.'

I felt a hand on the knee of my dungarees as if the woman were clawing for something. Then the hand went crabwalking up my thigh to grab my hand. Dry old fingers with loose particles of scratching skin, but Troy and I are heading down towards the barrier of the woods, into the valley where I never rode before. In that wood there are fir trees blotting out the light, no grass, but pine needles. But the voice said that there was this child who ran away up the drive and the voice kept repeating this, but I had to stay away from it, keep out of it. Pig sick I was of hearing about it, of her asking me to concentrate.

'The car. I can't read the number. You might know what kind of car it is.'

Nor was I going to tell her what kind of car it was. That car went to the scrapheap years ago. She had my hand and wasn't supposed to see into the past.

'Stay with me, Olivia.'

I pulled my hand away. I am with Troy in the murky wood, feeling for obstacles. I'll have to get off and lead him, tripping, bumping against coarse-barked trees, feeling for a trunk with lichen crumbling under hand, twigs cracking under foot, birds flapping up, Troy pulling back and rearing with his hooves up, his great black head between me and the patches of light far above, his reins at full stretch.

All right. No. Well. There was this child. The hair was right. Maybe this child thought there wasn't anybody there because mother was in London, wasn't she? Do not remind me to remember that. I saw the car. I had to run, get lost because I'd seen the car there before and the man who stood on the far side of the willows. I was saying to myself: hullo hullo what's all this then?

Then saw my mother hand in hand with him, she posh in long black shiny boots. Then they'd gone. I'd been mistaken maybe. But I saw you, mother, at the upstairs window. You saw me. We never talked about it, but we looked each other in the eye next day. And Henry wonders why we don't share confidences any more, the schmuck. And here I was in that disgusting place with that woman pumping my hand with her prickling hands, her grating voice telling me I had to think.

The central heating radiators ticked and gurgled and the false teeth clicked. Outside the traffic came and went. 'There, then!'

'Oh thanks.'

'I need more help another time. You'll help me more another time, Olivia.' Saying my name as if she knew it wasn't my real name somehow. 'Believing is the only thing that makes it work, Olivia. Don't underestimate your powers.' She nodded. But she nodded all the time. She might have Parkinson's disease. I left the five pounds on the brass tray on the table in her hall.

Mother, I never shopped you. You had your pleasure and I dare say that you needed it. You once claimed that you didn't fuck until you fucked my father aged nineteen, so probably you needed to make up for lost time once you started. I bear that in mind. Fucking must have been important to you, dead important. Now it may be even more so since you haven't many fucking years ahead of you. If Henry doesn't come back, I can't really see you fucking anyone else. One must be realistic, mother.

I'm in the workroom at night. I'm taking sketches out of his wastepaper basket. I'm putting my hands on them, holding my hands over them, testing my powers. But nothing comes. The face is like my mother's face, but more like the face of the woman at Waterloo. Has my mother unscrewed these sketches

185

and considered them and still drawn blank? I'm also checking through my mother's wastepaper basket. I do that every night by the way.

Jane said: 'Oh dear. I'm sorry that it didn't help.'

'No sweat,' I said.

'Have you heard about Mr Forbes' twins?'

'What about Mr Forbes' twins?'

One of them, it seems, is tiny and not all that strong. The trouble is, Jane says, that when you get one big strong baby in a womb and one weak one, the big one draws more sustenance through its placenta and cramps the little one. 'It's a case of nothing succeeds like success,' Jane said.

THIRTEEN

Call Alison Harrison, previously known as Frobisher, née Leadbetter. And did you, Mrs Harrison, on the day in question commit adultery with said Henry Harrison? And did you see the prisoner, Petra Frobisher, walk past while not acknowledging her presence in the drive in the rain, obviously distressed? Oh, no, Mrs Harrison, please do not distress yourself. You're not on trial. Please – water for this witness and a chair. Oh, witness would prefer gin, would she? Certainly.

The prisoner, I claim, my Lord, has further evidence and is withholding information which may help in the search.

'Withholding?' I said to Patrick. 'Of course I'm not withholding anything.'

He's taken to coming round in the daytime now, I found him there with Stella this lunchtime. I think he fancies her somewhat from the way he was eyeing her.

Later he was saying that the police will be pretty useless and will only post Henry as a missing person, but since my mother won't agree to hiring an investigator, Patrick has copied passages from this book he found, *How to be a Private Detective*, or words to the effect. He brought this file round. My mother came out of the workroom, looked at the papers, put them down and went away again. So did Stella – go away with Patrick I mean.

Then a woman who'd commissioned a wallhanging came in and I knew it was the one my mother is working on, so I told her that my mother had been away and then ill.

She said: 'People who are in business for themselves should not go away without completing commissions.'

She went pretty red in the face and freaked out, clutching her handbag under her arm, like a machine gun. She was built, as Henry would say, like a Sherman tank.

After she'd gone I picked up Patrick's papers. If you want to find a missing person, you must describe them accurately, the book says. You must give details of their height, build and complexion, eyes, nose and teeth.

I also sold a lampshade, a painting done by a loony woman who lives on the Isle of Wight and I talked to a man who didn't buy anything, but had just come back from Kuwait, which is where Mr Forbes would have gone to teach and often says he wishes he had. This man was telling me how he'd bought orientals in Kuwait much cheaper than we have them in the shop.

'Of course you did,' I said, which was what Henry would have said. When the man had left I said to myself 'Daft pillock and the best of luck to him,' which was what Henry would have said, except maybe not to himself.

People's builds are either stout, medium, thin, erect or stooping. Their faces are long, round, broad, smiling, sullen or wrinkled. Their complexions are fair, dark, pale, sallow, fresh and so on. You should also describe people's voices.

The man who didn't buy anything had just left and his coat must have caught this rocking wooden doll which was made in Russia. It went on rocking. I remember Henry saying when he first began to sell these dolls, that he felt like that – never truly static unless left absolutely alone. To which my mother pointed out that he mostly didn't like being alone. At which he got angry at being picked up for illogical remarks.

It was sunny outside and people were wearing thinner coats again. In the town I'd seen people buying paints and things for decorating houses with, also plants for gardens, seeds and that and Grobags. We always buy new flowers for the shop on Tuesdays and I'd bought all white daffodils like I saw Vivienne arranging in the cathedral. My mother said: 'However much were they?' but didn't listen to the answer.

Sometimes in the shop when there's not much to do, I get out this silver box containing the opals Ginny bought from Cooper Pedy in Australia. I was thinking that I could go to Australia to stay with her when I got my money. She lives near the beach in Adelaide and it's nearly always warm enough to bathe there. I could go there instead of Colorado maybe. Although last night round at Bentley's we were talking of this Scottish island we all want to visit to see if it could be a good place to avoid the holocaust. Bentley's worked out that it's the safest in regard to prevailing winds carrying fallout.

When Ginny went to Cooper Pedy she told me you could buy opals direct from the men who mined them. The opals are not always milky, though their shades are mostly green and blue. Ginny said you had to bargain with the men. I could describe Ginny's voice because it's husky and a bit Australian, my mother's voice because it's upper class and clipped and Patrick's voice because it is the same.

The opals: Ginny used to say you could see the sea in them. Australia was beautiful, she said. More than America, it was really God's Own Country and the wine terrific and the gin not that expensive, so I was like mentally in Cooper Pedy drinking wine when Mr Forbes came into the shop. I looked up and saw him standing just inside the door, gazing up at the hangings.

I'm still not sure what he came about. At first he handled toys on the low brass table, setting the rocking doll going again. Then he strolled around with his hands in the pockets of his tweed suit, which was quite a nice suit that I hadn't seen before, with a waistcoat to it. Underneath he wore a check shirt.

'You wouldn't by any chance be working on an essay, would you?' he said.

'Well, sort of,' I said, closing the file which Patrick had brought.

Mr Forbes wandered for a few seconds more. I watched him fairly carefully. It struck me that by noticing the shape and size of him, I might hit on something we could use describing Henry. What was the difference between the way Mr Forbes stood and the way Henry stood? How could he be recognised? What salient features had Mr Forbes?

'Nice day,' I said. His most salient feature, I was thinking, was his thick hair, dark but not as dark as Patrick's or my mother's hair in former days. Perhaps he had fair hair as a kid. His thick hair and his heaviness, broad shoulders. There's a solid look to Mr Forbes, which made me think that that's what's missing with Henry – a solid look.

'So this is it?' he said, with a gesture referring to the shop.

'Yes, this is it,' I said.

'You could always work here,' he said.

'How do you mean?' I said, but guessed that he meant that if I didn't get any A Levels or qualifications I could work in the shop for a living. 'That wasn't the idea,' I said.

He kept on stroking textures and touching things. He played with some of the puzzles on the central table for a bit, but everyone did that. So had he come to reprimand me or to make sure that I babysat for him one night? He fiddled with the onyx chess set, looking full of concentration like he knew good moves, ploys and everything.

I kept on making notes with the file half open, but saw he was on tiptoe, creeping over to me, head down, like he goes on the prowl between desks in the classroom, creeping up on people. Then he whispered as he came close, so close that I could smell his aftershave: 'Shop!'

'Talk about witty!' I said. 'Can I help you or are you just looking around?'

I often plan what I am going to say to Mr Forbes when I

know I'm going to see him in class, but as he'd come here in this unexpected way, I felt a bit confused. He went and squatted down beside the table, rocking the doll again, so maybe he had come to buy a present for his older kid.

'There are such things as extenuating circumstances, you know,' he said. As far as voice goes, Mr Forbes talks more like people of his age, like people in their early thirties with a touch of cockney in the accent, more like Michael Caine, although he doesn't look like Michael Caine one bit and is tons younger.

'Extenuating circumstances what for?' I said and thought that if you could pinpoint people by describing famous people that they looked like, Henry would be nearer Michael Caine than Mr Forbes would be. Mr Forbes would be nearer David Dimbleby perhaps. My mother watching TV the other evening said: 'Oh, he's got such nice thick hair!' which she always says very boringly when he is on.

'Extenuating circumstances for work undone,' said Mr Forbes. He's really nearer Robert Redford if you stretch a point. He stood up leaving the doll still rocking and came to the near side where the caftans and so on hang on a rail. He riffled through them very slowly, looking at the price tags. Maybe he was buying something for his wife since she'd need new clothes having been pregnant.

'I haven't any extenuating circumstances anyway,' I said and wondered who had told him that I had.

'All right,' he said, but sat down on the high stool near the jewellery counter near me, seeming to be peering towards the closed file of papers on the cash desk, then seeming to inspect his fingernails.

It wasn't like it is in class. No arguments, no jokes, no sarkiness. Embarrassing in fact, although I've often fantasised myself alone with him. In spite of the smoking rule, I took a cigarette, lit it up and held the packet out to him. He shook his head. 'I wish,' he said, 'I wish I could get you lot to get it into your thick heads that it does matter to some people how you do.'

191

He was sitting hunched up on the stool and his hair came over his collar when he ran his fingers through it like he does in class when irritated, and he wrinkled up his nose as usual. His nose is flat and straight and his forehead low.

'I know it matters,' I said, but my voice didn't come out right. 'I know it matters on account of you have to have good records, don't you, of success and that . . .'

He put both hands up to his head in a mock despairing gesture. Maybe it was not so mock because he stayed like that for some time, hunched up and rocking himself as if he had had a body blow. His ears which showed themselves to me from where I sat were flat and unremarkable.

'I expect you wish you were in Kuwait,' I said.

Getting down off the stool, he went and picked up the rocking doll and put it on the desk in front of me. When he took money out of his wallet I saw a photo of his kid, all blonde curls.

The money was banged down on the cash desk and I gave him change. I took the doll and wrapped it in some tissue paper, then put it into one of our bags which are vermilion, the colour of the shop front, with gold writing on. I realised that he hadn't taken the joke about Kuwait too well and felt pretty kind of sniffy and was wiping my nose on my shirt sleeve. Then felt he was looking at me, so I checked out of a corner of my eye and he was looking out of the window. I don't know why I can't bring myself to ask ordinary questions like: 'How are the twins?' It should be easy enough.

You'd say his nose was certainly flat. You wouldn't say his mouth dropped at the corners, but his chin is dimpled. I heard myself say: 'What did you expect? Miracles?' and he did just about smile faintly before he left. But he left in quite a hurry and I was remembering the time in class he said he wished that he was Sergeant Troy who swam out off the coast wanting to get away from it all, but lamenting that he never would; Mr Forbes, that is, lamenting that he couldn't be like Troy.

In the film they showed it from a distance, Troy taking off his clothes, Terence Stamp taking off all his clothes and his white

192

body going down into the greyish sea. A long shot it was I think. The beach was pebbled since it was not far from Portland Bill and you have to go down such beaches slowly, treading carefully.

Jane gets these books on astrology and reads everyone's signs. Mr Forbes, she says, is a Scorpio, a water sign, so it figures he might like the sea. Jane says of Scorpios that there is intensity, deep feelings, passion. Henry is a Scorpio as well. I said they had a lot in common, didn't I?

I'd done it all wrong hadn't I? I suppose it would be a miracle if I'd done it right. But there was no time to kick myself about it, since the phone rang.

She asked by name for Henry and I said: 'Hang on' as if I was about to fetch him. Quick thinking, that. I wondered if my mother had heard the phone. 'Can I take a message and he'll ring you back?'

'No, no, no thanks.' It was the one who used to ring last autumn – there's no doubt.

My mother came out of the workroom. 'Who was it?'

'Someone – you know – wanting Henry. She rang off.'

My mother fiddled with the white daffodils, picked up the can to water them, letting water trickle over the edge of the container. 'A voice you recognised?' she said.

'I've heard it somewhere, yes.'

'These daffodils must have been awfully expensive,' she said. But she'd been about to ask when I had heard the voice before or where. And I was about to say: 'You thought he was with this woman, didn't you, and now we know he isn't with this woman, don't we?' But no one said anything.

My mother went back to her wallhanging, closing the door.

When Stella came back from fetching Daisy from school I dashed upstairs and used the phone there. I said to Patrick: 'Henry's not with another woman. I can tell you that.'

There was a silence. 'Then I was right,' he said. 'He went away from something, not towards it.'

193

On my bike I was thinking of other people Henry might be said to resemble: Michael Caine? Corin Redgrave? David Hockney, Kirk Douglas of course, but none of these are really near the mark. Since then I've thought of Woody Allen. Yes, I know Woody Allen's tiny and Henry's big, but if you stretched out Woody Allen and gave him light hair, took off his glasses, made him larger round the waist and with long legs . . .

That was a thing we did together once. We went to see *Manhattan* and we talked about it afterwards. We all went, except for Daisy that is. Afterwards we argued quite a bit about it, about the end where Woody Allen gets his comeuppance from Mariel Hemingway who plays the younger girl. She says it's his own fault that she's leaving him because he has two-timed her with Diane Keaton. My mother said she felt Woody Allen had deserved that ending.

I expected Henry to sympathise with the Woody Allen character, but much to my surprise he didn't. He said everything was right about the film and everyone was lovely in that film and both the women in the main parts were stunning and sensational and that that was how life should always be completely unresolved and leave it there.

'If only it could be,' said my mother which rather spoilt the mood of things.

So I was looking down the drive of Rad Cottage. Don't underestimate your powers, dear, the woman said. But I was finding locked doors and grimy windows, Rad Cottage waiting for the hand of Henry to improve it, but no way was he there. Doves rose fluttering, rising in droves with whirring wings, seeming to dive off the window sills, swooping close to my head so I felt the down-draught of their wings, then settling back in rows on window sills again. Like *The Birds* of Hitchcock's which I dreamed about the other night. Clutching each window sill I looked in, peered in and pressed my nose against the glass. In the kitchen there was still the old wooden draining board and peeling wallpaper which had been ours.

My mother called to me that day and there he was. I put out my hand to shake hands in case he felt obliged to kiss me. I'd seen the red car again and didn't need introducing anyway. In the car there was this parcel on the back seat, gift-wrapped, indicating that he'd bought me a present. Surely he wouldn't be as daft as that. And my mother had been so incredibly careful not to suggest that anyone was getting a new father or anything like that. Surely he wouldn't be daft enough to bring a present.

Such a very casual meeting, so carefully casual that everyone was dead nervous sitting round the kitchen table, Henry making jokes like there was no tomorrow for making jokes, reminding me of a bus conductor on the King's Radlett run who wore his cap on the back of his head, called everyone darling and fancied himself as a comedian.

Everything was OK as long as you kept on laughing in the dark kitchen at the back and, although the jokes were really funny, it got harder and harder to laugh. Mother, you were looking from me to Henry and from Henry to me as if you were watching Wimbledon, and your grey eyes reflected his green.

'Knock knock.'

'Who's there?'

'Pregnant?'

'Pregnant who?'

'Pregnant Nixon,' which shows how long ago it was. Most of the jokes were better than that.

Did I leave too soon? There wasn't any need to prolong it, was there? Troy had arrived a few days before and Giles and Gerald were helping me to get used to him. Or was I supposed to break a normal pattern and sit around? I was not on approval, was I? Nor was he. He had arrived. Before there was normality and afterwards there wasn't. Or was there a new normality, where you and I, mother, looked at each other and understood?

Today Troy was easy to catch, almost docile. I slapped him and white clouds of ungroomed dust flew up in the sun.

Walking on up towards the gate into the stable block, he came behind me like an obedient dog.

Henry liked me for those first weeks at Rad Cottage after he'd moved in. Or seemed to like me. Of all the things I should remember, it should be the first argument we had. This might have been about me not helping with the washing up and me pointing out that he didn't help with it that much either. It might have been one of a dozen issues of a domestic nature.

All I really remember is that, whatever it was, it led to their first argument, which I overheard. The strongest memory is of Henry sighing one of his deep, shattering sighs and remarking that the honeymoon had been remarkably short.

FOURTEEN

When I was nearly ten my mother, pregnant, stood on a pebbled beach with the bump that was to be Daisy pointing towards France. I'm pretty certain it was France, but the bump was Daisy definitely. The beach was steep and I crawled down towards the sea, suddenly having had this idea of crawling between my mother's legs into the ripples at the sea edge.

My mother was probably cooling her feet which were swollen with the heat and pregnancy. She wore this tent-like sundress and a sunhat and dark glasses.

It was a time when Jim and Lily were staying and it was mostly a fun holiday. Jim and Henry between them showed me how to dive off a raft a few yards out from the shelving beach. Jim is a kind of bonus person, excessively warm and friendly to everyone and always keeping Henry in a buoyant mood. I've always thought of him more as a brother to Henry than a friend.

I was tall for my age at nine and most people thought I was a good deal older, so I suppose it was an especially childish thing to do to decide to crawl between my mother's legs, not to mention Freudian as well.

It was a still day and the sea was oily-surfaced as I cat-walked down to it with the sun in my eyes, so the sun must have been low and it must have been late-ish in the afternoon. The sun in my eyes and my mother's legs in front of me, and at the moment when I was about to dive beneath the tent-shaped dress, someone yelled my name out from behind me up the beach. Feet pounded down the beach crunching shingle, moving pebbles, but I'd already touched my mother's ankle and my mother screamed.

A small clammy hand, perhaps mistaken for a sea creature, and my mother fell sideways, saving her huge bulk with one hand. Henry helped her to her feet and sat her down. Then turned to me and took my wrist and dragged me along the beach, nearly wrenching my arm out at the socket, scraping my thighs on the pebbles. Then he let me go and looked down at me like I was some kind of unspeakably lowly sea-worm who had hauled itself on to land.

He left me and I crawled a good few hundred feet along the beach from everyone. Then I sat and picked up stones and threw them into the sea one after another watching the widening circles of ripples, the dip they made, the sea getting more and more oily grey and glassy like gloss paint as the sun went further down. I never looked along the shelves of pebbles until Jim came and sat beside me, saying things like 'You'll be all right, kid,' patting my knee and telling me that Henry was a daft bugger and so on, but how much Henry loved my mother and how my mother and Henry were the best thing that ever happened to the two of them and things like 'You're going to be something else, kid, you are, something special you are going to be.'

Then I remember a breeze getting up and Jim saying that the day was going to spoil itself, like he said today when I got back from Rad Cottage and he was in the shop.

These days he bearhugs me and asks me whether I have boy friends and tells me not to do anything he wouldn't do, but would like to do. It's simple stuff, but makes me feel good and I tell him about boy friends, saying I have several: 'Several – you know how it is . . .' and he says, 'That's right, my love . . .'

198

He was standing in his overcoat pacing up and down the shop. When he stands still he always stands with his head on one side when looking at you, always with this friendly and enquiring look as if what is going on with you is of the utmost importance. That is why he's such a good salesman, my mother says, in spite of the recession in fitted carpets, about which he is very worried naturally. Although he sometimes says: 'You can keep your Isfahans and Baluchistans – I'll stick to Axminsters,' or Wiltons, or whatever it is he sells. 'They'll see me out.'

Today my mother was at the desk, half sitting on it, sitting on her hands as she does these days, her bottom having lost so much weight it is probably uncomfortable to sit on.

'So how are you, my love?' Jim said to me.

She'd made a pot of tea and was clutching her own teacup and smiling, but he was looking at her when she wasn't looking at him, as if assessing her. Sometimes he leaned across the desk to her and held her wrist and said things like: 'I've been telling you, my love, you mustn't worry about him. He'll be back.' And she, amazingly, kept smiling at him and saying: 'Yes, I'm sure he will.' While I was standing wanting to tell him he must do something, but waiting till he'd left and planning to follow him out to his car and tell him how things were with everyone.

Then he said: 'And I hope the little lass will be better soon. Just a temperature you say?' so I stood there gaping.

My mother looked at me as if to say: don't speak, don't move, and said to Jim: 'Yes, just a temperature.' Then she changed her tone and spoke to me: 'Oh, Petra, by the way' – her voice was up a tone or two. 'Oh, Petra, by the way, do just pop up and see how Daisy is . . .' but she was telling me with her eyes to go and fetch Daisy from school. But first I checked that Daisy wasn't actually in bed and ill. Then I got on to my bike again.

The school's out past where Jane lives, out past posher suburbs where Forbes lives as well. Daisy was climbing on the railings waiting with other kids, but I couldn't take her home just yet.

She'd got a new knock knock joke, but I told her to shut up and walk towards Jane's house with me. The day had spoilt itself like Jim had said and there was this wind getting up. It blew Daisy's hair wildly away from her head.

Jane's house is newer than other houses in the street and of paler brick with a smooth lawn in front and a flagged path. A big picture window looks out at you. Behind it is always Mrs Robinson and her accompanying smell of baking.

Daisy thought it all was a terriff idea, especially as little Eddie Forbes was there for her to play with. She, like Mrs Robinson, went bananas over him.

The Robinsons' house is a house where Jim's trade flourishes, fitted Wilton everywhere and the sun when it came out again for a moment was pouring in everywhere. In the kitchen there is a patterned extra-strong man-made fibre carpet.

Mrs Robinson makes cakes. Vivienne arranges flowers. Jim's wife Lily makes the pastry sometimes when she stays with us. Some people manage without education, don't they?

The blonde kid Eddie was tearing round on a little tricycle, pushing and pedalling himself with his red sandals across the Wilton. I noticed that he had his father's dimpled chin.

It wasn't bad waiting there. Daisy and Eddie watched *Playschool* while I admired Mrs Robinson's new micro-wave oven that will make cakes even faster for her. She demonstrated and I saw the cake rising like you might see plants growing in a stopframe film. I used to come here frequently years ago whenever things at home were difficult.

Mr Forbes didn't seem surprised to see me there. I was sitting holding Eddie on my knee and I stood up to hand him over. I said, 'I haven't done my babysitting turn yet,' and he said: 'Oh, nor you have,' as though he was thinking of a hundred other things.

When he'd gone I rang the shop. Stella told me that my mother was hysterical.

'Has Jim gone though?' I said.

'Yes,' she said.

'I'll be home,' I said.

Daisy was complaining all the way home in the fading light that she would like to have a baby brother like Eddie and complaining that she'd missed the news and would miss *Nationwide* if we didn't hurry.

'For Christ's sake who wants to hear the news? Who wants to hear about bombs, Daisy? Come on! Move!'

She'd heard a joke about a neutron bomb, she said. She told it and it was pretty feeble. It was getting towards rush hour and the main road packed with shooting cars and trucks and people sheltering in bus shelters.

In the bedroom my mother was drawing in breath between sobs, her hair all over her face. Not a pretty sight in the light of the bedside lamp. The purport of her crying was that if someone as good and trustworthy as Jim was lying to her, then she was not worth the truth.

'But you were lying to Jim,' I pointed out.

It was the first time we had talked about Henry's absence and even now she wasn't really talking about it, only going on about herself and being unworthy. She had dozens of used Kleenex strewn around the pillow and the bedclothes.

'But you are worthy,' I said. 'You are generally known to be incredibly worthy by nearly everyone. Remember how Karen was always saying you were the nicest person in the world.' Then I remembered that it was Henry she'd said it about, but let that pass.

My mother bawled again and put her head into the pillow and seemed to be saying that it was bloody awful being worthy or being seen as worthy. Stella was with Daisy and the shop was closed. 'Shall I get Patrick or Gerald or even Mavis or the police?' I said.

The curtains were drawn and she was still dressed and the wind was banging the window which was slightly open, so I shut it. 'You think he is with Jim?' I said.

201

She said something like: 'Men talk to each other. Men tell each other all the things they don't want women to know about.'

'I suppose they do,' I said and was considering how many times she and I said things we wouldn't want men to know about. 'But on the other hand . . .' I said, but she was yelling at me, telling me to get the hell out of it and lock the door after me. I hadn't heard her yell at anyone like that since she used to yell at my father and kick Noggin the spaniel all over the place.

'You're going off your head,' I said. 'Why don't you get right into bed.' I pulled the duvet out from under her, dragging it out so that her legs flopped on to the sheet. She lay dead still, curled up like babies are supposed to lie in the womb; she looked pathetic, so I said, 'That was a pretty nifty lie you told to Jim. I shouldn't wonder if that doesn't do the trick.'

She kept her face away from me: 'I said: get out!'

'Sometimes,' I said, 'when I am really fed up or whatever, I try and remember nicer things, imagine I'm in places that I've felt good in . . .'

But that didn't help either, although it made her move her head to stare at me, which showed me her face messy with tears and creases and as if she was deciding if I was really as bad as Henry always said I was.

'Well – interesting things at any rate,' I said. Her tearful face reminded me how Henry hated people crying and suddenly I sympathised with him.

Her voice was chokey and off key: 'I'll tell you one important thing,' she said.

My feet were aching and my legs were aching but I didn't want to sit beside her on the bed. I don't need telling the important things. She shouldn't tell me the important things. Her head stayed turned away from me, her hand was spread, fingers splayed out showing her rings and her nails with their chipped varnish. I leaned across her and moved the flexible stalk of the bedside lamp to make it point towards the ceiling –

202

to stop it shining on the terrible mess her hair was in and how the roots were showing white.

'So what is the important thing?' I said, not because I wanted to know but because it might be therapeutic for her to tell me what it was.

'Avoid the bloody guilt,' she said. 'Avoid the guilt because once you have got it, it is arseholes to get rid of, isn't it?'

I was standing with my arms folded. I said: 'That's OK. I can cope with it.' But I was remembering being in here when she came back from hospital and seeing Daisy in the frilly Leadbetter bassinet that I'd been in once long before everything. Running in to see the baby, coming back from school to see it, but sprawling on the bed like she was sprawled now. Then hearing the door opening and knowing it would be Henry and hearing it shut again and looking round and seeing he was not there after all. He'd gone out again because I was in there. Rather he had not come in because I was there. But my mother's face, when I looked at it, wasn't intent on showing me the baby, but only noticing that Henry had gone out again.

Daisy was ever so easy to get to smile. I'd come in here, see them on the bed with her, getting her to smile, both holding her. My mother, seeing me, would leave off chucking Daisy under the chin, pat the bed invitingly and get her own smile going for me, but the smile was the wrong smile and took too much getting going. I would touch Daisy too, trying to get her to smile, and while I was doing that Henry would leave the room.

His flesh could never be conjoined with mine. Like on the bed, the touch, the cuddle, the connecting circuit between Daisy and me and him and my mother could never be completed. Like my finger under Daisy's chin, my mother's hand on my back, means that Henry's hand had to be removed in case the circuit was too heavy for the wiring. Like if he didn't move his hand the whole of the electricity in the shop and flat would fuse.

Daisy said tonight: 'Stella smells and I am rather sick of everything.'

'Maybe Stella can't help smelling,' I said.

'We watched TV and there was a deodorant commercial so I asked her if she used one.'

'You'll learn that everything stinks in time,' I said.

Henry makes up stories for Daisy about imaginary planets where there are no clocks and people sing and dance in sunny weather all the time. He used to tell me those stories before she was born. I can remember some of them. 'Shall I try telling you a story now?' I said.

'You wouldn't know the proper ones, would you?'

'Sod you, then. Go to bed.'

Stella was standing in the kitchen, tapping the draining board, not smelling particularly as far as I could tell. I took my mother a gin and tonic but she was asleep, so I drank the gin and tonic and had to offer Stella one. Then she had another and began to tell me all about her desperately unhappy marriage.

Patrick came and he and Stella went on about desperately unhappy relationships they've had, Stella saying that she'd always been terribly honest with her husband and always told him if she slept with anyone else until she realised that upset him the same as if she hadn't told him. Patrick was saying things like 'You can't win, can you?' Their eyes were meeting cautiously and when I left their hands were getting nearer and nearer across the table. I guess she was only telling Patrick about her infidelities in order to show him that she could be unfaithful and was ready to be with him at the drop of a hat. Flutter flutter eyelashes and you only have to say the word, sort of thing.

I left because they were going on about Henry again, saying that they both knew him well enough to know that he could never stay alone for long, remembering the time my mother was in hospital with Daisy – how lost he was and how Stella had to come and cook for him and Patrick had to stick around to drink with him. So it stood to reason, they agreed with their heads getting closer, noses almost touching, lowering their voices, that Henry was with someone else.

Yes, I wanted to shout, he is. He's almost certainly with Jim and Lily now if he's anywhere and still alive.

'He must have been desperate,' I heard as I left the room.

Patrick said: 'We men . . . we're hopeless, aren't we?'

'I don't think so. Not at all,' said Stella.

'The most available, I dare say,' said Patrick.

'The most available what?' said Stella.

'Woman, of course.'

I banged the door of the lounge but stayed in the corridor and heard: 'My theory is . . .' Patrick was saying, 'my theory is a combination of pressure from this end – from the younger generation at a guess – plus availability of another certain person who might have otherwise been nothing but a passing fancy. We men, you see, are like climbing plants sending tendrils out – catching on the the nearest firm surface . . .'

Stella would be loving it, but there's nothing firm about Stella. Even her bones are soggy at a guess.

Bentley's settled on the Hebrides, the Outer Hebrides, he says, for our pre-holocaustian evacuation. We were smoking and I got quite high. I began to talk about the stupidity of all of us going somewhere safe to carry on civilisation when those of us who are not gay don't want kids in any case. Wouldn't it be better if we took some people who wanted kids, like Jane, say, or like people who had kids already.

'Oh yes. Oh yes,' they all said. 'Mr Forbes, is it? Fertile Forbes, is it?'

'I only said I was going to babysit for him tomorrow night,' I said. 'For Christ's sake what's wrong with that? You want to make something out of it? Right. Make something out of it then.'

But otherwise the evening was quite matey. I was really high. 'Guilt is the secret of the universe,' I said. At the time I was gazing at Bentley's ears and noticing their complexity: the whorls, curves and recesses of his clean little ears which are set close to his head. I was remembering how we might even have to describe Henry's ears.

I was thinking also about Bentley's neck where it went down white and soft into his shirt and thinking what a pity about his gayness and I'd have to have a bloke or someone with their arms round me before too long or I'd go bust or crack or go bananas.

'Guilt,' Liz was saying, 'needn't exist. It's like only indoctrination.'

FIFTEEN

I was at Patrick's and I had Liz with me again. At lunchtime. Stella was there as well and they were saying since it was Thursday, Friday would be tomorrow and other jewels of wisdom. They were making up the file and the descriptions, finishing them off themselves. And I said 'No. Why you?' and they said 'Your mother isn't up to it.'

'She's OK. She is perfectly OK today and anyway I think you ought to give him longer than tomorrow.'

Stella touched me on the shoulder. Daisy's right. She does smell. She smells of old unwashed clothes and I can't think how Patrick can stand being near her. It is possible that they spent some of last night together. Today they were at his desk, her leaning over him, brushing against him. He knew I was monitoring this. The wind had gone round south probably and it was generally warmer though wet.

Stella kept her hand on my shoulder and said, 'Listen, Petra, honestly we think . . .'

How could any Leadbetter have to do with people like this, I was thinking.

'We think it's better for . . .'

'My mother's right. He will be back.'

Liz was leaning in the doorway. She said later that she'd never seen anyone look daggers like I was looking at Stella, as if I wanted to nuke her, Liz said.

'How do you know for sure?' said Patrick. Very wily that.

'I know. I just know. Or if he doesn't get back before tomorrow, he'll be dead . . .'

Patrick looked shocked, blind-eyed, cleaning his glasses. 'Bit over the top, aren't we? Bit what's called over the top today! Come on, Petra.' He was trying to assert himself, pathetically, in order to impress her.

'I'm sure there's someone else, someone else my mother is trying. She was ringing up early this morning.' Which was a lie, but necessary. 'It was only last night,' I said, 'that she got a bit desperate on account of, you know, managing the shop without a lot of help and that. My mother's perfectly all right.'

Stella moved off, sighing as I raised my voice. Patrick was patting the air as if he could smooth me down at a distance. He told me I was screeching. Stella shrugged her shoulders and went to a bookshelf where she held up a book and said: 'Oh Patrick, this is so interesting. Oh I do so love books . . .'

His eyes were darting everywhere like the bleep on electronic table tennis or squash when you turn it up for a high-speed game.

'You mean there have been developments?' he said.

Liz had gone to get a book as well, this big one with pictures in it of black naked Africans dancing with spears and she was nudging me to make me look at the big swinging dicks of the Africans.

'So could one know what these developments are?' he asked, looking sideways at Stella to see if she was watching him being manly and commanding.

'I'll tell you later. Or I'm sure my mother will. I'll tell you if he isn't home by . . . let's say . . . tomorrow morning.'

'You understand, don't you,' said Patrick, 'that you'll have to answer possibly unwelcome questions – in the unfortunate event that . . .'

'Obviously,' I said. 'But I'll take the file.'

'That won't be necessary,' he said.

I was looking into Patrick's eyes, standing my ground, making it clear that I meant business. I can look into Patrick's eyes for longer than I ever dare look into Henry's eyes. He handed me the file, picked it up and handed it to me rather than have me snatch it from him and make him lose his dignity, which he had lost years before because of not finishing things he'd started like his PhD.

'Thanks,' I said, and walked out, walking with head held high for as long as I needed to. Right out through the shelves, past Stella who was pretending not to see me or to feel the movement of air as I passed. Right past her, my head staying high, right out into the corridor with Liz following.

It is always dark out there on Patrick's stairs, and cold, and the way down is difficult to see. I don't know how he expects any customers with stairs like that, piles of books there tripping you up. Though I was sitting half-way down in any case. Feeling knackered like I'd fought and won a battle.

'Knock knock,' said Liz.

'Who's there?'

'Oliver.'

I must have told her last night when I was high – or some other time – that Henry used to call me Oliver.

'Oh, Christ, Oliver!' I said and began to sniff and run at the eyes all over Henry's file. It was a tatty pale brown file, not new like the bright coloured ones you can get at W H Smith and places. It was second-hand and old and Patrick had crossed out 'Invoices 1980' and written 'Henry Harrison' in red ballpoint pen.

One time he called me Oliver was on my last birthday and we went on this picnic to the monument. We walked along the chestnut avenue. He hates real country and made both Daisy and me hold hands with him when we got to the monument on this very clear warm day. Nature made him nervous. I mean natural things made him nervous and he'd rather be in the car

209

on a motorway or in a pub any day than on grass on a hill. But I held his hand; it was OK that time.

On Patrick's stairs I was snivelling, remembering things. Liz's hand is the most amazingly light hand. It was on my shoulder, seeming, this hand, to weigh nothing, running down my arm, me sensing it even through my padded jacket. On my wrist her fingers were still cold from the rain we'd been in earlier.

It was ever so warm at my birthday picnic for April and really too hot for the polo-necked riding sweater he had given me.

'Jeez, Oliver,' he said, imitating Ginny's Australian accent. 'Jeez, Oliver, that sweater suits you!'

He said he'd give me a driving lesson, so we went back along the chestnut avenue to the car, still some of the time holding hands. We got in the car and he said: 'Drive!'

'What me?' I said. 'I'm only just sixteen; you must be joking!'

But we went on a grassy track which is private land and for once he didn't make a crack about the Leadbetters owning everything. 'Mind that celandine!' he said. He was high like he sometimes was with energy that seemed to come from nowhere into him and then into other people. 'That caterpillar you just ran over will never be the same again,' he said. 'They are even now arranging a requiem mass for it. All the caterpillars in the country will come together and mourn.' Then he said I should come with them on holiday. Then he told me I'd be a very good driver one day. We were driving down a thickly wooded track at the time. Then he went back to talking about the holiday and I nearly committed myself to saying yes. Then he said it was nice to be a real family for once, wasn't it?

The trouble was that you couldn't say 'no' to that, but if you said 'yes, isn't it?' he would take you further, lead you further up on a spiral – like a bird rising on a thermal – where it wasn't your earthbound Leadbetter nature to go and your mind would burst with excitement and you'd go loony and do something shatteringly wrong and spoil it all.

'Christ, Oliver,' he said as I got up speed and the car was

bumping over tussocks. 'However have I put up with you all these years?' and then, 'If it wasn't that I was so potty about your mother . . .' and he went on about how marvellous she was, how he didn't deserve her, how he worshipped her and how much pain we caused her, the two of us. 'We mustn't make her bleed, must we?'

This afternoon – was it only this afternoon? – I panicked suddenly. Supposing he wasn't at Jim's and I'd committed myself and my mother to revealing all to Patrick. I left Liz and did the only thing I could think of.

The crummy little room: I was back in it. It seemed brighter – perhaps because it was mid-afternoon this time and the sun shone in directly, falling on the picture of the soldier. The clairvoyant looked much older than she did the other day and much more tired. Perhaps she had been having a few tiring visions in the two days and, like Bilbo Baggins, having given out so much, had begun to fade.

It will be important not to fade in life. I am determined not to fade. By thirty I may start to fade, but now I come to think of it, the odds against my reaching thirty are long, and, if I do, I will be so amazed that fading won't matter so much.

This time I took a toothbrush and a sketching pen. She looked with some disgust at the toothbrush and I'm not surprised – I suppose anybody's toothbrush is suspect. My mother once defined being in love by saying that, if you felt like using someone's toothbrush, then you were in love with them. So really she may have been using Henry's spare toothbrush while he's been away. In which case it wasn't a very sensible thing to have brought.

The woman moved some knitting and sewing from the coffee table and spread a lacy plastic cloth, while I sat there where I'd sat before and kept on thinking about Henry's teeth and how when he gets toothache, my mother gives him oil of cloves and has long since ceased trying to persuade him to go to

211

a dentist. He moans and makes baby faces and she rubs his head. Perhaps it will be for her like losing a child. His tooth-ache seems to go off in the end. But never having been to a dentist, and if his body has decomposed when found, they won't be able to recognise him, there being no dental records in existence. What am I saying? He is at Jim's.

'You're going to help me this time, Olivia?'

'Of course.'

'There's been no news?'

'No, nothing.'

She was reaching for my hand. I gave it to her. She kept looking at my wrist and saying I was not relaxed. 'You have to give.' She stroked my wrist. I shut my eyes. Her fingers were warm and scratchy like they were before.

'Your name's not Olivia.'

She had been prying. Must have been. I blinked. 'No, actually it's not.' This came out as a kind of croak. She stroked my wrist and squeezed further up my arm. I couldn't stand much more of this.

'It doesn't matter what your name is,' she said. 'The main thing is that you're going to help me this time much, much more.'

I had to think of elsewhere pretty fast, so brought to mind the driving lesson on the track, but then remembered how later Henry and I went back to my mother by the monument. It was really amazingly sunny for April and my mother was sitting there saying if only all the summer could be like this.

'There'll be France, remember,' Henry said. 'Don't forget about the holiday. We're all going, aren't we? Petra and I have been talking about it.'

Sometimes I do think he is mad, was mad. Then I saw my mother looking at me, telling me with her eyes I was going to Colorado, wasn't I? And me telling her with mine that I knew all that. And she telling me that we wouldn't say anything just now, would we, so as not to spoil things. And then Henry going off and standing with his back to us looking down at the

212

patchwork fields and the wide view south and not speaking on the way home.

'I see the dark-haired woman again,' the clairvoyant said.

I kept my eyes shut, trying to escape from the image of Henry by the monument, but couldn't seem to think of anything, except that there were thunderclouds coming up as well.

'The dark-haired woman in a different house this time. A tall house this. She's standing on the stairs. The lights are on upstairs: a door is open. There is the light-haired man again, coming out of the lit-up room. He's carrying a suitcase. My dear, I do believe he's coming home to you.'

Keep looking south over the view and the flat lands: blank out Henry standing there and backtrack to the sun and thunderclouds. Forget the silence in which he knew we could communicate.

'You know this house?' the woman said.

I shook my head. Why ever had I come back here? I should have stopped to reason, shouldn't I, that if he was dead, no one would ever know anything and things would go on being like they were. And if he was alive and at Jim's, then he'd be on his way back in any case.

'The woman is trying to detain him, dear, standing on the staircase trying to block his way. She thinks she can keep him. She is pleading with him. She is making promises to him . . .'

I tried to think of Mr Forbes and how I'd soon be babysitting for him and what I'd wear, etc. And since that failed I tried to make myself stand up and leave, but the voice went on about the woman pleading. 'Oh deary me, isn't she cutting up a fuss about it? She's not the sort of person whom a man like that would stay with . . . oh no . . . not the sort of woman for a good man to stay with, not with an ugly voice like that. No pride, dear, some women have no pride . . .' She gripped my fingers even harder, her finger-bones on mine as if there was no flesh between, digging in and working at my joints.

'There's another figure here. I can't make out what sex it is. A figure in the shadows with hands over head, over ears

213

perhaps, trying not to hear the screeching voice. No wonder, dear, it isn't a nice scene at all . . .'

In the room the clock was thudding in its muffled way. Let him be dead, I was thinking. Let him be dead. I mustn't stay here. But I couldn't get my hands away.

'No, the man is telling the woman that she mustn't make that kind of noise, mustn't make these promises she can't keep. He is leaving now. He doesn't like her this way: she mustn't promise what she can't fulfil and shouldn't fulfil. Ah, what a good man he is – so sad for him – men sometimes have to remind women of their responsibilities . . .'

Opening my eyes, I saw the photograph of the soldier on top of her television. The sun caught the silver frame and reflected into my eyes. I twitched and closed my eyes; sparkling shapes danced on my eyeballs.

'The light-haired man is outside now. It's cold. It's a kind of balcony with steps down from it and the woman's standing there still shouting at him, yelling that she'll make everything all right for him. The other figure is down there in the shadows still, shivering . . .'

My ears were ringing, starting to ring. I tore my hands away from hers and held them over my ears. She went on talking. So much for her need for help from me.

'He's gone. The woman's leaning over the railing. Her hair has fallen over her face. Her hand is over her mouth. The kiddie inside is calling her. I wonder what the person standing in the shadows will do . . .'

The person standing in the shadows left. The person had heard enough. OK, so the person had come back for a suitcase and a dustbin bag and was not going to hang round long enough for any promises to be fulfilled. 'I'll write and ask him if she can go there . . .' was the operative phrase, 'go there for good . . .'

That old woman's face: powdery; eyes closed but tears burbling out. 'Isn't it lovely that he's coming home to you, that you will welcome him and Mummy will welcome him – you'll all hold out your arms and welcome him. We'll all hold out our arms and welcome him, won't we?'

I was going. I was going anyway. Putting the money down on the table and going anyway, leaving her saying in her singsong voice, leaving the voice and the picture of the soldier: 'Home is where the heart is truly, dear. Daddy's coming home and you needn't worry any more and Mummy will stretch out her arms and welcome him . . .'

I was by the door.

'He's coming home as people must. Men have more to give than they can give to one woman in their lives, but still remain devoted to their families. It doesn't mean their wives have let them down or children have, because the nicest wives and children don't let people down and there's forgiveness and . . .'

I'd gone.

I don't have to tell, do I? Anyone knowing it can make no difference. The court is in my head and not in the hands of that old woman. Or in Patrick's. Whatever happens I don't have to think about the promise which was made, because it's another unfulfilled one, isn't it? I check the post, incoming and outgoing. I check as many phone calls as I can. What she promised, what he told her not to promise, has not been done. And if he's dead, will never need to be done.

I don't believe she'd do it. It was the last thing, wasn't it, he told her when he left. 'Don't do it, Alison.'

I'd been sent for by Uncle Gerald. I was standing next to him looking into the paddock and telling him I was sure I'd shut the gate yesterday.

Uncle Gerald didn't seem to be believing me, but said the chances were that some farmer or someone in a remote cottage had taken him in and would be getting in touch, but I kept thinking of Troy galloping down the shallow spur from the monument and away towards the New Forest, although it would be thirty miles at least to get there and dangerous roads to cross, even motorways.

At least, I was thinking, he was easier to describe than Henry. Lost. One black gelding. Fourteen and a half hands. Answers to name of Troy and shitbag and lousy bastard. His teeth suggest the age of twelve.

'No point in looking at the moment,' said Gerald. 'It's getting dark.'

SIXTEEN

Another thing that Henry said to my mother before he left: 'I am not leaving you. I just need time.' He copied Daisy's habit of saying everything twice and said it twice, three times in fact. 'Trust me' may have been his last words.

Another thing: thinking of Troy this time, as I came back down on my bike from King's Radlett at dusk; it was after the birthday picnic that I rode Troy in that thunderstorm.

Another thing: I *would* have gone to France with them, but we'd had Ginny and some other bad scenes by then.

And I've missed the true story of the Trip to Rome, the Bad Scene at the Wedding of a Distant Cousin and a zillion other culminations. I've also missed the good scenes that we have at Christmas and the medals that I've got for those. Once he actually made the medal, moulded it in modelling clay and painted it gold: The Order of the Opening of Harrison's. I have it still.

He also bought for me this very bicycle on which I coasted down towards the town this evening and on which I would ride up again at dawn to begin the search for Troy.

And another thing my mother said, yelled out at Henry as he

went off with his suitcase. 'No, *you* trust *me*,' she shouted. 'You trust me to do what's best for everyone for once. It won't hurt her. It's me whose mind is cracking, isn't it?'

'Perhaps it will have a chance to heal,' he said.

I'm sure I've remembered everything now.

Mr Forbes said: 'Hullo, Petra, going riding?'

I'd gone in riding clothes since I might have had to ride Troy some of the way home. I had the yellow polo-necked sweater on.

He had his coat on. The house wasn't like Jane's in the parallel street, but older, taller and a semi. The walls inside were dead dull, painted browns and dark greens. Evidently Mrs F is into miserable colours.

'All well?' he said.

'Not really, no,' I said and told him about Troy being missing and he didn't seem to know what to say. Being anxious to get to the hospital I suppose, he didn't have time to think whether to be just sympathetic or comforting.

He was showing me the kitchen and the coffee cups and all that and telling me that Tracey when she came last night finished the chocolate digestives, so he'd bought some more, a new packet of these.

'The telly's there!' He came behind me, steering me into the sitting room with his hands on my waist. 'Pointless asking you if you are going to work or read. My resolution has been not to ask any of you what you were going to do.' He took his hands away from my waist and bustled off to draw the curtains. 'You will be glad to hear that babysitting ends as of Saturday. They're coming home.' He came back to the telly saying: 'See! Switch on! Switch off! On! Off!'

Not a very big telly, I was thinking. With the way things were in this house, it might even have been black and white, but wasn't luckily. You never know with unmaterialist people like the Forbeses seem to be.

'Now, music!' He was at the record player – not even a stereo. 'No wages if you break a record.' The records were a

218

grotty collection, classical and jazz, though there were some Beatles, a few Rolling Stones and one Genesis. Their sleeves were faded and the corners squashed. Jane's often said that people have to make sacrifices if they want a family.

Forbes also took me upstairs to show me angelic Eddie sleeping with his little hand curled over one cute ear.

'Little bugger,' he said. 'Threw his tea up all over me. Don't worry though. He's OK now. Tough as old boots. He'll sleep through anything.'

Then he sort of stood looking at me with his head on one side, seeming to be waiting for me to make some apt remark or ask some question about my duties.

'You're really choked about that horse. Do you want to go home after all?'

'No, it's OK,' I said. 'It's OK honestly.' And it was OK: there wasn't anything to do about Troy. The reason I was standing silent was that I was remembering I hadn't been home at all and for all I knew Henry might be back. Or that there might be news of him. That, but as well I was thinking I should say something polite to Mr Forbes somehow, something warm and friendly maybe. 'You'll be looking forward to them coming home?' I said, but my voice sounded hopeless and wrong – a bit like Jane's voice or her mother's voice – or even like Vivienne's voice echoing in the cathedral.

'Ah well,' he said.

Back downstairs, I was staring at a desk with piles of files on it and all the books around the room, most of them new – I mean not second-hand. No wonder they didn't have a lot to spare for furniture. The shelves looked like he'd made them himself and seemed to bend under the weight of all that reading matter.

'Of course I'm looking forward to it, yes,' he said. 'With baited breath,' he said, but changed the subject. 'There is a bit to drink,' he said. 'My celebration bottle – haven't touched it since the twins arrived.'

Then he seemed to think he had to reassure me that he was

looking forward to his wife and babies coming home. 'I mean who wouldn't be looking forward to it?' he said.

The celebration bottle was Bull's Blood red wine and about half full. Mostly at home if we don't finish a bottle of wine we throw it away, but when I had some later, this wine of Forbes' tasted not too bad.

And I remembered, drinking, how Henry had, once when happy, poured a glass of wine for everyone and said: 'To the only family I've got!'

For a time I sat, hands folded between my knees, on a hard small armchair watching telly. It was pretty chilly in there. He hadn't said to light the gas fire and it didn't seem to be an automatic lighting one, but I had a match. I hadn't asked him if it was all right to smoke. Tracey and Susan and Maxine all said they'd smoked, however. They had also said there was nothing to do except watching telly since there weren't any magazines or anything.

It was a re-run of *Life on Earth*, this episode about those male frogs going at it, like probably Patrick and Stella were again, since I'd seen her going into his place after work when I passed on my bike – that meant my mother was alone. Let copulation thrive again, I thought. There must have been a thousand frogs on that log all belting away. First time round I watched it with Henry who said: 'That's the difference between men and women – indiscrimination!'

'Thank you so much, my darling!' said my mother.

'How do you know that women don't feel like that sometimes?' I said to Henry and he said he didn't want to have the programme spoiled for him by arguing. I could have quoted Thomas Hardy on sexual appetite.

In the whole of Forbes' sitting room there was nothing that we'd sell at Harrison's. Quite a way sub-Habitat it was, although the Forbeses can't be broke because they go abroad in the summer, camping usually. After the holidays you always have to hear about the Forbeses' camping holiday when they get rained out or flooded or sunburnt or whatever and it sounds hilarious but must be pretty horrible at the time.

Soon I went up to check on Eddie who was still lying, fingers curled, hand thrown back, on his side and breathing easily and lightly, although I could only just see his face from the passage light. He had this toy lamb at the bottom of the cot. Then I crept out again. Everything was extra neat everywhere. They don't have anyone to clean for them, Jane says, so Forbes must have done it all himself.

His wife's called Janet. He's called Sam. Sam and Janet I was thinking. Knock knock, who's there? Sam and Janet. Sam and Janet who? Sam and Janet evening. Get it? Some enchanted evening. One of Henry's.

The twins are to be called Peter and Stephen. There was a picture on the mantelpiece above the gas fire of the two of them just after they'd been born. So Mr Forbes must have been at the birth with his polaroid and holding her legs or whatever fathers are supposed to do at births. In the picture the babies were all covered with blood and stuff and you could see the hands of two of the nurses supporting them, also covered with blood. The babies' flesh looked shiny and rubbery like skinned chickens' legs look and one was definitely more chickeny than the other.

Actually I felt quite tired all over again and sat back down on this soft sofa, curling up but still shivering slightly. There was another photo of Mrs F, Janet, in bed after having the twins, her face pink and shiny, but I suppose what might have been called joyous. Can't remember my mother looking very joyous after having Daisy, but she was comparatively elderly and had to have forceps and other nasties.

Jane says that records show that there are always thousands more boys than girls born just before a war. 'That doesn't make sense,' I said. 'If boys are born now and there's about to be a war, or in our case a holocaust, then the boys born now wouldn't be old enough to fight and in any case there wouldn't be any fighting.'

221

'God or whoever is in charge of these things in theory,' Jane said, 'isn't to know that, is he?'

'Like in theory,' I said, 'the prime mover sets things going in an order and can't keep up with developments perhaps.'

When the frogs had finished, I turned the telly off and got up to look more closely at the picture of Janet Forbes taken immediately after giving birth and decided that she wasn't at all dishy, but looked friendly and intelligent, which I suppose is rare and not a bad thing to be as long as you don't get caught up by someone and ensnared by twins. I thought of how I could look friendly and intelligent when he came back. I also thought of having some of his Bull's Blood and what I'd be doing when he came in.

The others were right. There wasn't a single magazine, except a pile of colour supplements I'd mostly seen before. So I went towards the books. Endless books (almost as many as Patrick has in his shop), going half-way round the room; those shelves: the trouble was he hadn't put up enough brackets to support all these Shakespeares, Lawrences, Conrads, Brontës, Austens and more books than I ever realised Thomas Hardy wrote. And poets, dozens of them. We have books in our house, but this was ridiculous. He'd never transport all these to Kuwait, I was thinking.

Maybe there's a natural urge or drive in me to make me go through desk drawers. I found these files, quantities of them with his name on them and B.A. after it. Inside the files were notes written in red ink which seemed to be about the different set books he taught and were mostly things he'd said to us in class. And drawings too. Like in the *Far From the Madding Crowd* file there was a sketch of what must have been Fanny Robin hanging on to the big dog, leaning over it with her stomach just not dragging on the ground. And there was one of Bathsheba in the hollow in the ferns with very full lips and open cleavage and huge breasts with Troy's sword just about to slice at her. She looked more like Marilyn Monroe than Julie

222

Christie, I'd have said. 'Stap me,' I was saying to myself. 'Filthy beast,' I was saying in my head. 'Cheeky bugger,' I was saying.

The house was dead quiet, same as the road outside and every move I made seemed loud. So I lit the gas fire and me and it were the only things making a noise. In front of the mirror above the mantelpiece I stood and rubbed my lips and practised making them look fuller. Then I had half a glass of Bull's Blood. Then another half glass. After all he'd been gone much longer than the one and a half hours he'd said he would.

I made the files look like they hadn't been touched and washed my hands at the kitchen sink, then used some of his bottle of Vaseline Intensive Care on my hands and rubbed it well in, then lay down by the gas fire, listening.

About the names they've chosen for the twins: there's this joke which was the only good joke I heard in America. Polish jokes in America are like Irish jokes here. Anyway there's this Pole and he's married to this Greek. Greeks are not much better than Poles in America. Anyway this couple have this baby and they can't think what to call it and they think and think and finally come up with 'Zorba the dumbshit'. I told Henry that joke. Just after Christmas, it must have been, when we were on good terms. And did he laugh? Talk about laugh! Following upon which we discussed racial jokes which he is good at, though as I've said before he isn't really racialist I don't think. But he said he would fight if he had to and I said what was the point of fighting but he said he'd fight for my mother and Daisy and even me if I'd believe that. Which I don't know if I did or didn't. But this I can say about Henry: if there was the holocaust tomorrow he'd be back if he could get here if he's still alive. 'But you think everything is awful, so what would you fight for apart from people?' I said. And he told me people who hadn't got ideals like I hadn't any ideals would never understand in a zillion years. And I said I had ideals but couldn't explain them. And Patrick said 'ideals' was only a word we've got used to using.

I reckon Mr Forbes would be one who fought. Like it could be a miracle if he didn't fight.

On the ledge under their coffee table there was this photographic album, full of pictures of the Forbeses on holiday and Eddie from the age of nought, Mrs F looking ruddy and joyous in the labour ward again. And one of Mr F on the beach, which reminded me of the pebble one we went to with Jim and Lily, Mr Forbes taken from the back by someone on the beach, looking as if he was imitating Terence Stamp as Sergeant Troy – as if he could with his solid frame. He was imitating the diving action. His back was white and a good deal wider than his hips which were held in tight by these stripy trunks, but his legs were really a good shape I decided.

I kept on listening for the car and kept on thinking that I'd heard it. Then I think I had a cup of coffee sometime and another half glass of Bull's Blood or so. I think I went to check on Eddie several times. Then Liz rang and said was I coming round to her place and I said I thought that was tomorrow and she said my voice sounded peculiar. She said she'd been watching the frogs too.

I think I thought for certain Forbes would be back by closing time and wondered what excuse he'd make. The others said he never was out that long.

In the end I was back in the low chair, hands between my knees when he came in. He looked like he'd been drinking and threw himself into the soft sofa with his legs stretched out. 'Life's a sod, isn't it?' he said, looking round the room as if to check what I'd been doing.

'Don't look so guilty,' he said. 'You're a weird one, aren't you?'

I told him Eddie was OK. He told me that the twins were OK.

'Isn't it quiet here?' I said.

'Make us a coffee,' he said, 'and stop looking guilty.'

I went and made the coffee and when I came back he said, 'But you probably don't believe in guilt.'

224

And I said 'No', but wanted to qualify it because I wanted to say the right thing at that stage. I tried smiling, but he yawned again. Beer makes people sleepy, more sleepy than wine I think.

'I ought to get my coat and go,' I said. Maybe the girl who got it together with the physics teacher had more guts than me. Maybe she was more of a Cool Hand Luke. I said 'I've got my bike' and 'I had some of your wine' and one or two other not very memorable remarks and he kept staring at me but didn't say 'Yes, get your coat' or anything. I was sitting there almost getting a headache with the tension of it all.

He leaned forwards. 'Life's better from behind a desk, isn't it?' he said.

'I don't know what you mean,' I said.

'Some people need the herd to survive or to excel,' he said.

'I was watching *Life on Earth* again tonight,' I said.

'I was talking about you, needing the herd, the group, to play your butch game in . . .'

'In *Life on Earth*,' I said, 'I saw the frog bit . . . did you see the frog bit the first time round?'

'Give me your hand,' he said, reaching across the coffee table like the clairvoyant was always doing. 'I'm very tired,' he said. 'I drank and shouldn't have left you here so long, but thanks for coming. Why do you keep on going on about the frogs?'

I swallowed. 'I suppose I may be dropping hints,' I said. 'Frogs take to everyone, you see, regardless of who, regardless of sex or anything I mean . . .'

'It's the frogs that are the trouble, get us in the troubles we are in. I'm very tired.' Henry used to say 'tired and emotional' as a joke about people being drunk.

Mr Forbes' hand was warm and soft as if he put Vaseline Intensive Care on it several times a day. 'Come on . . .,' he said, 'off you go.'

Every man smells totally different, Mr Forbes in fact of baby powder which wasn't cancelled by the beer, though I could

225

taste that on his lips. Jane says he always buys Johnson's baby powder. Soft. Talk about soft! I discovered all this in the hall when he was helping me on with my riding mac and then holding me up against him, swaying and knackered, tired and emotional, so I felt I was supporting him but that he wasted it. You know when it's urgent. 'Do me a favour,' he was murmuring.

It seemed that there were no canyons in between us. It was like the place you sink into when you fall.

'Do me a favour,' he said again. 'Get on your bike and get the hell out of here,' he was saying. He's not that much taller than me. Then he said into my ear: 'But do me another favour and babysit again tomorrow night.'

'OK,' I said and tried to work out how I would make sure to miss class again tomorrow in case he changed his mind and tried to tell me so. I told him that the next day, Friday, suited me equally as well as tonight.

The lights were on, blazing out over the yard as I put my bike in the shed. The curtains were not drawn and the shadow of my mother's figure was thrown on to the cobbles. I can usually tell when something's happened, like dozens of times I've guessed it has happened and I've been right. But this couldn't be the big event, could it, because Henry has always seen to it that the curtains were completely drawn.

My mother was back on the long settee when I came in, really white-faced and getting up and coming towards me, putting her arms around me so that I began to cry without her saying anything. I hadn't even had a chance to tell her about Troy being missing.

But someone had rung Gerald up. Someone who has a cottage about three miles from King's Radlett. South – so he was going south. Troy must have needed to scratch himself and pushed against this sharp stake this man had since he was making a fence. It was a springy stake and gave way suddenly. He is, was, strong. He is, was, heavy.

'I suppose it didn't kill him outright?' I said.

'No. The man shot him.'

'How come he had a gun handy?'

She knew she had to tell me. 'No, actually the man had to get the vet who did it and then recognised Troy and got in touch with Gerald.'

'So there was a bit of time, wasn't there?' I sat down away from my mother. She was bawling and saying: 'I hate anything like this. I really hate things like this happening. When it isn't anyone's fault.' Her crying was totally different from the way she cried the night before or two nights ago or whenever it was she was in bed with all those Kleenex spread around.

But I was thinking that that image of Troy stuck there waiting to be shot was worse than anything – any image I'd ever had come into my brain. Other images you can make yourself forget. Other images you can clean out of your brain. Other things you can brighten or dull by the way you think about them. Or you can make yourself into a different person who doesn't mind about those images.

'Have a drink,' she said, my mother said.

I shook my head.

In the workroom, snivelling into bits of her cotton waste and everything. In the workroom checking in the diary since that has become a regular thing I can't seem to go to bed without doing. In the workroom finding nothing new in the diary, but finding a letter from my father which hadn't been there last night.

So she can't possibly know that I go there at night.

This was not intended for my eyes.

I could hear her walking about upstairs, probably wondering what to do about me crying downstairs.

I didn't need to read much. My father's writing is rather round and childish. Half-way down the first page: 'Yes,' he wrote, 'I do understand, although Petra has never, I assure you, spoken directly of this problem. After some consideration,

227

Laura is agreeable. Of course it won't be easy for her . . .'

So how was my mother going to break this to me, I was thinking. She wouldn't do it for a good few days, I was thinking. Not after Troy, I was thinking.

But when had she written to him? Here was the answer at the top. 'Dear Alison . . . re yours of the 14th Feb.' St Valentine's Day. She must have posted it the morning after Henry told her she was to do no such thing, the morning after she said it must be her decision in the end because her mind would crack. Too late, sneaky mother, it has cracked. No wonder with all that guilt, uh?

What a pity. What a waste when Henry said he left to let your mind heal over!

Not easy for Laura, uh? Then another fine mind will bite the dust.

The black dog is a bitch in fact and now she is on heat. I was explaining this to Daisy when I took her in the park just before five-thirty which was the time Patrick was going to the police. 'That's why all those dogs are after her,' I said to Daisy.

'Knock knock,' said Daisy.

'Who's there?'

I said I'd keep her out for at least an hour in case the police wanted to see my mother or come round to the flat or whatever.

'Luke,' said Daisy.

'Luke who?'

'Luke there's another dog after her. I made that up myself.'

On the station side of the park you find this paddling pool which is only filled in summer, but there'd been some rain. Over there the trees are young, thin-stalked and staked and labelled and with wire round them to keep dogs off. I ran towards this area, running fast and hearing Daisy shouting, 'Don't run so fast. It isn't fair. It isn't fair.'

My mother would be waiting in the kitchen with the file. She was giving Henry every chance to turn up in the nick of time.

Daisy will soon be old enough to find her own way to the pool and the swings beside it and the seesaw and the mini-roundabout and play with other kids there. And, before long, I shall be old enough not to be sent anywhere against my will. I wonder if my mother's thought of that.

'Knock knock knock knock,' Daisy was shouting.

I see in my diary that lighting up time was 17·56 tonight. The lights came on around the play area just as a train sounded in the distance. Down at the pool the black dog caught us up followed by four other dogs. There was, as I'd expected, some water in the pool. The dog leaped in, so did the other dogs. Then the five of them came towards us and shook themselves and Daisy screamed as drops of freezing water splashed her.

'What on earth am I supposed to do?' Her chest was beginning to heave.

'Just say piss off or find a stick to throw for them.'

Doesn't my mother realise that if he comes back and discovers she has sent me away, she will have done the thing he didn't want her to? That great love he protested won't half be tested in that case. Hasn't she realised that it's written that she has to live with both of us, cracked or not? Catch 22, mother. Catch 44, mother. Catch 88.

I left Daisy throwing sticks. She might learn. She might have to learn. I got on the mini-roundabout, pushing it with my foot to start it whirling. Being on my own, I could go as fast as I liked and not worry about anyone else falling off, whizzed by the centifrugal force with the street lights streaking together. Then the black dog jumped on too and pointed its nose to the sky: I held it by its collar. Then at high speed we both jumped off and the roundabout went on round with its metal shafts clanking. I was still giddy with the world spinning with me at its centre.

The train hooted for the second time and the black dog bounced into the pool again, nosing its way through the water, making a bow wave, with a huge stick in its mouth. Daisy pelted away again. I shouted at her that it was no good being scared. Of anything. I caught her up at the edge of the circle of lights and dragged her away from the playing area on to the grass

229

again. She opened her mouth to scream. I held her by the collar of her duffle coat, my face close to hers. 'If you utter one sound, I'll shake every tooth out of your head!'

Then I turned on the dogs. The black one had sunk to the ground with its paws stretched out in front of it. The other dogs kept their distance, grouped in the twilight. Everything stayed quiet and still except Daisy's legs were twitching. From that part of the slope you can hear the doors of the train slamming and the train move off again. Because it was so nearly dark, the blackbirds had stopped twittering.

Daisy's mouth began to open: 'Wait!' I said.

My back was to the station, but I knew because I can feel Henry approaching through my back even if my back is turned towards him, through my right arm if my right side is turned towards him, through my left arm, leg and everywhere if that left side is turned. Etc. And if he came down hanging from a parachute, I'd feel it through the crown of my head. He's always there and always will be there. I'll always know exactly where he's standing and what he'd say in any circumstance. I'll always measure what I do against his views of life, and when it's what he would approve of, I will want to tell him I have done that thing. And if I've done the thing he'd say I shouldn't do, I'll need to justify that too. Even though I'm miles away, I'll think about the justification of that act. I'll justify it to him, if not in person, in my head. Maybe there's no prime mover, but there's Henry there, the shit. Call Henry Harrison. I only have to call him, you know.

Daisy's face held close to mine: 'Do exactly as I say and go back down the slope. Towards the station, Daisy.'

'You come with me.'

'No. Walk, Daisy. Wait on this side of the road.'

'Where are you going then?'

'Babysitting.'

He will be in the kitchen when I return later after everything I've done or have not done. He may or may not be clasping my mother's wrist across the table.

230